LEDGES

A Novel

By

Michael Frederick

Novels by author:

White Shoulders

The Paper Man

Missouri Madness

Shy Ann

Summer of '02

Autumn Letters

Places

For KIRA

Acknowledgments

Special thanks to Mariam Kirby and Just Your Type, LLC,
for your assistance with this book.
This edition is possible because of your
sharp mind for detail.

I want to thank my loyal librarians for buying
my books and supporting me for the long run.

Thanks Tony for your art.
Cover Design by Anthony Conrad

Spring Fever

April, 1959.
Des Moines, Iowa.

The school clock high on the sixth grade classroom wall clicked as the minute hand paused, then pointed to 11:55. Ben Smith could see the red second hand's circular sweep for the first time. It moves too fast, he thought, dreading the lunchroom teasing in store on his first day wearing glasses.

He hated them. The thick lenses and heavy plastic frames bore down on his nose, making dents that marked him as a four-eyes even if he hid the glasses in his lunch box.

Last week after school, his mother had taken him to the eye doctor. "Myopia," the doctor had informed them as they sat in the darkened examination room. "Legally blind."

Ben could see some things clearly without the ugly glasses. When he put his chin on the frame of Dr. Doolee's weird examining machine, Ben could smell fresh Listerine on Doolee's breath. And the doctor had swiped the tops of his black shoes on the back of each skinny calf before ushering them into his office, his avid gaze on the mother's face, not glancing at the son.

Michelle Smith's curvaceous figure was adorned in a secretary's business suit, too chic to have come from an Iowa store. Doolee looked into her almond-shaped hazel eyes, shadowy below her stylish beehive hairdo, and wet his lips.

Michelle looked away. "He hasn't been able to see the blackboard," she said. "And he's had accidents and tripped over things."

Ben rolled his eyes at his mother, not wanting anyone to know that he had stepped too close to a teeter totter at the park and received a red knot on his forehead.

"As I said," Dr. Doolee commiserated, "without correction, he's blind. But I can fix that in a jiffy."

Yesterday, after the doctor adjusted the frames to fit over Ben's ears, his first steps outside Dr. Doolee's office on a downtown Des Moines sidewalk made him woozy. His legs seemed longer. The length of his stride seemed farther away and awkward, as if walking downstairs in the dark without a feel for the next step.

Leaving the curb, stepping down into the street at the green crosswalk beside his mother, required effort to keep from swaying sideways and crashing into her.

"You look so handsome and smart," his mother had said.

Ben had frowned.

"No, really! They do look good on you."

Ben was not one to whine or vent his true feelings if they might cause his mother worry. He knew his mother had enough problems raising him and his two sisters on her secretary's salary at the paint company. The $96.90 monthly in child support from his father didn't cover much. Ben knew all the details of his mother's life-good and bad. She never kept anything from him.

As they walked to their olive green Ford sedan, Ben didn't like what he saw with his new vision: Men's heads turned and they stared at his mother. These were men with or without their wives, obviously attracted to twenty-nine-year-old Michelle. Twenty steps away and closing, their eyes scanned her up and down, as if Ben's feelings about it

2

didn't matter, as if he didn't understand their lust.

This is terrible, Ben thought, thinking of the things he saw so clearly now with his new eyes. These were things he'd just have to get used to, like the nasty remarks he was sure to hear when he wore his glasses to school the next day.

Michelle glanced at her office clock at noon. Her boss, Mr. Cook, was still on the phone with a customer. She covered her typewriter. Her thoughts were on her paycheck. She had asked three weeks ago to get paid at lunch instead of five o'clock, in order to go to the bank. She was too proud to mention the real reason.

Mr. Cook had slipped her check beside her typewriter just before noon three weeks in a row, the last two times without being asked. Cook, a seventy-year-old New Englander with a sharp eye for business, knew that many a customer spent more time in his store since Michelle had come to work for him. Placing her desk in the middle of the store near the register was no accident.

At 12:02, Cook heard Michelle's sigh. Any man with a pulse would respond to it. Then Michelle cleared her throat softly, looking his way. Before he could think, he was opening a drawer and handing Michelle her check with a smile, as his phone customer gabbed on and on about a paint job.

Spotless black high heels hurried across the street into the bank. Minutes later, she was behind the wheel in Cook's parking lot praying she had enough gas to start the car.

Two blocks over and out of gas, she coasted right into the service station, where in her haste she had time for the attendant to pump only two dollars' worth.

As Ben turned the corner and entered the lunchroom the scent of goulash on the day's menu was a welcome change from yesterday's wiener links. His sister was there in the same spot as always, at the last lunch table in the corner closest to the accordion steam furnace that hissed when on and clanged when not. Her lips curved in the same smirk that she wore at breakfast. Ben knew she had been planning all morning to upset him in some petty way, or worst of all, embarrass him in front of his classmates. That was the real problem. Ben, for some reason, had the ability to blush on a dime. His sister, Pam, only ten months younger, was one grade behind him. Pam purposely made a practice of turning her brother's face into a hot tomato.

She looked innocent. Chubby, she wore her pixie-styled, dark brown hair combed behind her ears then curving back toward her face. Her big brown eyes widened and seemed to say: Who me? I didn't do a thing.

Ben sat down at the table.

"Betcha a quarter she's not here by twenty after," Pam greeted him.

"I won't bet. My luck you'd win," Ben said.

"As always." She grinned.

"Shut up," Ben muttered, as the first students headed with their food-laden trays for tables, splaying out to sit as far away as possible from the Smith kids.

"Those glasses make you look weird. I liked you better when you squinted."

Pam's impression of Ben squinting caused him to blush. He could feel his ears turning white hot, and a hundred pair of eyes focusing on his burning neck. Ben reached down to his sister's thigh and pinched her hard through her dress. She yelled, "Ouch!" increasing attention their way. Pam started to giggle, pointing her finger at Ben. His embarrassment seemed so funny to her that soon Ben was holding back laughter, pursing his lips tight. Pam could always get Ben to laugh at himself. That made the blush fade faster.

At 12:22, the sound of Michelle's high heels turned

every head around as she waved to her kids, motioning them to come up to the serving counter to get their meal. Michelle smiled and thanked the elderly women of the kitchen staff while she paid for three bowls of goulash. She gave Ben three nickels for the milk machine.

The room emptied steadily, until mother and kids sat alone eating fast with three minutes to go until the next bell marked the end of lunchtime.

"Grama Merle's coming over tonight," Michelle said.

"No. I hate it when she baby-sits," Ben argued.

"That's because she snores," Pam said.

"Do you have to go out?" Ben asked.

"I have a date."

"With who?" Pam demanded.

"His name is Dutch."

"Dutch. What kind of name is that? It's a paint," Ben said.

"That's Dutch Boy, dummy," Pam observed, polishing off her goulash by wiping her bowl clean with wedges of white bread squeezed in half between her chubby thumb and index finger.

Ben craned his head, eating close to his bowl. His mother took a new dollar bill from her purse and placed it on Ben's tray.

"After you pick up Debi, you can stop and get ice cream."

"Thanks Mom," Pam said and smiled as they returned their trays.

Ben refused to take his mother's hand, as Pam did, while Michelle walked them to their classrooms across the hall from each other. Pam always got a kick out of her class-mates' and teacher's star-struck reaction to her mother. Pam understood that that kind of attention was a good thing for girls. Ben loathed it. On his way into his classroom Michelle caught him.

5

"Ben, I didn't get my kiss goodbye."

"Mom, not now."

Michelle smiled and said, "I love you." That was Ben's cue to repeat her words. Instead, he smiled and waved goodbye, nodding to convey his feelings without being heard by his peers.

On her drive back to work, Michelle was thinking about Pam, how last week her teacher had asked Michelle to stop by school after work to discuss Pam's progress. Mrs. Ruckman wanted Michelle to consider having Pamela skip two grades, moving into the eighth grade in the fall because she was doing eighth grade math already, and her language skills were high school equivalent.

Michelle didn't have to think about it long. She compromised. She couldn't do that to Ben. To have his sister pass him by a grade would devastate her sensitive son, and Pam would miss out on too many social interactions with kids her own age. Michelle told Mrs. Ruckman, "One grade, not two. It might be good to have them in the same grade, learning together, since Ben sometimes asks Pam for help with his homework. But I'll have to see how it goes."

Michelle made the last remark with such final eyes that Mrs. Ruckman dropped the matter of two grades without argument.

Back in her car Michelle admitted to herself that she had blindly done to two of her children what her mother had done to her. The distance between the two women was such that Michelle both thought of and addressed her mother as Edith. Now, guilt assailed Michelle, causing her to roll down the car window to get more air. Years ago, Edith had told her if she read out loud during her pregnancy, she'd produce a brilliant child. She had. Pam. Ben and little Debi were mere bookends compared to the volumes she read out loud while carrying Pam. Edith had done the same thing with Michelle's sister Victoria. Victoria had gone to college and was given the best clothes, along with her mother's best wishes. Michelle got average grades, hand-me-downs, and her mother's tongue lashings about failure, stubbornness, and worthlessness.

Ben was smart, too. But it was Pam to whom Michelle had read for eight months, often as much as eight hours a day, while Ben slept in his crib in the other room.

Newspapers, magazines, novels by Thomas Wolfe and D. H. Lawrence, chapters from Melville and Fitzgerald, books borrowed from the library on math and science. Michelle read without understanding most of it. Poetry by Whitman and Frost were Pam's lullabies, just to prove to Edith she could have a bright child. Her entire life, Michelle had been looked at instead of listened to.

Arriving at the paint store in a car rusting out from the bottom up, she felt poor and stupid. On her walk to the back entrance, Michelle started to cry, tears marring her perfect complexion, overcome by remorse for what she had done. For what she hadn't done for Ben and Debi. She had played the ugly game of favorites. She would have to let it go, breathe it out, forgive herself, and do what she could to make life happy for all of her children.

Sisters of Mercy Day Care was a four-block walk for Ben and Pam. Usually their mother picked up three-year-old Debi after work, leaving Pam and Ben three blocks to walk in the opposite direction toward home. Ben walked several steps ahead of his lumbering sister, who wore a steel leg brace from heel to just below her left knee. Pam had been born with only a trace of a heel cord. Doctors had said she'd never walk without a limp, and if she continued putting on weight she'd end up in a wheelchair. She wore the brace only while walking to and from school. Still, it made her an object of ridicule and the target of taunts outside the classroom.

It was not shame that prompted Ben's lead on his sister. He was giving her all the sidewalk space she needed to swing her braced leg sideways, out from her hip, and forward with each arduous stride.

The first green buds of spring were showing on gray/brown birch trees that stood like frozen pretzels, thawing to life after a cold winter. Pam's brace produced seasonal sounds. In summer it creaked like a wooden cupboard door swinging open. If humid, her own perspiration seemed to quiet it, giving it a smooth movement that made her feel like running, at times, for a dozen steps or so. Now, her tongue stuck out of the corner of her mouth, as if she balanced the weight of the world with every step. The brace rubbed against the sole of her black and white orthopedic shoes and scrapped the concrete-the sounds absorbed by her painful laugh that made Ben hate her. For she had the power to choose pity or laughter. It all depended on her whim, while those chocolate brown eyes were rounded so large they seemed to push away all bordering whiteness. If not for her snide laugh and her stubborn vengeful temper, wielded against Ben more than anyone, he would feel sorry for her, and do anything to put a smile into those sad eyes.

Halfway to the day care, Ben turned back to Pam and stopped. Her brace was making its winter sound. Seeing the brace clearly, after years of nearsighted detachment, was daunting. He realized that Pam would welcome rest and stand beside him, stopping the sound of metal gouging into sidewalk, resonating like a hammer striking blows step after step. Ben stared at the thick, green knee socks covering her calves

"What flavor of ice cream are you going to have?" Ben asked.

Pam pushed up the sleeves of her green, wool sweater and looked down at her brace.

"I don't know yet."

"I'm getting licorice."

"You always do," Pam said, listening to kids' voices closing-in behind her, ready to respond if anyone made fun of her.

This time, they walked by with barely a glance. Too bad, Ben thought. It was time to get his sister fired up. When she was mad she didn't focus on her leg pain.

"You're in a big hurry for ice cream," he said, "forget to stuff yourself at lunch?"

"Shut up!"

Sisters of Mercy was a block away by now. Ben continued to push her buttons.

"Seems to me," he said, "if you get fatter, your leg will hurt more."

"I'd rather be fat than blind, any day," Pam retorted.

"Dad wears glasses," Ben countered, knowing that she adored their father.

"Yeah," Pam agreed, dragging after Ben, "but his glasses look good on him."

"Shut up."

Ben flashed back to a memory of his father: His new brother or sister was due to be born any day. He was in a waiting room in a Wichita, Kansas, doctor's office. Ben watched the white, starched leg of his father's Navy uniform nervously fidgeting up and down, pumping like a Kansas oil drill, but faster. First Class Petty Officer Kenny Smith's black Navy shoes reflected an onyx glow, but his face reflected despair. Michelle had made it clear the night he got drunk and raped her that their marriage was over. Then she discovered she was pregnant. Michelle informed Kenny that they would stay married until the baby's birth and the Navy covered her hospital expenses. Reluctantly, Kenny had moved out of the house.

Pam had been there, too, sitting on the floor near Ben,

looking sad, her coloring books untouched. She had covered her leg brace with the hem of her red dress. Ben wanted to get away from his father's pain, so he picked up a crayon and began filling in the page. Pam went over to Kenny and he lifted her onto his lap, continuing his leg-thumping while Pam laughed at the bumpy ride. Kenny held onto her waist as he leaned forward to blow bubbles on her cherubic neck. Pam's laugh had changed after their father moved out, no longer the whole body laugh Ben remembered.

The scrapping of Pam's brace as she climbed the seven steps to the day care entrance brought Ben back to the present. He waited at the top of the steps holding open one of the massive double doors and inhaled the scent of pine from daily mopping.

This Catholic day care was the best in Des Moines, costing their mother sixty dollars of her monthly $96.90 from Kenny. Though a dilettante Methodist, Michelle was one of a dozen mothers with a Methodist or Lutheran child at Sisters of Mercy.

Ben had spent a summer here. Pamela, as she was called by Sister Mary, had been here for a year. Pam would not have climbed those seven steps if not for the possibility that Sister Mary might be there to give her a welcoming hug and kiss. Pam certainly would not go through such pain just for Debi. If Pam had known Sister Mary was busy in her office, she would have gone straight to the ice cream store, saving herself five blocks of endless sidewalks, let alone those cursed fourteen steps to the door and down again, for nothing.

Ben thought of the place as a prison for kids. Every morning: Oatmeal. Oatmeal and toast and margarine. Then the empty bowl would be filled with warm milk and the marble-sized chunks of leftover cereal floated to the top. You had to finish your milk. Sometimes, some poor kid would vomit this disgusting breakfast back into his bowl, leaving it for all the other kids to see and smell.

The nuns' power came from silence. Just the pallid, scowling mouth bordered by ghostlike garb, gave all the kids the creeps. Debi called all the nuns nuts. Tiny as a three-year-old could be, Debi Smith was a mama's girl. She cried easily and often. She only spoke when forced to by fear. The Sisters of Mercy let her nap as long as she wanted. For that was the way to keep the whining and crying for her mother to a minimum.

Debi came running to Ben, seeing him as the vehicle to mommy. Debi's light brown hair, adorned with a pink barrette most days, seemed always matted and moist from her long naps. Friday, payday, was the one day Ben picked up Debi, while their mother did the grocery shopping after work.

The Smith kids were on their way to buy ice cream when a white taxi slowed beside the trio. Ernie, the cab driver, a little man with black, greased-back, short hair, leaned over and swung open his back passenger door. A non-filter cigarette hung from the corner of his mouth.

"C'mon kids, I'll give ya a lift!"

Pam got in first, dragging the steel brace through the door with the rattle of metal on metal. Ben helped Debi onto the seat, then got in and slammed the door.

"Mom said we could stop for ice cream," Pam said, smiling into Ernie's face in the rearview mirror.

"Ice cream!" Debi repeated excitedly.

Ernie cocked his head toward Ben to gauge if Pam's claim was true, which caused Ben to produce his crisp dollar bill.

"Let's get you kids some ice cream then, by golly," Ernie said, tossing his spent cigarette out his open window wing.

Ernie told the kids it was okay to eat their treat inside Road Dairy. He waited for them, finishing two more cigarettes and informing his dispatcher that he was on a fifteen minute break when a call came in for his cab.

Pam enjoyed her chocolate cone more, knowing she had a ride home. But Debi's tiny licks and dabs at her chocolate chip cone ticked Pam off. She despised Debi's ability to make a good thing last longer by having the willpower, at age three, to make it so. Making the differences between them even more pronounced-Debi was skinny and had her mother's hazel eyes.

"You have to eat faster, or I'll eat it myself," Pam threatened.

Debi's cone vanished.

A few minutes later, Ben watched Ernie drive away from their white, two-story apartment house. The cab turned the first corner and sped off to pickup the next fare. Pam and Debi waited at the top of the stairs for Ben to unlock the apartment door.

"Hi Ben," a shrill voice called from down the hall.

Ben waved to Marie, their seventy-five-year-old landlady, whose eighty-year-old Polish immigrant husband, Al, still worked as a handyman and maintained the building.

Ben opened the door into their small kitchen. Pam went right to the refrigerator.

"There's nothing in there! Mom's bringing groceries," Ben reminded her.

Pam found a jar of mayonnaise and, with a tablespoon, twice she filled her mouth with the white greasy spread. Ben turned away, filled with disgust.

The apartment's two bedrooms were small. Ben and Pam shared one room. Debi slept with Michelle in her slightly bigger room. One bathroom. A rather unique living room area was furnished with a maroon sofa and matching armchair with a blond coffee table and end table. There were no windows in this room. Michelle left the room when the kids fought, claiming she felt closed in and tense without air.

After his mother parked at the curb, Ben carried in the bags of groceries. Michelle undressed in her room with Debi at her heels, whining for her supper. Michelle had taken time to have her hair done at the beauty shop and Debi was even more demanding than usual.

"Mommy's going out," Michelle told Debi.

"Why does Grama Merle have to watch us?" Pam complained. "She drinks and smokes all the time."

Michelle wrapped her aqua robe around her naked body, not wanting to lose the day-long feeling of anticipation of her date with Dutch tonight. He had called her at work and said he'd be over at seven, telling her they would have dinner at Rancher's Steakhouse around 7:30.

After putting away the groceries, Michelle plopped hot dogs into a pan of boiling water, where they started to bloat. Cream-style corn heated on another burner. With supper underway, she ran her bath water, adding Debi's pink bubble bath, and opened a new package of nylons.

In the living room, Debi and Pam argued over who had to sleep with Grama Merle.

"Ben! Stir the corn please!" Michelle called. "And set the table for three! I'm not eating!"

Why can't Pam do those things, Ben thought.

He collected plates and glasses from the cupboard above the sink, pulled silverware from its drawer, and automatically set the table for four, before realizing his error.

Pam came into the kitchen without her brace, having stored it for the night under her twin bed in a boot box. She was careful to put the lid on the box so she wouldn't see it until needed.

The kids were bickering at the kitchen table as usual, when Michelle slipped into her hot, bath. She was thinking of better days in Wichita, Kansas. Just divorced, Michelle had been soaring with confidence as she took control of the

13

twin-engine aircraft from her instructor and coworker at Cessna. Sinking into the warm water, Michelle recalled the perfect freedom of soaring above the clouds.

Michelle's new boyfriend, Bob Booth, had been up to his waist in new oil strikes in Western Kansas and was the main reason Michelle took up flying. Booth, a handsome silver-haired man, a self-made millionaire, was thirty-three years older than Michelle. Floating in her bath water, her long legs elevated, touching the cool porcelain tiles with her toes, she thought of the hundred-dollar bills Booth would hand her to buy a new dress, a necklace, shoes with matching handbags, even toys and clothes for her children. She recalled all the nightclubs and fancy restaurants, where Wichita women flaunted their mens' wealth during an unprecedented era of new money and prosperity-the likes of which Wichita had never seen. Michelle had dolled-up in the prime of her youth and beauty and had it all. Attention was never more lavished upon her and her alone.

Three minutes of respite from the chaos at the kitchen table were gone. She could hear the kids arguing over portions of weenies and corn, and Ben yelling at Pam that dipping potato chips in mayonnaise was gross and sickening.

Pam had been swallowing fury with every bite of her meal. Her anger had been growing over the two days and nights since her father called to say he had remarried and soon would be stationed in Korea. Pam had looked at a world map in school and found Korea. So far away, she thought. She wished she could go with him. But that was impossible. Over her mother's dead body. Goading her brother gave her release.

Michelle rushed out of the bathroom in her robe, stomping-mad, toward the kitchen. Pam smirked at the trouble she expected for her brother. As the oldest, their mother always blamed Ben first, then sorted out who was the real culprit.

"Ben, you've eaten. I want the kitchen cleaned before Grama Merle gets here!"

"Pam has to help," Ben said.

"I don't feel so good, Mom," Pam whined.

Michelle felt Pam's forehead.

"You are a bit warm. Get into your pajamas and get under the covers in my bed," Michelle said.

Pam grinned at Ben, then dragged one more potato chip through the heap of mayo on her plate, cramming the whole thing into her mouth as she left the table.

"That's not fair! She's not sick. She's fakin' so she won't have to do dishes," Ben cried.

"Ben, do as I say!" Michelle said.

Michelle sat next to Debi and cut her weenie into tiny bite-size portions. It was just a matter of time before Debi threw her inevitable tantrum, so Michelle thought she might as well get it over with before Merle and Dutch arrived.

"Mommy's going out to dinner with a nice man," she said.

"No!" Debi denied.

"Yes, and Grama Merle is going to stay with you."

"No Mommy! No!"

Ben and Pam covered their ears when Debi's wailing took off sharply and stayed there for a good three minutes. Pam hightailed it onto her mother's bed. Ben started filling the sink with soapy dishwater, while Michelle sat unmoved beside Debi until the siren wore down to a tolerable cry.

"You want me to bring you a treat?" Michelle asked.

Debi nodded yes and the scene was over. Michelle took Debi by the hand into the front room where she sat her in the easy chair with her blanket and allowed her to suck her thumb.

Through the open kitchen window, Ben heard Grampa Dick, Michelle's father, bark something to his third wife outside on the sidewalk.

"Grama Merle's here," he announced.

"Turn on the porch light for her," Michelle said.

Grampa Dick drove away, not forcing his arthritic legs to attempt the Smith stairs.

Up the steps she bounded: 4'9" and ninety pounds, seventy-two years of piss and vinegar. Her steady hand, covered with lumpy purple blood vessels, frail skin clinging to bone, gripped the handrail with each upward step. Ben watched from the window with horror. This was no endearing granny, the kind you'd help across the street with an arm around her shoulders. Merle's black vinyl purse held a 1/2 pint of vodka and three packs of Viceroy 100s. A six-pack of Hamms was brown-bagged under her arm. Her black metal glasses rode oval cheeks smeared with vermillion rouge, as an undertaker might camouflage a customer. Her black hair streaked with shades of gray looked like a spider's web wound atop a skull meant to frighten the kids. Her one good quality: Grama Merle had an Irish laugh so contagious it must have kept her ugly parts from scattering everyone else in sight.

Ben opened the door for her at the last possible instant.

"Hello Ben."

Merle's chicken lips puckered. Ben closed his eyes just before contact, never failing to feel the wrinkled, cold facial skin sag against his cheeks during that quick peck.

Debi came into the kitchen with her thumb and blanket corner in her mouth. She took one look at Grama Merle and started wailing all over again. Michelle came in wearing high heels and a blue, mid-length, strapless dinner dress. Her breasts were tan and visibly firm behind the low-cut front of the dress. This would be her first all-night stay with Dutch on his farm. Michelle kissed Merle on her cheek, ignoring Debi's crying.

"Don't you look spiffy," Merle said.

Michelle smiled and said thank you before returning Debi to the living room, where she turned on the black and white TV set.

Merle stashed her beer in the fridge, then draped her sweater over a kitchen chair.

"Where's Pammy?" Merle asked Ben, who was washing dishes.

"In Mom's room."

Merle whispered to Ben, "Leave the dishes, I'll do 'em later." Then she headed into Michelle's room to check on Pam.

Ben removed his hands from the dishwater, wringing the yellow dishrag before hanging it over the faucet.

Pam lay on her side facing the bureau mirror. Merle's spindly, cold fingers tickled the bottom of her bare foot and brought a giggle and smile, then Merle bent down to kiss Pam's forehead.

"I don't feel good," Pam said.

"What's the matter with ya?"

"I don't know."

"Some hot chocolate sound good?"

Pam nodded yes, knowing Grama Merle made hot chocolate with both miniature marshmallows and whipped cream at her house.

"We don't have any marshmallows," Pam said.

Merle winked. "I brought some."

While Merle was busy in the kitchen, Pam watched her mother, who was standing before her dressing table mirror, touching White Shoulders behind each ear, on her neck and wrists.

"How do I look?"

"You look beautiful. You always do. How come you look so pretty and Daddy married someone else?"

"Oh, Pam, you should be happy your father found someone."

17

"Why can't I go with him?"

"We have talked about this a hundred times. I'm not going to discuss it now."

Michelle slipped on the mink stole Booth bought her in Wichita. Her gaze went from her image in the mirror to Pam, whose brown eyes widened at her mother's beauty. Merle, Ben, and even Debi gaped when she sought them out for approval.

As Merle skimmed the cocoa, craving a beer or a shot, a Viceroy burned in a black plastic ashtray on the kitchen table. She picked up the ashtray and carried it along with Pam's cocoa into Michelle's bedroom.

Ben's eyes were on the baby blue '57 T-bird pulling up to the curb.

"He's here."

Michelle came to the window and watched Dutch's lanky 6'3" frame climb from behind the wheel. He looked strong to Ben. Not as old as his fifty-two years, at this distance. The sound of his mother's quick feet back to her bedroom mirror told him this was a special man and no ordinary date.

Irving 'Dutch' Beal's shiny butterscotch boots, worn with brown slacks, matching jacket and a string tie, were about to mount the first step up the front stairs. Ben focussed on Beal's brown crewcut receding above a rugged face. The many lines cut deep under his eyes and into his jowls told of many hard years spent running his 600-acre farm northwest of Des Moines. Beal carried a brown bag in one hand. The powerful hand concealed the shape of the bag's contents. Ben opened the door before Dutch reached their landing.

"Hi there. You must be Ben."

Ben pushed his new glasses up his nose a bit and gave Dutch a courtesy smile.

"I hear you kids like ice cream."

Another smile. Dutch handed Ben the sack containing a 1/2 gallon of chocolate chip ice cream.

"Make sure you share that with yer sisters."

"I will."

Michelle came out of her room wearing her stole, smiling into her date's approving green eyes.

"Hi." Michelle smiled.

"Hello."

"He brought us ice cream," Ben said.

"I see that." Another smile at her date.

Merle came out of Michelle's room holding Pam's hand. Ben showed the ice cream to Pam. Dutch introduced himself and politely shook the old woman's bony hand.

Merle asked, "Want a beer?"

"Sounds better than ice cream. But I'd better pass." Dutch flashed cigar-stained teeth and Merle's cackling laugh filled the apartment.

Michelle feared Debi might scream her head off, now that her date was a reality, but the chocolate chip did the trick. Debi hung back, afraid of Dutch. However Pam's hungry eyes on the ice cream brought Debi into the kitchen for her share.

"Merle, there's aspirin in the medicine cabinet, if Pam's temperature goes up. Dutch's number is under the phone by the fridge, if you need to reach me."

"Oh, we'll be fine. Get out of here. Go have some fun for God's sake."

Michelle kissed the kids goodbye and was out the door with Dutch without another big scene-to Michelle's relief.

Merle poured herself a treat on ice, while the kids enjoyed their ice cream, each content for the moment on this spring night in the heartland.

The evening went well at Rancher's Steakhouse.

Drinks and dancing after prime rib. Scotch and water for Michelle. Bourbon shots for Dutch. Three rounds, he figured. The huge dining room was packed. Dutch was greeted respectfully by several farmers and middle-aged men who ran agriculture-related businesses. "Hello Dutch! How are ya?" "Hi Dutch. Haven't seen you in a long time. Gotch yer corn in the ground?"

Back at their tables their curious wives asked about Dutch Beal, and the beautiful, young woman with him. "Is that his wife? She must be half his age."

The men answered pretty much the same. "Don't know. He's one hard workin' man. Gets his corn planted early."

After three and a half hours as the most-watched couple in Rancher's, it was time to leave. In the parking lot Dutch glowered at an old, white pickup in the process of parking too close to his prized T-bird. As if in slow-motion, Michelle saw the driver open his door and ram it into the T-bird's front passenger door. Dutch's face reddened to bloody mad. The truck's driver was drunk, stumbling toward the steakhouse entrance. Dutch ran his rough hand over the blemished door, feeling the metal under the paint. Beal's voice cut through the silent parking lot.

"Yer gonna fix this door."

"It's just a scratch, Beal!" the man bawled, removing his cowboy hat to smile at the woman in mink, who released her arm from Dutch's when she felt him tense and move forward. In moments Dutch had the man's head in both hands, bouncing the man's nose and forehead on the pavement. Michelle's scream for Dutch to stop was the only thing that saved the drunk's life, now lying motionless, gurgling air from his bloodied nose. Dutch picked up the man's hat and jammed it onto the pickup's radio antenna, where it sat like a severed head on a medieval pike.

A few blocks out of the steakhouse parking lot, as

Michelle began to breathe normally, the blue veins of anger were still pulsating on Dutch's temple.

"I hope you didn't kill him."

"He's an asshole with no sense."

"You know him?"

"He owns a junk yard in Ames with his old man-who's just as dumb as he is."

Michelle sat quietly, thinking about Dutch's temper, and the strength it wielded. She was not afraid of him. She felt protected and safe knowing he could handle himself if trouble came.

Flat and winding on Highway 17, the drive north at 75 mph in the quiet T-bird led to a paved turnoff headed toward the Beal Farm. Then out of nowhere, surrounded by miles and miles of level ground, darkness like a void of nature loomed in the background where Dutch turned onto a narrow gravel road. Michelle wanted to ask what the darkness concealed, but now they were headed away. She felt as if they'd turned just in time to avoid some hellish abyss. Surely, she thought, it could be explained during the day. Besides, she had a headache from the incident at Rancher's mixed with all the Scotch she had consumed.

Dutch flipped on his high-beams and pointed to a grove of tall trees ahead on the left, where a lone light bulb glowed in the central farmyard. The light cast a silver, shadowy solitude upon a group of farm buildings and the large, two-story farmhouse. Michelle thought it odd that no lights were on inside the house, not even the front porch light. She shifted her mink over her shoulders, for the April rains sat 12 to 14 inches in the ditches bordering the gravel road, wafting a cool fog onto the T-bird's glass.

Michelle dipped her nose onto her stole's right shoulder to smell the cigar and cigarette smoke from Rancher's. The absence of cigar smoke in the car impressed her. This was a man who could take care of beautiful things and himself, she thought. He turned onto a dirt road that fringed the massive yard, neatly spaced with pine and oak trees. About forty yards away, was a white-graveled road that looped in a circular drive before the darkened front porch.

The dirt service road turned right at the cattle yard and barn, opening to the large central farmyard where that lone bulb burned atop a telephone pole standing in the middle. On the left was a three-stall garage with a fifteen-foot ceiling for tractor and combine repairs. To the left of that, a storage shed housed two Farmall tractors. On the other side of the hog yard, an empty chicken coop stood farther back, behind a 200-gallon elevated gas tank. Rounding the corner they passed a feed house and propane tank. Ahead, the white farmhouse appeared dull gray in the pale glow of its back porch light.

A massive, red collie/retriever mix wagged its tail in the T-bird's headlights, prancing back and forth in greeting. When Dutch shut off the engine, the quiet was deafening: too early for insects, too late for birds and animals. It was the lonely time of year for a bachelor farmer.

Dutch turned to Michelle. "I was married twenty-six years ago. My wife left after eight years. No children. No love lost," he said wryly. "The solitude and weather got to her. She left for California, no cows there, but plenty of people." He laughed. Michelle smiled.

The dog cowered lovingly at his master's boots as Michelle stepped onto the wet ground, driving her heels into it, forcing her to walk on her toes. When the dog started over toward Michelle, Dutch said, "Duke." The dog turned back.

"His name's Duke?"

"Go lay down!" Dutch ordered the dog.

Duke sulked toward the back porch. When he reached the brick patio he circled twice before lying down, eyes

22

steady on Dutch and his guest. Michelle followed Dutch to the porch, dodging mud puddles dug by Dutch's over boots as he strode to and from his morning and evening chores. The smell of cow and pig shit and silage was so heavy that she breathed through her mouth until she reached the red brick. There, Michelle scraped away wedges of mud clinging to her high heels at the edge of the patio. A tipsy laugh came out of her as Dutch unlocked the porch door.

Dutch flicked on the overhead light inside the porch. Michelle slipped out of her heels, staying on her toes on the cold, olive green linoleum. Dutch proudly opened his new freezer's door, showing his guest the white, locker-wrapped cuts: ground, chops, T-bone, sausage and bacon, and roast beef. This display of frozen meat showed her he could feed an army-or perhaps her kids.

Past a curtained, glass-topped door was more cold linoleum. Dutch turned on another overhead light that revealed a spacious, high-ceiling kitchen, all white: the floor, the walls, the lace curtains, the sink, stove, countertops, and refrigerator. The kitchen table was chrome-legged, its surface covered with a faded, checkered red and white cloth. It stood near the windows that looked out to the west service road on which they entered the farm. The other window faced out to the central farmyard and that lonely light. A wall telephone was mounted five feet high, with a thin Boone telephone directory wedged behind it.

"This is nice," Michelle said, then added, "You know, I could fit my entire apartment in this kitchen."

Dutch lit a tipped cigar from his shirt pocket. Smoke drifted over his glossy-green eyes, eyes creased with wrinkles from ten thousand man hours of sun, wind, snow, hail, and everything in-between. He had been with women over the years since his divorce, but only a select few had been brought here. Michelle was the best of his possibilities. And more stunningly beautiful than any woman he ever hoped to court.

"Bathroom's in there," Dutch said. "Kinda small for this big ole house."

Dutch led Michelle into the large living room, passing over the home's only heat source, a grated floor furnace the size of a card table. He turned on light switches as if he were opening a museum to view a painting just for a few minutes. Michelle took off her stole and carried it over her arm to the center of the room.

"The paneling looks like antique walnut," she said.

"My granddad put that in years ago," Dutch said, flicking his cigar's ash onto his palm.

"How old is this house?"

"About a hundred and ten years old. The foundation was laid in 1850, ten years before the Civil War."

Michelle saved her comments about the furniture, notably the two plum-colored sofas on faded beige carpeting, the two blond coffee tables and one corner table. A 30" Zenith black and white television in a brown case crouched catty-corner below a west window. This was the only window downstairs from which you could see traffic on the distant paved road. The curtains were a dull, dark brown. Much too dark and not a match for anything in here, Michelle thought, smiling at Dutch, now tagged as a typical bachelor as he stood near his favorite chair, a black vinyl recliner.

Behind him were sliding oak doors open to the master bedroom. Dutch turned on a lamp in the bedroom to show Michelle his antique roll-top desk.

"That's beautiful." She draped her mink over the back of the desk's castered chair.

"I do all my book work here."

Her body followed her eyes over to the double bed covered by a jade-colored comforter. She sat on the edge of the bed and yawned behind her hand.

"Tired?" he asked.

24

"I'll be alright-if I can get out of these clothes and into something more comfortable.

Dutch was happy to open his cedar closet exhibiting his robe hanging from a peg. It was thick, royal blue cotton. She hooked it over her index finger and carried it hanging behind her back on her way to the bathroom. She left Dutch a seductive smile and hope for the future.

Ben stared at the crack of light under his bedroom door. Debi had wanted the hallway light left on while she slept in her mother's bed. As soon as Ben opened his door he could hear the loud snoring of Grama Merle. Wearing only white briefs, and without the aid of his new glasses, Ben walked into his mother's darkened room, passing the ugly, agape mouth that Merle turned up to the ceiling. Her mouth became a chasm of flabby, wrinkled skin while her dentures soaked in a plastic container on the night stand beside her overflowing ashtray.

Debi lay tucked against Merle, her back to her, in deep sleep after an entire day of worry. Pam's face looked hot, but not seriously so. Ben gently placed the back of his hand on his sister's hot forehead. Her brown eyes fluttered, her dry lips pursed for water.

The refrigerator light made visible the telephone and Dutch's phone number on the wide-ruled page of notebook paper. Ben wet a washcloth at the sink, then put two ice cubes into the cloth before dropping two more cubes into a glass of tap water. He hurried back to Pam's bedside. This act of service to a family member in need gave Ben a sense of satisfaction, like being grown up. He pressed the cold cloth to her bangs; her pug nostrils flared from the chill. He lifted her head slightly and gingerly poured the cool water onto her chapped lips and they parted. As she gulped each swallow, Pam's fevered mind unreeled an eleven-second dream.

Little Pammy sat next to her daddy on the front seat of his red convertible. He lowered the top after they parked at the lake facing the water. Here, he removed his wedding band from his left hand and placed it onto Pam's small palm, squeezing her hand shut and covering it with his, then kissing the top of her head.

It was a dream. Not a memory. Fragments of life. A collage of things assembled by a mind stuck at 102 degrees. Awake and well, she never remembered it-her brain's way of protecting her.

Ben dabbed Pam's cheeks and neck with the ever-colder washcloth. He knelt beside her to hold the cloth on her forehead after putting the water glass on the night stand. Above Merle's snoring, Pam mumbled something that included the word Mom.

"Mom'll be home soon," he whispered real close to her ear. "In the morning. Another sip of water?"

Pam nodded yes. After another sip, he said, "You sleep now. Sleep."

They lay under the comforter, asleep an hour after making love, when the first ring from Dutch's phone woke Michelle. She thought of her kids. Dutch, naked-white, got out of bed and headed for the kitchen. Michelle counted four rings before she heard Dutch's hello. Again, another hello, then his returning footsteps.

"Wrong number. Nobody there," Dutch said.

"If it rings again, I'll answer it," Michelle offered.

"Okay."

Dutch went back to sleep fast. Michelle curled up, closed her eyes and waited for the phone to ring, worrying. I shouldn't have gone out when Pam had a fever, she thought. Maybe Ben or Pam is afraid to talk to Dutch. Or it could be the guy Dutch clobbered at Rancher's. No, if it were the kids, Merle would call.

No more calls. Michelle slept.

When Michelle entered her apartment at nine the next morning she had already been up for four hours. Merle sat smoking a cigarette with her morning coffee. The kids were still asleep.

"That Dutch is a catch!" Merle blurted.

Michelle smiled.

"He's a real gentleman too!" Merle added.

"Kids okay?" Michelle inquired.

"Oh sure. Everything's just fine and dandy! You want me to make you some breakfast Michelle?"

Michelle joined Merle at the table. "I made breakfast at five this morning," she said.

"That's a farmer for ya," Merle cackled. "Has to get the chores done. Does he have a nice place?"

"Yes, it's quite a big farm. The house is real nice."

Michelle wanted to get away from Merle's cigarette smoke. "I'll check on Pam," she said and went into her room.

Merle gave Grampa Dick a quick call: "Come get me," she demanded, then hung up the phone.

Michelle stroked her hand down her daughter's cheek, smiling into Pam's sleepy eyes.

"Your fever's down. How do you feel?"

"Okay."

"You feel good enough to go see a movie?"

"Will you go with us Mom?"

"I have to do some things for Grampa Hutch."

Pam turned her head away, hiding her aversion to Hutch. Michelle kissed her eldest girl on the nose, then covered sleeping Debi up to her chin with bedding.

Considering she only had four hours of sleep, Michelle felt excited and energized, and satisfied, having been with a sure-enough man and serving him breakfast before sunrise. She had watched him tramp out in work overalls after sitting together over coffee, bacon, eggs, and fried potatoes. He especially liked the way she seasoned the potatoes with lots of pepper, and that she pressed off the bacon grease with a paper towel. He'd wrapped his work-hardened arms around her from behind and said he liked seeing her standing in his robe and thick wool socks at the stove.

He'd known she was at the window watching him walk across the farmyard as Duke led the way. Any man who had lived alone for so long, accustomed to the eyes of animals watching him, would turn to her gaze. He knew, also, that last night and this morning were tests for him to pass. When he had passed-if he passed-the children would come. Michelle was Dutch Beal's chance to roll back the clock. Just keep passing those tests, he told himself. He turned and touched the brim of his hat.

The muffler's obnoxious clatter announced the Smith Family's departure an hour after Grama Merle left with the twenty bucks Dutch had paid for baby-sitting. Ben liked to sit on the back seat so he could duck down, or lie on his side when they drove past his school in sight of peers. God forbid, if his mother should drive past the downtown Kresges, where all the older kids hung out on Saturday mornings to buy the latest 45 records: Elvis, Fabian, Frankie Avalon and Paul Anka. Ben would plead with his mother to take another route and, when she ignored him, would end up on the back seat with his face buried in shame between his knees.

Ben's blond head turned red at least once a week, riding in his mother's rusting 2-door with its farting muffler that grew louder with time and with the angle of the road's incline.

Their first stop was four blocks away at Edith's place. The short drive over to her mother's gray, two-story house on the corner was nerve-wracking for Michelle. She chewed on her lip and said to herself over and over: Keep calm and do not argue with her.

Michelle had been adopted at age twelve, after Edith abandoned her at the Boys and Girls Home. Edith had married seven times that her daughter knew about. Michelle's kids had heard the story at least a dozen times. Usually after a visit like this.

Pam was the only one glad to be at her grandmother's house. Michelle squashed her right front wheel high onto the curb. Ben made the mistake of laughing out loud. "Nice driving Mom," he said.

"Shut up, Ben," Michelle said, clenching her teeth and ready to swat him if he didn't wipe the grin off his face.

Pam was in high spirits, over her fever and braceless. Edith, a physical therapist, insisted that the brace on Pam's leg crippled her mind, and limited her use of the remaining muscle. Pam's leg felt like a feather compared to when she wore that contraption. Yesterday's long walk was still bothering her.

Michelle scooped Debi off the front seat and carried her to the sidewalk as Ben exited the car on Pam's side, wanting to ask his sister something. "Do we call her Grama Edith, Grama or what? I never know what to say."

"Play it smart. Don't say anything," Pam advised.

Ben and Pam followed their mother up to Edith's white-painted front porch. Michelle rang the doorbell, resolving to get along with her despotic mother.

Edith opened her front door wearing her gray/black hair pinned back in a bun, not a hair out of place.

"Wipe your feet good," Edith greeted them.

"Hello," Michelle said. "You're baking bread."

Edith never responded to what she called stupid questions or obnoxious small-talk. She had no time or patience for her daughter's senseless banter. "Take Benjamin and

Deborah into the kitchen for bread and milk."

"Come," Edith said to Pam.

Pam lumbered down the basement stairs following Edith. The gray cement of the basement floor and the air were comfortable because Edith willed it so. She had rigged a damper to divert her oven's heat when she worked downstairs. A black leather massage table was covered by a bleach-scented white sheet, tucked-in as tight as the grip of Edith's muscular hands.

Pam tugged the knee-high sock off her left leg and lay on her stomach on the table. Edith uncovered a steaming pot and tonged-out a wet towel. She let the hot water drip, then wrung it out before shaking it forcefully once and applying it to Pam's leg. Pam winced.

"Too hot?"

"No."

Edith wrapped the towel tight lengthwise, knee to toe. As steam rose into her face, she kneaded her granddaughter's leg with the same fierceness she used on her rye bread.

"Extend your heel slowly back and forth. That's it. Now hold it for a few seconds after you've stretched as far as you can."

Edith massaged the hot towel deep into Pam's flesh, nearly bruising against the bone with her strong, Quaker hands. Pam flinched.

"Grama, that hurts."

No compassion whatsoever would come from this woman. "You must sustain the stretch Pamela. Hold it!"

Tears fell from Pam's eyes onto the stiff white sheet.

"Stretch it. More! Hold it. More!"

Debi sat on her mother's lap with Ben seated across from them at Edith's kitchen table. All were chewing Edith's oven-warm, sweet, rye bread. They ate quietly, looking around at the iron order Edith created on and with-

walls. Every inch she herself had planed, painted, papered, plastered, sawed, spackled, shingled, hammered, carpeted, wired, plumbed and upholstered.

"Good, huh?" Michelle declared.

Debi and Ben nodded in agreement. Michelle got up to pour herself another cup of coffee, but decided not to upon hearing Edith's footsteps coming up the basement stairs.

While Edith scrubbed her hands at her kitchen sink she quizzed Michelle about her new boyfriend.

"His name's Dutch," Michelle said.

Edith gave Michelle a look that demanded his real name and some finer details.

"Irving Beal. Dutch is his nickname. He has a farm about thirty miles north of Des Moines near Boone."

"Beal. Beal," Edith repeated, thinking of how she knew that name.

"He has a nice home," Michelle said.

"Oh, you've been there?"

"Last night. For the first time."

"I'll bet you did," Edith said.

Michelle would have laughed if anyone else had said it. Ben knew what Edith implied, but quietly chewed his rye bread and accepted Edith's offer of a glass of milk. Just then, Pam came into the kitchen, sore in her leg and wary of her grandmother's tongue. Edith's hazel eyes, slitted and critical, were on Pam's bad leg.

"Pamela. Don't drag it like a club. Lift. Lift!" she said.

Pam joined her siblings, helping herself to two thick slices before the bread was gone.

"How old is this guy?" Edith inquired.

"Fifty-two."

"An older man. I'd like to meet this Dutch," Edith said.

"Why?"

Michelle had sworn never to argue with Edith in front of the kids because it produced nothing but a headache, never a resolution. So Michelle pulled back, mentioning Dutch's arm bothered him and maybe Edith could work on it.

Edith's front screen door smacked shut on tight hinges behind the Smiths. On their way to their next stop, Pam played with her mom's enmity toward Edith.

"Mom, you and Grama Edith should forgive each other."

From the back seat, Ben rolled his eyes and stared at the back of Pam's head, knowing his sister was being wicked, punishing their mother because of their next stop. The seven-minute drive downtown was not pleasant. It began with Michelle's reply.

"What are you talking about? Forgive. You have no idea what that woman did. She gave me up, put me in the Boys and Girls Home when I was just about your age. How would you like something like that? She did some evil things I can't forgive. I wore hand-me-downs with holes in my shoes while my sister had the best of everything. You kids have no idea."

As if this tirade wasn't bad enough with all the windows rolled up, little Debi started wailing and rocking on the front seat. The muffler, Debi, Michelle's unresolved anger-all mixed together inside the car's space like a venom.

His mother wasn't finished. Ben knew if she kept-on, she'd be a little calmer in the long run. And Debi wouldn't bawl her eyes out for near as long, afraid of the dark in the Des Moines Theater, if she cried now. Michelle caught his expression in her rearview mirror.

"What's so funny Benjamin Smith?"

"Nothing, Mom."

Pam fell silent as they neared the familiar downtown

parking space in The Corner Tap's lot across the street from the Hill Hotel. As soon as the engine was off, Pam asked if they could go on to the movies now. Michelle answered no into the rearview mirror that she had angled to her face while she slid on some red lipstick and circled a little coral rouge onto her cheeks.

"Grampa Hutch wants to see you kids."

"He can't see anything," Pam protested.

"You know what I mean. Besides, he's going to treat us all to lunch and treat you kids to the movies."

"Can't we wait in the bar, Mom, please," Pam begged.

"No."

Michelle took Debi's hand, then after a few steps picked her up and carried her on her hip, careful to not wrinkle her blouse and skirt. Michelle's shoulder purse swung awkwardly.

"Carry my purse, Ben."

"Have Pam carry it."

"Oh, never mind, then."

His mother's tone made him feel so guilty he wished he had just taken the purse and slipped it over Pam's head, as they crossed the street at the corner and made their way on the sidewalk to The Hill, an unmarked three-story building crammed between an office block and a mens' clothing store. The Hill was the scene of Pam's worst nightmare, a secret she hid from her distracted mother.

Last December, a few days before Christmas, her mother had left her and Ben with Hutch while she took Debi shopping for their Christmas presents. A single light bulb had glared from the middle of the room's 12-foot ceiling. The door to Hutch's room was always open, unless he was asleep, or out. Sixty-five-year-old, silver-haired Hutch had been sitting on a cushioned straight-back, wooden chair. One skinny thigh, in spotless gray slacks, was crossed over the other while he dialed the black rotary phone resting on his chipped walnut bureau.

Pam sat on a mushy cushion on a wide olive green armchair, sandwiched with Ben, behind them, an alley window with a view of cinnamon/black bricks and shadows seen through the dust-caked blades of a window fan. The window was closed, trapping the pungent pine disinfectant odor that always rode the air of Hill Hotel.

Hutch's room was located at the end of a long, dark hallway. The dirty carpet runner down the middle of the hall passed a dozen unmarked walnut doors that were most-always closed. Behind a few of the doors hookers served clients for fifty bucks, while Nels, a balding middle-aged bulldog, kept watch from the open door of the first room at the top of the stairs.

Nels called the clients and let them know Daisy, Penny, Alice or Micki were in for a few days, then on the way to Omaha, Denver, Kansas City, Chicago, or Minneapolis. Most of the clients were farmers and small businessmen in and around Des Moines, ranging from forty-five to sixty years old. Most never missed a Sunday in church with the Mrs. His bills were paid, his yard clean, his kids doing well on their own. Then one day he'd go to get his car waxed, or tuned-up, or something. Only he'd end up climbing the two dark and narrow flights, where, at the top and around a left turn on creaking oak floors, Nels would see him and push a buzzer to one of four rooms. A prostitute in a see-through nightie, a sheer kimono, or stretch pants with skimpy halter top, her hair artful, her makeup plentiful, greeted the man in the hall.

Hutch was the only full-time resident of the Hill. If he wasn't in, his door was locked, the skeleton key placed in his dress shirt pocket-the only key he kept on his person.

Ben and Pam sat in the chair marveling at how a blind man could dial the telephone by finger-hole counting so patiently. Hutch made call after call to his bar supply customers, retaining the detailed orders in his memory until transmitted by phone to the supplier.

"Hello, Teddy."

Anyone who ever heard Hutch's powerful, confident voice knew it forever-a voice mixed with keen intellect and caustic wit. His voice was his most valuable tool, besides those sky blue, sightless eyes that blazed any hour, day or night.

"My grandkids are visiting. Michelle's kids. Anything for me today?" Hutch barked.

Ben and Pam could hear the bar owner's voice bouncing off Hutch's elephant ear, naming the items he needed: two cases of stir stix, one case of plain white cocktail napkins, a dozen urinal blocks for the men's john.

"How are you fixed on tissue paper? Towels? Bowl and glass cleaner?" He always suggested things and usually got a few added to the original order.

"Thank you, sir. Goodbye."

Hutch's index finger would find the flashhook cradle, while he took just a moment to remember the order just taken before phoning another bar, the same two-dozen in downtown Des Moines that were his steady accounts.

His next call threw Pam off, leaving her anxious and with a sudden attack of gas.

"Mr. Morey. Yes," Hutch laughed, sounding like the devil himself to Pam, as she watched him stroke his free right hand with its long, slender fingers cupping his knee.

"I'm sending my grandson down. Pick out a dress shirt and a nice pair of slacks for him. Thanks, Morey," he said softly. Pam's leg started to ache under her brace. Her heart pumped fear. She stood up with Ben, when Hutch got up and walked with his hands raised to his dresser, where he found his billfold, felt for a hundred-dollar bill and handed it to her brother.

"Pam, will you stay here and help me with a few

things?"

Ben left the room so fast she didn't have a chance to pull him aside and beg him to stay.

Hutch was no blood relation. One of Edith's husbands. Pam recalled overhearing one of her mother's conversations. Hutch chased anything in a skirt, she'd said. Edith had booted him out of their house, divorced him, then, when he lost his sight to glaucoma, for fifty dollars a week over six months, she turned him into a self-supporting blind man. She taught him to walk using a cane, how to distinguish money, memory tricks, even little things like flicking his cigarette into an ashtray to prevent a fire, and cleaning his electric razor-all in the dark.

Without Ben's presence, Hutch stood with his white dress shirt open at the neck. Pam watched him walk over to his bed and sit on its side. He removed his black, shiny dress shoes and placed them in a shoe rack in the neat little closet across from him. The black rayon socks stretched up to his knees would have been hilarious if Ben or Mother had been there. He removed his slacks and shirt, then stood in his white boxers at the closet, returning his clothes to their proper hangers.

Hutch sat Indian-fashion at the head of his bed in his white, sleeveless T-shirt, boxers and socks and lit a cigarette from his night stand .

"Want a butterscotch sundae, Pammy?"

"Okay," she said, detesting being called Pammy.

Before she could get to the sweet syrup at the bottom of the sundae cup, Hutch had left the bed and felt his way over to her breasts and up her thigh under her red dress. She could not speak, only stare into those sightless blue eyes above flabby jowls gone slack, his lips wet and slightly apart.

"Grampa, No!"

She managed to stand on the chair cushion and lean

36

back out of his reach. Most likely, the messy butterscotch syrup that dropped onto his thin sock saved her.

When Ben returned, smiling, wearing his new outfit, Hutch was sitting on his bed smoking a cigarette, listening to the weather report from his bedside radio.

"Where's Pam?" Ben asked.

"Pouting in the ladies room...with no date for the ball," Hutch said, then laughed.

Ben saw the spilled butterscotch swirled in melted ice cream at the base of the chair.

"I'll go show her my new clothes."

"Just a minute, my boy."

Hutch butted his cigarette, then made his way to his dresser. He felt for the right amount in his wallet and handed a fifty-dollar bill to Ben. "Give this to Pammy."

Ben was envious; he would rather have fifty bucks for Christmas anytime instead of clothes. Excited to thrill Pam, Ben headed for the restroom around the corner from Hutch's room. Inside, he saw Pam's feet beneath the locked door of one of the wooden stalls.

"Pam!"

"What?"

"I've got a big surprise for you."

Ben slid the fifty, with Grant's face up, part way under the stall door, then pulled it back, teasing her. The door opened. His sister had been crying, but Ben was thinking about spending the money and didn't bother to ask her why she was so upset about spilling her ice cream on the floor.

"You know all the stuff we can get at the movies with this? If you tell Mom, she'll want to spend it on dumb stuff," Ben advised.

She wiped her eyes and sniffed hard. Ben handed the fifty to her.

"It's yours. Hutch gave it to you for Christmas.

Pam looked at the stiff bill carefully.

"Okay. But what if Hutch tells Mom he gave me this much?" Pam asked.

"By that time we at least get to splurge at the movies," Ben said.

"Yeah. Okay," Pam agreed.

She started to put the bill under the bodice of her dress, suddenly cringing from the image of the money touching her skin there-the same place those cold, boney fingers had been groping. Before Ben arrived she spent a good deal of time rubbing wet paper towels on her chest and thighs. Ben watched her stuff the fifty along the inside part of her leg brace below her knee where the leather strap had a slit just long enough to conceal it.

She never told her mother about Hutch; her mother needed the money he gave them and didn't need to know why. She had enough worries.

Now, standing at the bottom of the Hill's stairs, the familiar ache in her left leg seemed to intensify. Pam looked up and saw Hutch's white-tipped mahogany cane cradled on his gray suit sleeve like a candy cane as his sure feet descended the stairs, with Ernie, the cab driver, trailing.

"Hi, Michelle!" Ernie said, his voice amplified in the stairwell.

"Hi, Ernie. Who's that handsome man in the snazzy suit?" Michelle smiled, her tribe behind her against the glass door.

Hutch was grinning, his tongue visibly counting the steps as he negotiated them. He always seemed elated when Michelle visited him. He was proud to have her lead him into his customers' bars and to introduce her as his daughter. The charade made Pam sick to her stomach.

On the sidewalk, Ernie said, "See ya later, Hutch!" Then Ernie was off in his cab, running errands for the blind man.

Hutch and Michelle decided on lunch at The Corner

Tap.

"Ben, why don't you lead Grampa Hutch," Michelle suggested. She helped Hutch's right hand find Ben's shoulder; his other hand held his cane. Pam imagined Ben leading Hutch into an open manhole, or sidewalk freight elevator; a smile played at her lips.

Pam wanted to lead him around the block just once—during rush-hour.

The bartender at The Corner Tap placed an order with Hutch every other Saturday, though he didn't particularly like the blind salesman. Hutch was a man who took advantage of his loss and used the sympathy of others against them.

"Hi ya," the bartender said.

"Hello, Tommy."

"I need a few things."

Michelle and company took up nearly half the barstools, except for the one occupied by the lone regular slouched over his draught.

Hutch was ready, his attention focused, as Tommy recited his six-item list: stir stix, plain napkins, bowl and glass cleaner, concentrated floor soap and urinal cakes. Edith had taught him a memory technique that mixed humor with the bizarre. So now, Hutch imagined Edith standing naked atop The Corner Tap's roof, one foot in bowl cleaner, the other in glass cleaner, juggling urinal cakes, and sipping through a hollow stir-stik from a gallon jug of floor soap placed on a white cocktail napkin.

With the list lodged securely in his memory, Hutch introduced Michelle. "You've met my daughter, Michelle," Hutch said, hooking his cane on the lip of the bar to the right of his barstool.

"You bet. Hi Michelle."

"Hi, Tommy."

"What'll ya have, Hutch?"

Hutch stroked his chin lightly with his thumb, an unlit cigarette between his fingers.

"Johnny Walker straight up, with a side water."

Michelle ordered a C C and water, no ice, along with four loose meats, chips, and Cokes for the kids. While her mother ordered their food, Pam watched Hutch's hand stroke her mother's nyloned leg. Michelle made no effort to remove it.

"He's touching her," Pam whispered to Ben.

Ben leaned back, but couldn't see. Then he got his mother's attention, shifting his eyes over to the pool table.

"Ben wants to play pool," Michelle told Hutch.

But the food came and the Cokes were refilled.

In the dark theater's balcony, Pam wanted to tell her brother what Hutch had done to her last Christmas. But what could Ben do about it, she wondered, besides telling their mother?

Pam, oblivious to the dull movie, was seeing a better movie in her mind. She had called her daddy in Omaha, told him what Hutch did, and watched her daddy's reaction from her balcony seat, as Debi sucked on Good 'n Plenties next to her.

Her father stood at Hutch's locked door, reaching above the door, feeling around until he found a spare key on the ledge. Inside Hutch's room he found a small, rectangular, metal can on the dresser, picked it up and filled the bedside ashtray with lighter fluid.

Hutch wore his boxers and sleeveless T-shirt, his legs crossed under his pot belly, sitting at the head of his bed after washing down a shot of bourbon with a glass of water. Pam sat on her daddy's lap in the same ugly green chair where Hutch had felt her up the first time. Father and daughter smiled at each other as they watched Hutch reach for a cigarette and his lighter-the beginning of the climax.

Pam added new characters to her movie. Dutch was exiting one of the hookers' rooms, zipping up his pants-witnessed by her mother lingering in the hall-just as Hutch flicked-on his lighter, its flame moving in slow motion toward the tip of the cigarette between the blind man's lips. Ever so slowly they watched Hutch's right hand with the lit cigarette on its way to the ashtray. Hutch's slender fingers were blue and yellow torches for a few seconds, until his sense of pain blasted him out of bed. He burst from his room and ran down the dark hallway with his right hand ablaze, screaming, headed toward Michelle and Dutch's wide-eyed gape.

Pam laughed. Ben and Debi turned toward her.

"Shut up," Ben said.

Pam played the ending over and over, speeding up Hutch's flaming exit, adding shots of Hutch tumbling down the long Hill stairway and howling from his blazing hand.

On May Day, after spending her fourth overnight at the Beal Farm, Michelle dropped a bombshell on the kids. She told them that Dutch had invited them out to see his farm. They would all spend the night after having a picnic in the park next Saturday. Ben and Pam appeared happy, mainly because their mother was excited telling them how it would be a fun outing for them all.

Later that day, Doris Day filled the apartment with "Que Sera, Sera." Michelle sang along as she did her spring house cleaning with such romantic energy she didn't even ask the kids to help her. Pam had gone into her bedroom to think what this would mean to her and her daddy. She saw her life slipping farther away from the man she truly adored, the sailor in dress whites Debi called Popeye, the prince Pam imagined would rescue her from Hutch, from mean kids at school, and from any man who could take her mother far away to some farm and a stupid picnic.

Outside, Ben walked the patched sidewalks, circling the block counter clockwise. Dogwoods were blooming in front of a corner house on his first turn. The dirty city snow had soaked into the wet, black soil after a moderate winter. Green buds were showing on the stark, forked Elm trees that lined his path. Ben failed to notice.

Something else was on his mind. It was a feeling, an imbalance between rage and love: this love/hate a son feels for his mother when he is the man of the house, yet needs and wants so much to be protected and directed by her. Ben sneezed from the spring pollen several times before going home.

The next day in school, Ben felt too hot sitting near the steam radiator a few feet from his desk. On the way to school that morning, his legs had wobbled and felt weak under him. During the second hour in class his teacher tapped his shoulder to wake him up. Any other boy, she might have smacked his desktop with a ruler. Not Ben. He was Mrs. Kruger's pet and all the kids knew it. Besides Michelle, Mrs. Kruger was the only other person who didn't fault him for being a lefty.

During lunch Ben sat half-asleep with his head down on the table while Pam polished off his bowl of chili.

Ben felt chilled, then hot, and then hotter; his legs were on fire and aching against his jeans as he walked the dirty sidewalk stretched out before him. After lunch period, Mrs. Kruger had stopped him at her classroom door and told him to go home and get some rest.

His knees were buckling and his feet stumbling over the slightest crack in the sidewalk. His glasses were in the cowhide carrying case inside his shirt pocket. His pale blue eyes stared straight into the sun-two blinding moments melded in time, taking him back to a bleached-white summer street in a middle-class residential neighborhood in Wichita, Kansas, nearly four years earlier.

Kenny and Michelle had just divorced. Divorce was a rare and horrible word that meant his father was gone. At a ravine, neighborhood boys his age and older, were swinging perilously back and forth from a creaking rope tied to a tree limb high above them. The swing took them far out into a dark patch of shade a dangerous distance from the ground. All the boys were shrieking with glee as they left the bank, some barefoot, all brave, all with fathers at home.

A paralyzing fear kept Ben from trying the swing. He could not push through his fear and make himself do it. The other boys called him chicken and scaredy cat. Anger at his cowardice caused him to turn against himself.

The memory sent Ben spinning to the ground in front of their apartment house, in Al and Marie's yard. He lay exhausted on green grass, warm from a wind blowing from the south.

Murmuring in a fever sleep, too weak to make it up the steps and onto his bed, he curled his knees up to his chin. The breeze blew onto a hot strip of his lower back where his shirt had shifted from beneath his belted pants, causing him to shiver in the sun. His parched mouth kept asking, "Mom, where are you?"

Pam found her brother on the grass and got Al and Marie to help carry him upstairs, dress him in his pajamas, then cover him with his sheet and wool blanket.

Michelle took his temperature when she arrived home from work. 103 degrees. She sponged him with cool water, ignoring his fevered protests.

"Ben's real sick," Debi said, beginning to cry.

"He'll be better in the morning," Pam consoled her. "God will make him better."

While Michelle fought her son's fever, Pam recited the Lord's Prayer many times over, not just for her brother, before falling asleep beside Debi in her mother's bed.

43

The Spanking

Saturday morning. Dutch parked his T-bird outside the Smith apartment house just as they were all filing down the front stairs. Ben led the way, his legs still weak from two days in bed. Pam's brace had been stashed in the boot box under her bed. Edith had gone so far as to have Pam's doctor call Michelle and tell her the brace was not necessary except for strenuous exercise and, at this point, was a hindrance to her self-esteem.

Ben and Pam hesitated to approach Dutch, who stood smiling by his open passenger door wearing a Panama hat over his balding head. Michelle paused to pick up Debi's sweater, dropped on the last step.

"You feelin' better?" Dutch asked Ben.

Ben said, "Yes." Then hastily added, "Sir."

"That's a pretty dress." Dutch smiled at Pam.

Ben and Pam relaxed a bit, soothed by his smile. A big-face smile that deepened the creases touching his temples, a smile in his eyes. Dutch's physical appearance held Pam and Ben's attention. He was thin-legged in stiff, new jeans and rust-colored, round-toed dress boots. His long muscular arms with imposing biceps stretched his short-sleeved, gray and white nylon shirt to its limit.

Dutch came alive around Michelle. She looked beautiful to Dutch in her ankle-length, tan cotton pants above spotless-white Keds that matched her bright-white sweatshirt. But it was the change she had made to her hair that had him staring. Michelle the blonde. Her hair was now gold/yellow, spun up and angled back into a beehive, and covered with a sheer, yellow scarf.

She kissed Dutch in front of her kids for the first time, her pink lipstick leaving a sweet taste on the farmer's lips. Michelle removed the scarf, smiling at Dutch.

"You like it?" Michelle asked.

"Yes." Even though Dutch didn't much like change. Surprises even less.

Another test. Passed.

Debi sat between Ben and Pam on the T-bird's back seat bouncing her head back and forth, and sucking her thumb. Pam thought that it was good to have Debi as a buffer between her and Ben. Neither wanted to make trouble around this man. Dutch looked like he wouldn't put up with the teasing and arguing they were accustomed to. Driving north on Highway 17, three wide-eyed city kids listened to the conversation coming from the front seat.

"I called yer mother and made an appointment with her for tomorrow afternoon," Dutch said.

"Oh, that's good. How's your arm?"

Dutch test-flexed his muscular right arm, stretching from his steering wheel to the dash.

"It bothers the hell out of me if I'm shovelin' feed or pitchin' hay. A specialist in Des Moines said it's a damaged tendon."

"Is there anything you can do for it?" Michelle asked.

"He'd operate if I let 'im. But I won't let 'im."

Dutch turned his head to Michelle then back to the road that, with distance from the city, had become a black-top dividing line between the corn and soy bean fields stretched across the horizon in all directions. Michelle stopped herself from telling Dutch about her cold relationship with Edith. This wasn't the right time, she said to herself.

Along miles of country roads, Dutch pointed to every farm and isolated house, knowing every name and story therein. Thirty-seven miles from Des Moines, Dutch pointed ahead and to the left, across his tilled corn field and lush pastures, toward his farm. It looked like an Iowa city skyline to Ben. On the left stood the massive, white corncrib-the tallest building; it dwarfed the mud-splattered, red barn in front of it. The white, two-story farmhouse, secluded behind tall pines, looked much bigger than Al and Marie's apartment house, Ben thought.

As Dutch turned onto a gravel road, Ben noticed a dark silhouette rising out of the flat farmland. The oldest trees in Iowa grew there: giant maples, oaks, cottonwoods, and ash. Ben's only words during the entire drive erupted from his lips, his eyes gazing at the odd sight.

"What's that?"

"Ledges," Dutch said. "Ledges State Park. That's where we'll have our picnic. The Des Moines River sometimes floods the park in early spring, but it's open now."

"Oh boy!" Debi cried around the thumb still stuck in her mouth.

Michelle turned around and smiled widely at her youngest daughter, then reached back with one hand to flatten her fine, brown hair over exposed bald spots, the result of using her mother's scissors while playing beauty shop.

Ben had a way of knowing how his mother felt at any given moment, perhaps because he paid more attention than his sisters. He had never seen his mother so happy. After being given away to strangers by Edith, Michelle's priority had always been to keep her family close. The divorce had been devastating to her, the more so because she had been the one to demand it. If a man was in the picture now, a man who could bring security and a good life in the country-all the better. At that moment Michelle was thinking, surely, Dutch would grow to love her children in time.

Up ahead, fifty-foot Loblolly Pines and seventy-foot Live Oaks lined the spacious Beal front yard, freshly cut grass two hundred feet long and half that across. Dutch turned into his entry drive, a white gravel single lane, and stopped to check his mailbox. Ben turned to look out the rear window at a mammoth, bulging-eyed bull.

The farmer noticed Ben's interest. "Name's Lester," he said.

Lester was licking a salt block under a fifty-year-old oak in the near corner of his large, solitary pasture.

Dutch drove slowly, like a tour guide, but was only concerned that dust and white gravel not land on his baby-blue T-bird. He stopped outside the narrow entrance to the single-stall garage.

"Go ahead and get out here. I'll pull 'er inside."

Pam was the last to squeeze out of the back seat, just in time to be greeted by a dog nose stuck in her crotch.

Dutch ordered the dog back. "Duke! Down!"

The dog cowered in the dirt at his master's feet. Ben started laughing, which made Pam laugh. Dutch introduced his dog to the visitors one at a time while Ben and Pam patted its dusty, copper coat.

Following Dutch along the path to the back porch, Michelle carried Debi on her hip, not at all trusting Duke's devotion to his master, or the dog's interest in her baby.

"Kitty cats!" Debi exclaimed.

As the group neared the red brick patio, four feline rat-catchers, scrawny and coarse-haired, scattered, dashing into the dark cob house on the opposite side of the farmyard.

Pam followed her mother and sister inside the house, where they all removed their shoes on the back porch's cold linoleum. Ben strolled into the central farmyard, taking in the splayed arrangement of buildings: the outhouse; the shop and adjoining machinery storage building; a red gas tank on spider legs; behind the tank, a low-roofed chicken coop; hog barn and hayloft; a feed house near the turn onto the dirt service road; a silver-colored propane tank in front of one of the three fenced pastures where a hundred head of brown and white Herefords and their calves grazed.

Dutch and the girls loaded the cooler and picnic basket onto the bed of Dutch's red Ford pickup. Dutch spread a blanket on the truck's bed dotted with corn kernels and dirt clods. Ben helped Pam onto the tailgate, riding with her in back while Debi sat between Dutch and her mother, nestled close to Michelle's side, her thumb a slippery, red fixture inside her mouth.

The dust cleared when the truck turned onto the paved service road. The quick drive to Ledges under a cloudless azure sky was all too quick and exhilarating for city boy, Ben, who felt as if he were flying as he leaned out of the truck and let the wind blast his face.

The east entrance road into the park started to wind after passing a campground with picnic tables and a small public restroom. Ben craned his head forward to see the canyon entrance ahead, while Pam faced the pickup's tailgate, preferring to watch the landscape moving away.

Dutch explained to Michelle that Ledges was named for its sandstone walls, as high as 75 feet. "The cliffs are part of Indian lore," he said. "At Sentinel Rock, the Sioux, the Sac and Fox used to gather on the council ledge to boast about their bravery."

Pam was not as impressed as Ben with the miles of trails in the park. They were not for her. Her brother was already planning to know more of this hidden gem of nature by day's end. His failure to master the rope swing back in Wichita would surely be dashed out here, alone, made forever insignificant once he conquered the unexplored territory before him.

Dutch parked near a covered picnic shelter where they

could view Table Rock and Inspiration Point from their table.

While Michele set the table, Dutch went to work building a charcoal fire to an even glow at a barbecue grill. At his side were thawed hamburger and hot dogs, provided by his own pigs and cattle. Livestock he fed and watered, doctored and castrated, and bent to shovel their waste by the ton. If he could pass this final test, he would have a family again.

From a distance Pam watched how Dutch and her mother interacted. Her mother might marry this guy, she thought. He seemed like he might be an okay guy, but nothing like her daddy.

As the meat patties and dogs hissed on the grill, Ben was following a trail that led up to Inspiration Point. Ninebark shrubs lined the path, their golden yellow leaves would glow all summer. Just a hundred yards from the summit, the sound of the pickup's horn stopped Ben in his tracks. He hesitated, his breath heavy and rasping.

Then Ben was running toward the picnic area in response to Dutch's signal. Ben wanted the man's respect. And wanted to give respect, in turn.

The meal went smoothly, without mishap, except for a comment by Dutch to Michelle when Pam asked for a third hot dog. "You think she should have another one?"

Michelle compromised, telling Pam she could have the wiener without a bun.

He's not my dad, Pam said to herself. But just the same, she ate the hot dog self-consciously with her eyes averted, all the while wanting to comment on Ben's third hamburger that went without mention.

By the end of their picnic it had started to cloud-up above them, sprinkling much needed drops on the Central Iowa soil. On the return trip to the farm, Ben and Pam saw a baggy-trousered man clad in a yellow slicker walking in

49

the ditch near the park's front entrance. He wore a lopsided, dirty-white baseball cap pulled down to his ears. His head was down and shaking back and forth as if he was disgusted by the litter he was lifting in a gloved hand and stuffing into a burlap gunny sack.

Dutch's truck engine whined into third gear, moving away from the park's main entrance. The man with the negative nod watched until the red truck made its turn onto the gravel road that led to the Beal Farm. He had noticed children on the truck's bed and a pretty blonde woman on the front passenger seat.

Now his ever-moving gaze turned to the narrow leaves of a closed Gentian resting against the fold of a wet newspaper that he crumpled into his bag. His eyes were the same color as this late-summer bloomer, whose upturned blue trumpet flowers thrived in Ledges. The longer he stared at the green stem, the slower his head seemed to shake, while the rain came down in bigger drops, until ending in a short downpour. He kept on his path, gathering more trash as the clouds moved past the park. He thought he would work his way south to the Ledges border, then west across to Lost Lake, where he would check on something personal. He stopped again for a moment to reach inside his trouser pocket, making sure he hadn't lost the two AA batteries.

The rest of the afternoon was spent exploring the Beal farmhouse, surroundings all but ignored by a longtime bachelor. When Dutch opened the door in the kitchen's west corner that revealed a stairway, the air smelled stale and moldy. Dutch pushed a button switch that lit the single bulb hanging on a cord high above the dark stairway. The stairs hadn't had five people trooping up them at one time in a hundred years; they creaked and groaned.

Michelle had been given a quick tour of the upstairs on her second overnight. Now, she stood holding Debi's hand next to Dutch in the doorway to the room to the right of the upstairs landing. Pam and Ben stood behind them in the wide hallway. This room, painted pink, had been Dutch's sister's room thirty-five years ago. Nothing much had been done to it since then.

"This is where you girls will sleep tonight," Michelle said. Pam looked at the bare mattress of the four-poster double bed. It stood in front of five-foot high windows that looked out to the expansive front yard. Two walnut dressers had dust rings around the white lace doilies that hadn't been touched in decades. The floor was cold, varnished oak and without a rug. Pam wondered what this room would be like at night.

"You like it?" Michelle asked Debi.

Debi nodded yes just because her mother seemed to want her to like it.

Leaving the bedroom they faced a locked door across the hall.

"Is that the bathroom?" Pam inquired.

"My mother's sewing room. Bathroom's downstairs," Dutch said.

To the right of the girls' bedroom, another door opened onto the largest bedroom in the house, now used for storage, holding a century of memorabilia, furniture, clothing, old oil lamps, and odds 'n ends.

On their way downstairs Pam thought how she would hate having to limp down these stairs every time she needed to use the bathroom. Ben was glad his room was downstairs near the floor furnace. The long, narrow room that looked out to the back porch and central farmyard via two windows, one at the head and one on the left side of a twin-size bed. Oak sliding doors separated Ben's room from the master bedroom where Dutch and his mother would sleep.

Michelle really liked the front porch with its view of the front yard, though now it was sealed with storm windows. Dutch had to move his recliner back and closer to the master bedroom's entrance in order to open the door that led to the front porch.

"You ever drive a tractor?" Dutch asked Ben.

Ben's magnified eyes grew larger behind his glasses. "No, sir."

"Come on," Dutch said.

Michelle and the girls watched from the kitchen window as Ben's city legs climbed up and behind the wide wheel of a midget Farmall Tractor. Dutch stood behind the boy with his over boots secure on the frame above the rear axle. He pressed the button that started the little red tractor's engine.

"Push the clutch in," Dutch said.

Ben pushed in the brake pedal by mistake.

"No, that's the brake. Yer clutch is over there. You need to push in the clutch every time you shift gears."

Ben's nervous left foot used way too much energy. The black metal shifter terminated in a black knob bearing a confusing diagram of white numbers and letters, awkwardly placed and imposing to a lefty.

"Put it in first gear," Dutch instructed.

Ben could feel his ears redden and his glasses slipping, wanting to please the big man. Ben pushed the shifter and the tractor emitted a metallic scream.

"Don't grind the gears," Dutch said. Ben tried again, and again the tractor complained.

Ben was so wound up and nervous from the engine noise and Dutch's muscular body hovering over him he was bound to make mistakes.

"When I tell ya second, push in yer clutch. Here, put yer hand on mine on the shifter."

Ben's smaller, smooth hand felt the raw power in Dutch's right arm move through him.

"You'll shift?" Ben asked.

"I'll shift."

Dutch took over, calling out "Clutch," "Give it gas," and "Let out the clutch."

Ben steered them around the telephone pole in the central farmyard, picking up speed past the feed house turn, past the cattle yard, and onto the open stretch of dirt road that led to the gravel driveway, where a simultaneous "Brake" and "Clutch in" killed the engine.

The girls had moved from window to window, until settling on their knees on the sofa in the front room. They watched through curtains Michelle held open, via the front porch windows, as Dutch gave Ben the thrill of his life.

"Now, Ben, listen to me. Turn left here. No, not now! Okay, now!"

Out onto the gravel road they went, passing another gravel road on the right that ran alongside Lester's pasture. They were on the road that came closest to the south boundary of Ledges. In third gear and free to steer down the center of the road, they passed the Lay Farm and, across the road from them, the one-story house belonging to the Nagels. Then Dutch had Ben turn around, using reverse, and steer back to the girls waiting in the central farmyard.

"I drove the tractor, Mom!"

"Yes you did!" Michelle exclaimed proudly.

Pam was happy to see her brother so excited, but she knew that this day marked the end of the Smith Family. Her brother's opinions pulled a lot of weight with their mother, and the tractor ride would be the real clincher-as long as the night went well.

At sunset, they all followed behind Dutch, now dressed in forest green overalls and a battered Dekalb cap, as he fed his cattle and hogs. After the brief afternoon downpour, mud was so deep in places the hogs appeared to be crawling on their bellies to the trough. The visitors moved from the rusty metal hog gate to the other side of the barn, where Michelle observed the sun going down, and her son's eyes on Dutch's every move.

Debi, riding her mother's hip, pointed to the lumbering heifers and suckling calves, saying, "Cows and baby cows."

Pam's leg throbbed. Not from the walking or the lower temperature, but the way her mother and brother seemed so willing to defer to Dutch, who was little more than a stranger to her brother. What about me? she thought. What do I get out of it? I'll be stuck in a cold upstairs bedroom, in a pee-wet bed with a crying, thumb sucking siren who's afraid of the dark. The bathroom so far away. And the final insult: Dutch exerting control over her mother with one quiet question. "You think she should have a third hot dog?"

Michelle reveled in preparing supper: pork chops, mashed potatoes with her special gravy, and Dutch's sweet corn. The house smelled like comfort to the farmer, who hadn't been around a homemaker of Michelle's caliber since his mother. He felt alive again.

Sitting in the trayless highchair Dutch brought down from the storage room and cleaned, Debi was allowed to say grace, short and very sweet-another first since Mother Beal.

"Thank you for this food, God. Bless us all and make us good. Amen."

After a few bites, Dutch said, "Good gravy. Very tasty." Michelle beamed with pleasure.

Pam and Ben nodded, chewing and shelling their sweet corn like beavers on a deadline: butter, pepper, and corn cheek to chin; the barren cobs piled three and four on each plate.

Michelle's thoughts were on the highchair. Maybe it had been Dutch's, or his sister's, or both. She smiled at the man seated at the head of the table as if to say, You're doing good, honey. Keep passing those tests.

While Dutch and Michelle were doing the dishes, Pam and Debi bathed together in the small bathroom just off the kitchen, where every word spoken by the farmer and their mother could be heard when Debi wasn't splashing.

"Quiet. I can't hear," Pam whispered sternly to Debi.

At the same time, as the television played quietly in the background, Ben stood near the kitchen entrance listening just as his sister was.

"I want you and the kids to move in," Dutch said.

"What are you saying, Dutch?" Michelle smiled into his hooded green eyes.

"They'll be out of school soon. They might as well have the whole summer to get used to livin' on the farm," Dutch said.

Though separated by the length of the kitchen, Ben and Pam both held their breath. Pam, wanting her mother to wait. Ben, alive with the prospect of more tractor-driving, was ready to let his mother go to another man.

Pam waited for the answer. Whenever her mother paused and thought about something, it had always meant yes and final. Pam's heart began to pound as her mother paused now.

"I could sure use Ben's help this summer," Dutch continued.

"So you're saying we should get married after school gets out?"

He nodded yes, smiling and circle-drying a plate already dry. It wasn't long until they heard their mother crying tears of joy onto Dutch's chest. The struggle of raising her kids alone was over, Michelle rejoiced, and the good life promised to be theirs at last. One close family facing the future together in the center of Central Iowa.

Ben followed Michelle and the girls upstairs to watch his mother tuck them under the covers, and to find the light switches in new and dark territory. Dutch had said it was okay to leave on the hallway light their first night. Pam wanted the pink glass-domed bureau lamp left on too, but Michelle said no.

"Why?" Pam complained.

"Dutch said one light," Michelle said, making it clear to Pam who the real boss would be.

Ben's sibling mean streak took over as he began waving bye bye to Pam from the doorway, then half-closing the creaking bedroom door, throwing the room into a darkness that brought instant wailing from Debi, along with Pam's protest, "Mom, Ben's teasing!"

"Ben, knock it off, or you can sleep up here alone, and they can have your room!"

Ben's gaping mouth brought laughter and finger-pointing gotchas from Pam while Michelle consoled Debi, whispering close to her face, "Okay, sweetheart, just this once." The pink lamp would be left on with the hall light. Debi's crybaby howling was good for something, Pam thought.

For an hour after Ben and their mother left them alone, the girls cuddled together out of a deep sense of unease. The blackness outside the window looming through the faded pink curtains, bothered Pam more than Debi. Debi had a thumb to suck on, and Pam's body heat to warm her. Pam only had her wit and imagination-all useless to her now that her mother was determined to ruin her life.

Pam couldn't keep watch on the strange shadows haunting the room, or worry about what lurked behind the closed doors in the hallway. Her mind was focused on the creepy night noises seeping through the thin pane of glass behind the bed. The voices of two frightened girls singing "Jesus Loves Me" under the covers were not heard downstairs, where Ben could not sleep, either. In the front room, Dutch and his mother snuggled together on one of the farmer's ugly sofas.

The last day of school passed too fast for Pam and Ben. It marked the beginning of a two week stay at Grampa Dick's and Grama Merle's. The Smith apartment stood empty. Dutch had moved everything by himself in three full loads in his pickup. Now, their mother and Dutch would be off, driving in his T-bird to Las Vegas to get married, then on to La Paz, Mexico, to honeymoon.

Ben held Debi's grief-stricken face up to the front room window so she could wave goodbye to her mommy as the T-bird drove away. Pam's thoughts were elsewhere, happy to think that in just three days her father was driving in alone from Omaha to take them to Okoboji for two days.

Before Debi could throw a full-throttle tantrum, Pam took action, getting into her sister's face and smiling. "Guess who's coming to visit us?"

"Huh?" Debi's eyes widened and her mouth rounded in curiosity.

"Daddy! Yes. Daddy's taking us to Okoboji!"

"Obakogee!" Debi shouted.

"Yep," Ben agreed, bouncing her on his hip, dancing her away from the window, across the thick carpet and into the kitchen, where Grama Merle set a plate of cookies on the table and filled a milk glass for Debi.

The first full day at Grampa Dick's set the pattern: If Dick wasn't trimming his nose hairs or soaking his dentures, he lay all the way back on his recliner pretending to watch TV, if a baseball game wasn't on. Beer and cigarettes were consumed all day long by the retired couple. Merle, a nag and complainer, wrinkled from head to toe, smoked and drank like a field hand; however, Dick Groveland had some class about him. He smoked inconspicuously, holding back while the kids were in view. Merle, on the other hand, would salt the top of her Hamm's Beer can and give Ben a slug or two each day.

Merle cooked three good meals a day for Dick-her substitute for physical intimacy. Every night they broke out the vodka and Seven. Little Merle would get roaring drunk and laugh like a banshee at whatever filled the television screen. Then they'd retire to their beds in separate bedrooms.

The night before their father was to arrive, Ben and Pam were awake under the covers on either side of sleeping Debi. The double bed stood near the furnace in the Groveland's furnished basement. At the other end of the room, Merle's hanging laundry dampened the trapped air. Ben and Pam giggled about their father's visit, and eavesdropped on Merle's drunken tirade upstairs, carried to them through the heater's metal pipes.

"Those gawl-darn kids are drivin' me nuts!" she bellowed.

Silence from Grampa.

"All they do is eat, fight, and run all day long. I'm tired of it, Dick!"

Ben and Pam snickered at every complaint uttered by Merle, knowing she was not a blood relative. Dick married Marilla McGinty long after Michelle was born; she resented this unexpected invasion of her home.

"You hear me?" Merle whined.

"Yes, every word, dear," Dick replied.

"That Pam eats like a horse," Merle said.

Ben burst out laughing. Pam whispered, "Shut up. I can't hear."

"Debi cries all day for her mommy. And Ben steals money out of my purse!"

Ben had taken a couple of bucks from her purse, just yesterday, and spent it on pinball at the bowling alley. He'd thought he'd gotten away with it. When Dick didn't respond, Ben exhaled a sigh of relief. Dick hadn't believed his drunken wife. Merle's rambling went on and on, long past

58

the time the two got bored and fell asleep.

By noon the next day, Pam was riding next to her daddy in his red convertible with the top down. The car's trunk was stuffed with the kids' clothes and some of Debi's toys. Not knowing what they might want to do, Kenny had made sure the kids packed some good outfits along with their play clothes. Ben and Debi sat on the back seat, Debi with her thumb inserted. They were going 75 mph on Highway 71, headed north. For twenty miles Ken had been glancing down at Pam and gazing at his kids in back in his rearview mirror. Then he got the scare of his life: Lost in reverie, he didn't notice a four-way stop sign at the Hwy. 3 intersection, until too late. He slammed on his brakes, skidding through the crossing without another vehicle in sight. It scared Kenny to death. Just the thought of his kids hurt by his mistake knotted his stomach.

After a long silence, Pam asked her father if the gold band on his left hand was a wedding ring.

"Yeah, that's my wedding band," he smiled.

"Her name is Mary?" Pam asked.

"Yes, it is. Mary Smith, now." Kenny felt a moment's guilt as he realized how little he had told his kids about his life without them. He felt another sort of guilt as he admitted to himself that Mary could never take Michelle's place.

"Will our name change when Mommy marries Dutch?" Pam inquired.

"No. Not unless he adopts you."

"Why would he do that?" Ben demanded from the back seat.

Ken pushed his thick glasses up the bridge of his nose. "Sometimes it's better for kids to have just one family," he said.

"I'll keep my name, no matter what!" Pam declared, thinking that Dutch would never ever be her father.

"I hope so," Ken said.

Ken explained to them that the Navy was sending him to Korea. His new wife would be living in Okinawa, Japan, with her kids; he'd be able to visit when he was on leave. "I'll be stationed in Korea for four years," he said.

"We won't see you again for four years?" Pam cried, her brown eyes wide with shock, looking up at her father.

"I'll call at Christmas, and on your birthdays," Kenny promised. "And we can write letters to each other."

For a while during the long drive, Kenny felt that leaving the States was not the right thing to do, if it meant abandoning his children. Divorcing Michelle hadn't been his idea. And now the Navy was sending him to Korea, separating him from the four loves of his life. A couple of stupid mistakes and he had lost everything. His little rascals would grow up without him.

From behind his glasses he snuck a peek at Ben. His son's stoic expression reminded him of his own period of loss when he was around the same age. He had lost his mother; then his father spiraled down, moving into the bottle, dying young. Many heart-wrenching nights were ahead for Ben, he knew. But the ability to see only what he wanted to see came easy for Yeoman Chief Smith. In less time than he cared to admit, he thought only that he had a whole weekend ahead to spend with his kids. Any clouds rolled away, leaving a perfect, sunny day in early June.

"Who wants ice cream?" Kenny asked.

"I do."

"I do."

"I do, too!"

Dutch and Michelle Beal had said their I do's in a Las Vegas mini-chapel twenty-four hours earlier. Crossing the border at Tijuana, Mexico, Dutch's wire-rimmed butterscotch sunglasses gave the groom a remote look to

60

Michelle.

At the beginning of their trip, halfway across Nebraska, Dutch had noticed a red ball of fur in the ditch on Michelle's side of the road. No hesitation. He braked onto the shoulder, opened the T-bird's trunk and soon fired his 12-guage shotgun across the ditch toward the fence line. Michelle's ears were still ringing as her fiancé stood at the T-bird's front passenger window, grinning and displaying the bloody tail of the red fox he had skinned by the open trunk. Back behind the wheel with hands smeared with dried blood, Dutch was elated. He told Michelle, "I can get 75 bucks for the pelt. That'll pay for gas clear to Mexico!"

Pedestrians on the shanty streets of Tijuana, Dutch wore his sunglasses with baggy khaki pants and a white t-shirt into a crowd of street vendors, coming away with two pairs of sandals for himself and his new bride. They were headed to Dr. Jorge's office. An hour later, the abortion would be over and they could get on with their new lives, honeymooning in La Paz.

Dutch had wanted no part of raising children into his 70's. He had promised Michelle that the farm one day would be Ben's to run. She could live there long after Dutch was plowed under.

A few hours after the abortion, Dr. Jorge became concerned about Mrs. Beal's heavy blood loss and ordered her to a San Diego hospital. Dutch, tight-jawed and upset, harped on and on about the inconvenience as Michelle rode flat on the T-bird's back seat, bleeding and white-hot because of her new husband's callousness. As the miles crawled by, she grew faint. One thing kept her fighting against joining the fox in the trunk: She would not abandon her kids as Edith had done to her. Michelle mumbled, nearly unconscious, "Don't take me now, God. I have to live for them."

Kenny Smith, holding a fidgeting Debi in his arms, waited outside the fence surrounding the trampoline pits, as Ben and Pam bounced with glee on two separate units. Debi had whined, "I wanna jump on the tramoleens!" But Kenny had thought it too dangerous for his little peanut.

The Smith kids had been to Arnolds Park twice in the last two years. No other town in Iowa had so many fun things for kids to do. The amusement park there was loaded with rides, concession stands, and one of the world's top-rated wooden roller coasters.

After their fifteen minutes were up on the trampolines Pam began to complain of a stomach ache.

"You wanted that ice cream," Kenny admonished. Taking his girls by the hand, he followed Ben into a cement hut jammed with pinball machines and a jukebox. Ken held Debi aloft so she could watch Ben moving the flippers, trying to keep the steel ball alive. Pam dropped a coin into the jukebox. Doris Day's "Que Sera, Sera" made all of them think of Michelle. Ben lost his concentration. Debi cried for her mommy. Kenny thought of the time Michelle caught him with a date at the drive-in movie while she was pregnant with Ben. Pam hated her mother for marrying Dutch and wanted this time with her daddy to last forever.

Ken was smart enough to leave their hot dog lunch until after their roller coaster ride. Before heading out of the amusement park to their reserved cabin on Okoboji Lake, Ken noticed a poster advertising ballroom dancing. Suddenly Kenny saw himself surrounded by pretty girls in summer dresses, dancing the night away.

The sun was still up when Ken unlocked cabin number nine's paint-flaking door. One room with a half bath-a dollhouse for eight bucks a night. The mushy double bed with squeaky box springs took up half the cabin's space. No rugs covered the cold, curling linoleum floor. Kenny had brought two blankets with him, remembering the last time here with the kids. Debi had wet the bed that night. Kenny's pajamas had been soaked so thoroughly with her urine he thought he'd peed the bed himself.

After hauling their stuff into the cabin, the kids spent ten minutes bouncing and playing on the bed before heading out for dinner in a nearby town, Spirit Lake. At the fish restaurant, Pam took her sister into the restroom. Alone at the table with his son, Ken explained to Ben that he wanted to take Pam to a dance for a couple hours.

"The dance will last way past Debi's bedtime," Ken said. "I need you to stay with her."

"Pam can't dance. Her leg hurts too much to even climb stairs," Ben countered, not particularly happy to be a baby-sitter.

"She'll be just fine. I think Pam'll really enjoy it," Ken said.

Ben understood that Pam was the one who would miss their father the most. Grudgingly he said, "Yeah, she will."

Ben and Debi ended up going along to the Arnolds Park Roof-Top Garden that night because a noisy bunch of teenagers checked in next door to their cabin. Putting Debi to bed early was no longer an option. On the drive over to the dance, Pam, in a yellow polka-dot dress and black patent leather shoes, sang in a clear, soprano voice, "Oh, this is the night, it's a beautiful night, and we call it bella notte..."

For some reason Ben was annoyed with his sister's delight. Perhaps because it would last only for the moment...or the night. Her happiness would soon be over. Eventually, Ben would be alone with her sad, brown eyes-always searching, wanting, craving this moment that only Dad could give her. This evening would be lost in the swarm of lonely minutes, hours, days and nights-forever gone. She sang the theme from Lady and the Tramp the whole way to the ballroom. Ben stared at just another night of darkness out of the convertible's window, refusing to sing along.

"...look at the skies, they have stars in their eyes, on this lovely bella notte..."

A Glenn Miller-era band in white tuxedoes played from the stage before two hundred couples on the dance floor. As the evening progressed, Ben's lap became the pillow for Debi's slumber on two folding chairs at the far end of the dance floor, where a long row of chairs stood empty against the wall.

Kenny was teaching Pam some 1940's dance moves. Watching the two, Ben realized he could never say what was on his mind. He had been thinking hard during Pam's joyous moments that neither he nor his sister had any close friends. And how would he ever make any friends stuck out on that farm?

For an hour, father and daughter jitterbugged at the edge of the dance floor closest to Ben and the sleeping child. During a break they sat on chairs spaced two away from Debi so not to wake her.

"How'd I do, Daddy?" Pam asked.

"You did terrific, sweetie! How's your leg feel?"

"Fine. Can we dance again? Please?"

"Sure. How about you, Ben? Do you want to dance with your sister?"

"No thanks." He pointed at Debi draped across his lap. The real reason for declining was the fact that dancing with Pam would make him feel even more of an outcast.

Their time together was half over. Ken resolved to do his best to make these few days a wonderful memory for his kids. He told himself, they know their daddy loves them. That thought kept him from feeling sorry for them and himself. But the memory of losing his mother hovered at the back of his mind-along with ever-present guilt. Ken Smith was creating the same loss for his children that he had endured. Why does this happen, Kenny wondered, watching Ben sitting there with his thick-framed glasses heavy on his nose, looking bored-and the spitting image of himself.

Late that night in their spartan cabin, the Smith girls slept nestled against Kenny, while Ben lay awake facing the wall. His father snored sonorously. The girls exhaled through slack mouths, as if their father's low rumbles had taken them deep into sleep. Ben lay listening to his father's breathing-the rhythmic rising and falling tones telling him that father and son now followed different paths. Ben whispered, "It's okay, Dad. I'll keep your name. And see that the girls do, too. I'll take care of them and you'll be proud of me. Don't worry. I love you."

The next morning, before noon, the glacial blue waters of Lake Okoboji were too cold for swimming. At a picnic table in the shade of a large elm twenty feet from water's edge, they shared a bag of potato chips and bologna sandwiches. Debi was balanced on one of Ken's legs happily eating her sandwich. Ben had finished his, and was throwing rocks into the lake: plunk, plunk, plunk.

Pam could not eat with her usual zest. Her chin quivered. Tears fell.

"Daddy, take me with you to Korea," she begged. "Mom will let me go, if you say it's okay. Why can't I go with you?"

Kenny chose to be stiff and stern rather than break down in front of his children. "Pam, you have to stay with your mother. She would never let you go halfway 'round the world. Anyway, you'd be living in Japan with Mary and her kids, not with me."

Ben overheard their exchange and realized that his father was fighting tears.

"Pam," Ben said, "quit your whining. You know Dad has to go. You're just making it harder for him."

Ken was never more proud of his son. His boy had said it all for him.

Ben's remark angered Pam, as Ben knew it would. But that was the only way to save himself from witnessing his father's heartache.

When thwarted, Pam could be ruthless. She lumbered up from the picnic table and walked away with an exaggerated limp, extending her left leg out way too far. Her pretense disturbed her father. He looked away, remembering an afternoon at a public swimming pool in Wichita.

The night before, Michelle had informed him that she would be divorcing him after the baby's birth. Michelle and Pam were lying on their stomachs, sharing a large beach towel. Kenny overheard Michelle explaining to her daughter, "Pam, it's more ladylike to raise one leg up like this. Pam watched her mother's shapely left leg bend at the knee, lifting her bare foot into the air, where Michelle allowed it to sway slightly from side to side. Kenny noticed the eyes of the men around them drawn to his wife. Then Pam imitated her mother and painfully raised her left leg, too. Her calf muscle was atrophied and the scar tissue on her heel an ugly sight. The men quickly averted their eyes to avoid being caught staring at a deformity. Kenny had lost it right there, burying his head under his arm, sobbing quietly and unnoticed.

The remembered sorrow was too much for Ken. Tears streaked his cheeks.

"Ben. Pam. Come here," he called. "I need to talk to you."

Ben and Pam sat across from their father, while Debi smacked her lips, still working on her sandwich, oblivious to the emotions flowing around her. The two older children watched their father cry-long-held tears that looked frightful and pathetic.

"The hardest thing I ever had to do was leaving you kids," Ken sobbed.

That was it.

Maybe this awful sadness was punishment enough, Pam thought, as she sat beside her father. She leaned into his side and said, "I love you."

Ben sat there awkward and weak, while his father removed his glasses, pinched the top of his nose between his thumb and forefinger, then blew his nose on Debi's dirty paper napkin.

Pam gave Ben a look, one that said she had topped his mature words earlier. Ben turned away from them all, gazing toward the other side of the lake, where the houses looked new and clean, and removed from all trouble. He murmured to himself, "Hurry up, Mother. Come home."

In San Diego, Michelle had spent two nights in Mercy Hospital, though needing two more. Dutch was hot about the cost, reluctantly forking out three hundred and fifty bucks to the hospital. And thirty-five more for prescriptions.

"What a honeymoon!" Dutch complained.

Michelle bit her lip, resisting the urge to let him have a piece of her mind. Quiet rest would allow her to heal faster. His complaints about her condition transitioned into complaints about his sore arm. He decided to see Edith, for sure, when they got back home.

On the return trip from Okoboji, Ken turned east on Hwy. 30 at Carroll, announcing a surprise side trip.

"Let's drive by your new home. I'd like to see the farm."

Ken had two reasons: He wanted to inspect the place where his children would live while he was stationed so far away from them. He knew he would pause a thousand times in the days ahead to wonder what they were doing and what it was like for them living on a farm. And second, their time together today would be extended by an hour or two.

On their approach to Boone, where Ken planned to stop, gas up, and get directions to Ledges State Park, he announced, "Here's Boone. This is where you'll be going to school."

All three kids looked for a school building that was not yet in sight.

"You kids know who's from Boone?" Kenny asked.

"Who?" Pam and Ben spoke in unison.

"Mamie Eisenhower, the First Lady. Her house is near here, somewhere," Ken said.

"Can we go see it, Daddy? Please?" Pam asked.

"Sure. I'll get directions when we get gas."

At the station, Ken put down the convertible's top before heading for 709 Carroll Street. He drove slowly, enjoying the kids' heads turning left and right in search of Ike's wife's birthplace.

They ended up touring the small, single-story house, tramping through roped-off walkways, gaping at the furnishings of a real-life famous person.

In his quest to introduce his kids to a bit of history, Ken forgot to get directions to Ledges. He asked the elderly tour guide, who described a shortcut that sent them on a wild goose chase, ending up on a gravel road that dead-ended at Lost Lake, a few hundred feet from the east bank of the Des Moines River, southwest of Ledges. Lost Lake was a pond and not on the map he pulled from the glove compartment.

Ken shut off his engine, and parked in the center of the single lane gravel road. He took a good look at his Iowa map, asking Pam to help him find Ledges. Ben resisted saying, she can't read a map. Keeping quiet, he turned his attention to the thick grasses and weeds that obscured his view through the barbed wire fence beside the lane. Through his lowered window he heard a barely discernible sound. Music. That's music coming from there, Ben thought, scrambling to his knees to stare in that direction.

Pam relished the smell of Old Spice on her father's neck as she watched him finger-trace their drive from Boone on the map.

"Dad?" Ben said.

"Yeah?" Ken replied, squinting at the map.

"Do you hear music?"

They listened.

"I do," Pam said.

"Where?" Ken inquired.

Ken's gaze left the map to follow Ben's pointing finger toward the fence line. "I hear something, yeah. Maybe somebody's fishing nearby with a radio on, or having a picnic."

"Can I go see?" Ben asked.

"Me, too!" Debi cried.

"No," Ken replied behind a snorting laugh. "Maybe they want some privacy."

"Please, Dad? If I see someone, I'll come right back," Ben said.

Any other time but this, Ken would have stuck to it and made his son mind his own business. But guilt made him indulgent.

"Okay, but just a few minutes. And don't bother anybody, or sneak up on 'em."

"I won't, Dad."

Ben swung off the back seat onto the gravel road, leaving Debi behind, pouting. Ken and Pam listened to the faint music coming and going with the light breeze that moved Pam's bangs on her forehead. Both turned their attention back to the map.

The soil, close to the river, was rich and black under Ben's sneakers, and clotted on his soles before he reached the fence covered with lush, green Walking Ferns. A dozen yellow butterflies went airborne at his approach.

The top wire was neck-high to Ben, its barbs rusty orange and dull-sharp, hanging slack from barn wood posts, rotted and leaning every which way from seasons of wind and rain and isolation.

Peering over the fence, Ben discovered an old country cemetery. Every grave marker lay flat, or leaning askew from the churning soil, where choking weeds thrived until the winter kill. The music was distinct now. And what he saw in the back corner of the cemetery was as thrilling as if he'd seen it in his wildest dreams. Goose bumps tickled his naked arms. Ben wanted to rush between the wires and run to it with all the energy of boyhood. And he wanted his family to see this sight.

"Dad, you've got to come see this!"

"Come on back, now!" Ken called.

Ben had never disobeyed a direct command by his parents, or any adult-but this time, he shouted over his shoulder, "I'll be right back, Dad!"

It was easy for Ben to fit his skinny legs and torso between the wires, then stand on the other side unscraped. He ran with the fear of stepping on weeded-over grave sites long forgotten, and the sound of his father's car door slamming behind him. Ben ran toward the silver star atop a five-foot tall Christmas tree. The tree was decorated with red, green, blue, and silver balls, its branches hung with little presents wrapped in shiny paper and wearing colorful bows.

Ben stood still, breathing hard at the edge of the small family plot-a section of mowed and manicured grass, perhaps ten feet by twenty-five feet. The music was coming from a red, hand-size transistor radio at the base of the tree. The tree's stand was weighted to the ground with cement. A toy train stood idle on tracks that circled the tree. Fresh silver tinsel had recently been hung on the tips of the branches.

The music was the haunting part. Not the kind of

music playing, which was barely loud enough to hear; rather, the feeling that whoever did this believed the music could be heard by a person or persons buried here. Just then, Ken came up to the edge of the plot and stood beside Ben, quiet and unconcerned about his son's insubordination. His eyes were wide behind his glasses, scanning the same things his son had seen, with the same feelings of silent wonder. For this moment, he and Ben shared something that many fathers and sons miss-the chance to be boys together. Deep down Ken knew he needed the sharing more than his son ever would. This was a moment they would never forget. Not the painful moment of separation soon to pinch his heart, but this: Christmas in June in a remote cemetery, where some gentle soul chose to honor a life or lives lived.

Looking at two markers made of sandstone on each side of the tree, Ken read out loud, "Rainbow" inscribed in letters now barely legible at the top of each headstone.

"That must have been their last name," Kenny said. "Strange there's no date of birth or death, or a first name." He looked around at the cemetery. "These are pretty old graves."

"Why would someone leave music on, and all these presents, and a Christmas tree?" Ben asked.

"I have no idea. It sure is strange though."

Ben felt tempted to open some of the gifts. But his dad said, "We'd better get back to the girls."

Walking back, Ben expressed his curiosity. "I wonder what's inside those wrapped presents?"

"Maybe nothing," Ken smiled, ignoring his muddy shoes and the mess Ben would surely leave on his car's back seat floor.

Ben related all the exciting details at the cemetery to Pam and Debi from the back seat while Ken found his way to the gravel road that led into Dutch's farm. Ken stopped on the road, ready to back out if Ben and Pam objected to satisfying his curiosity. But they reassured him. "We want you to see the farm, Dad."

On they went, slowing on the white gravel drive at the front of the farmhouse where Duke prowled toward them. The big dog growled and barked so ferociously that Ken feared the dog would jump inside his convertible and attack them, if he didn't speed away. With the dog running after them in a cloud of chalky dust, Ken circled out of the drive and onto the road. Duke cut across the yard to bark close enough to Ken's wheels he worried he might hit the animal. "Oh God," he swore under his breath, "just what I need. Kill my ex-wife's new husband's dog!" For a quarter mile Duke gave chase before stopping in the middle of the road, panting. Ken was thankful for the episode with Duke. Between the dog and the cemetery there would be no room in his children's thoughts for mourning his upcoming departure.

Pam clung to him in the front seat before he drove away from Dick and Merle's. The goodbyes were said. Kisses given. Then he was gone.

Late in the afternoon, after time seemed to drag slower than at any other period in their lives, Dick, Merle, and three beaming children literally jumped for joy on the front porch as the bug-splattered T-bird honked and parked against the front curb. Now ten shades darker in contrast to her blond hair, the kids were all over Michelle's tan body, capering at her feet, all wanting to be held and kissed to seal the reality of being together again. Michelle's eyes filled with tears, then let go a river of pent-up emotion.

Dutch had been burned red beneath the Mexican sun while deep-sea fishing off the Baja coast. He left on his sunglasses, his eyes sensitive and strained after so much sun and driving. The Iowa farmer had patched up Michelle's feelings for him, blaming the fear he experienced at the possibility of losing his new bride for his callous behavior. "How could I face your children," Dutch had said, "if I brought you home in a coffin because of complications after an abortion I asked you to have?" His teary-eyed sincerity worked on Michelle. Then he listened for hours as Michelle described her life in Wichita, including all the details of her love life. When she finished, he said, "I've heard it all and never want to hear it again." He took her hand. "A new life is ahead of us, now," he promised.

"Did you miss me?" Michelle asked each child, then kissing them after each voiced a resounding "Yes."

"Did you get the postcards?" she asked them.

All nodded yes, pushing close to Michelle in her four-dollar Mexican leather sandals.

Dutch stood back from the reunion, feeling awkward and insignificant, staying out of their space by walking up to the front porch where Dick and Merle smiled as widely as a couple of carved pumpkins. Their day had finally arrived, too.

Debi rode her mother's hip. Ben and Pam followed her up to the porch, where she couldn't help but laugh at the relief on her dad's face and Merle's frazzled appearance, like a mouse attacked by three determined cats.

"I'll bet you two are glad to see us," Michelle observed.

"Oh, Michelle, we had a great time," Grampa Dick denied.

The whole scene gave Michelle the biggest laugh she'd had since leaving the elderly couple waving goodbye from the same porch. Michelle began laughing all over again upon seeing her children's belongings all packed and waiting just inside the front door.

Dutch stood near the front door, anxious to get his new tribe under his roof, because Michelle had argued him out of stopping at the farm first in order to check on his ani-

73

mals. To Michelle, their honeymoon had ended that first day in Tijuana.

Michelle and the kids waved goodbye to Dick and Merle from the baby-blue T-bird driving away under the summer sun.

Closing in on the farm, Ben broke his silence from the back seat, speaking excitedly about the Christmas tree in the cemetery near Ledges. Ben resented the way Dutch only spoke to Michelle, glancing sideways to her, not looking once at Ben in the rearview mirror when he explained the mystery.

"Gene Rainbow. He's a character. Works for the state as a part-time groundskeeper in Ledges and cleans school buses for the county. He fell off the railroad High Bridge when he was a boy. It messed up his brain or somethin'. His head shakes back and forth like this day and night." Dutch demonstrated to Michelle.

"Why the Christmas tree in the cemetery?" Michelle asked.

"His parents are buried there. Keeps it goin' year 'round."

"That's strange," Michelle said.

"Is his last name really Rainbow?" Pam asked.

Dutch nodded yes. From Michelle's lap Debi pointed out the window exclaiming, "Rainbow!" For the first time the new family laughed together. Pam was hoping it wasn't the last, as she scanned the black soil rows of Dutch's cornfield. Soon the fields would match the green of Ledges' leaves, tall against a blue background of sky and invisible winds that blew warm and constant in June.

After shadows and nervous giggles and heads under blankets, Pam and Debi made it through their first official night in their new home. Michelle was up with Dutch at 5

AM to make her men a breakfast of eggs and bacon, toast and fried potatoes.

Dutch had turned on Ben's bedroom light, then stood over his sleeping stepson and woke him, his voice guttural and low, and to Ben, foreboding. "Ben. Get up! Time to do chores."

Ben was up on his feet, his body not ready for movement, before he was aware of his new surroundings. He stood squinting and blinking at Dutch, not sure what to do next. He couldn't find his glasses, all the while fighting the urge to crawl back under the warm covers.

His city clothes-unblemished jeans, spotless short-sleeved T-shirts and Keds-were out of place on the farm. Ben's clothes had never felt so cold on his skin; compared to his bed, the house seemed as frigid as a Des Moines winter. He'd never dressed this early, with the view outside his bedroom windows still dark as night.

"Ben, you have to dress warmer than that," Michelle said when her boy gingerly walked into the bright kitchen. Dutch was outside filling Duke's bowl with dry dog food from a fifty-pound bag kept just inside the open cob house door.

Michelle went into Ben's room where the overhead light still burned within its opaque white, glass dome. She came back into the kitchen and found her son looking out at the darkness in the central farmyard. She handed him his heaviest sweater.

"You should have a coat to wear for doing chores. I'll see if Dutch has something that will fit you."

Ben seemed upset. From the stove Michelle inquired, "What's wrong?"

"Nothing."

Dutch came in from the porch, closing the door quickly behind him. He stood in his jeans, flannel shirt and thick white socks. He removed his worn, green Dekalb cap; his face appeared long and spoon-shaped below his receding hairline.

"Ben, what's yer bedroom light doin' on?" Dutch snapped, in a harsh tone that scared Ben.

"I left it on, Dutch, when I went into his room to get him a sweater." Michelle explained.

Dutch strode into the bedroom and flicked off the light, then returned to a plate laden with his breakfast. Ben ate quietly, thankful his mom had saved him from Dutch's quick temper.

"When yer not usin' a light, don't leave it on," Dutch said.

"Okay," Michelle said. "How is it? Your breakfast?"

"Good," Dutch said. "Real good."

"It's real good, Mom," Ben agreed.

The farm was in good shape even though Dutch had been gone for two weeks. He had turned his fields for planting corn in late April, when he first began dating Michelle. He had started his planting in late May and had finished before leaving on his honeymoon. It was his habit to plant in early spring because the soil was always in excellent condition then. The success of his farm was but the reflex of its fertile soil. Dutch Beal had long been known to produce the best crops in Boone County. Farmers around him agreed that he ditched and fed his soil the best. Not that Dutch was a farmer who loved and nurtured his soil out of a sense of Middle West patriotism; but rather, farm values were based on soil fertility. Dutch Beal would never be a greedy soil robber, would never over-farm his land. He was too smart for that.

The sun was far below the horizon behind the Beal barn, where morning wind gusts bristled Ben's neck hairs as he tiptoed behind Dutch, avoiding pig shit every other step through the dry and clodded hog yard. They stepped up into the barn onto a wood floor slippery with straw and dung. Dutch flipped on a switch inside the barn's sliding door that lit three, 60-watt bulbs at the low ceiling and handed Ben a pair of stiff, soiled work gloves.

The noise of waking hogs, gigantic sows grunting and snorting at their master's return, increased to a frenzy at the back of the barn. The herd of swine lay massed together in a sea of black, white, and mixed American Landrace. Dutch took up a barn shovel and scooped a load of dung from the floor, tossing it out into the barnyard before handing the shovel to Ben.

"Here ya go. Scoop some of this shit out of here."

The stiff gloves, the shovel and the motions required to wield it were as alien to Ben as the hogs themselves. He watched Dutch move into the herd, swatting and kicking them hard with the toes of his zipped-up boots, yelling, "Get up! Move! Up, you bitch! Get out of the way!"

Ben continued to watch while he scooped and shoveled, starting as close to the door as he could to save steps back and forth.

Dutch took a wide-scoop feed shovel from a rack near the feed bin and shoveled sweet pellets from the bin into the trough, occasionally smacking an unruly boar or sow with the shovel's handle. Dutch's callous tactics seemed cruel to a city boy, though the hogs were never injured. That would have cost Dutch money.

A stream of younger hogs, teenagers, shouldered their way into the barn, wary at first of Ben, dodging around him.

"Ben!"

Ben jumped, caught watching the new arrivals scurry past him.

"Put five or six scoops into that trough. Spread it out a bit." Dutch handed him the feed shovel and moved out the open door to check on the hogs' water supply at the other end of the hog yard. Alone with six tons of hungry pork, and their constant backbiting and squealing, Ben spilled his first shovelful of pellets onto the floor when a barn swallow winged out of its mud nest just above his head. Kneeling, with the shovel held flat to the floor, Ben picked-up and slid the pellets onto the scoop, afraid Dutch would see the spillage. He pushed his glasses up his nose and dumped the pellets into the trough. He could hear Duke whining just outside the gate, wanting to join his master as Dutch fed the cattle.

Pellet powder mushroomed into Ben's nose after each shovel load into the trough, causing a sneeze attack that startled the biggest sow into flinching-up its pink snout to investigate for a second or two.

"Was it like this or like that," Ben wondered, trying to stow away the feed shovel. "Handle up or down?"

Ben was back shoveling the barn floor, when an old white pickup parked outside the hog yard gate.

A man in shoulder-strapped, navy-blue overalls with the legs tucked inside knee-high rubber boots climbed out. His cap was angled sideways over the plain, round face of a Dutch/German in his late 30's.

"Hi. I'm Jim Vanderhaus."

"Hi," Ben replied.

"Dutch in there?"

"He's outside somewhere," Ben said.

The man walked away toward the sound of a small tractor starting in the cattle yard on the west side of the barn. Ben recalled that Vanderhaus had fed and watered the animals for Dutch when he was away. Ben felt stupid for not telling the man his name. His mind, fearing Dutch's reaction if he returned to find Ben's chores not done, had already forgotten the man's first name. Was it John? Ben wondered. He didn't know for sure.

The sun was shining into the barn doorway by the time Ben thought he had the floor scooped clean. At the hog yard fence Ben watched for Dutch to signal him, or something, but Dutch had cut the tractor's engine and was chatting with Vanderhaus while Duke waited nearby.

"How was Mexico?" Jim asked.

"Hot as hell some days," Dutch said, climbing down from his tractor to talk with his friend.

"I reeled in a 300-pound spearfish after two and a half hours," Dutch said.

"Really? How'd you land him?"

"If I hadn't been strapped in, I'd've been wet for sure," Dutch laughed.

The men laughed and talked more about Mexico, the cost of things there, and the value of the peso. Then they moved on to the current market prices of cattle and hogs.

Ben thought it odd Dutch didn't mention his new family. Only that he would sell Michelle's car to the man for four hundred bucks. They shook hands on the deal, then went back to their day's work. Ben, undecided about whether to call out to Dutch, or go over to him, loitered beside the barn. And the big problem: What to call him? Dutch? Dad?

Not done with his chores after all, Ben spent another hour sweeping out the barn with a worn house broom, and made a friend who he named Jerry, a two-month-old, thirty-pound white pig who ate sweet pellets from his hand.

Michelle's hazel eyes had looked out from the kitchen window at least a dozen times to catch a glimpse of her son at work with the man she had chosen. Years of watching her mother shed man after man taught her that Dutch was the sort of male she could not change. Her husband's issues seemed to center on money. She would talk to her children and caution them about leaving lights on and doors open.

It will all work out, she sighed to herself. She began scouring the kitchen sink with Ajax, then the countertops and stove. This was the first time she'd done heavy-duty cleaning seeking another's approval. She needed rubber gloves. Her long nails, professionally manicured for her wedding, would have to do without occasional luxuries until she could gauge her new husband's tolerance and temper about such things.

Now, she went to her purse and took the last of the medication prescribed in San Diego. The blue pill was a mood elevator. Pep pills, the doctor had called them. She swallowed the last pill with iron-rich tap water from the kitchen sink. She'd see how she did without them for a while.

Michelle woke the girls for breakfast at 8 AM. They had lain awake late into the night, frightened by unfamiliar squeaks and howls, huddled under the covers, whispering about ghosts and monsters, evoking tears from Debi and fear induced gas from Pam. The girls ate their breakfast wearing pajamas and slippers. Debi ate like a bird while Pam filled herself with a second helping of her mother's fried potatoes.

"We're going to have to start our diets soon, Pam," Michelle said, diplomatically including herself in the impending famine.

Pam rolled her eyes, still chewing a last bite of toast she'd swirled with egg yoke and leftover catsup. "I know. I know," she said.

With a full belly, Pam looked contemptuously at her small-framed little sister. Debi's light brown ponytail was cute, and arranged by their mother, who took pride in her perfect figure. Debi nearly always left half the food on her plate untouched, and later suffered no hunger. Her sister's eating habits were an affront to Pam.

"Your brother's helping Dutch do the chores," Michelle said.

"What chores?" Pam said.

"Feeding the pigs and cows. Things a farmer has to do

to keep things running smooth."

The next day, in the afternoon, Pam and Debi were upstairs in their bedroom cutting out paper dolls from a book and arranging them to stand inside their paper doll-house. Pam resented the matching shorts and T-shirts they were wearing. She loathed the heavy orthopedic shoes she had to wear, while Debi pranced around in ballet slippers. Michelle had told her girls they must wear shoes upstairs, because the worn floorboards were full of splinters. Today the temperature in the bedroom was near ninety degrees, and Pam was feeling the heat more than her sister.

"I'm going outside," Pam announced.

Debi followed Pam downstairs, but stayed with her mother who was washing the front porch windows with vinegar and water.

Inside his huge shop, Dutch lay on his back on a creeper under his pickup changing the oil. The truck was hoisted by overhead pulley chains. A fan on a tall stand blew toward the open overhead door, keeping the temperature bearable.

Ben had not been wakened for chores this morning. Now he worried that his new step-dad was unhappy with his work. He stood for a long time near the feed house across from the hog yard. There he printed his name in the dust in bold letters with the heel of his shoe. Pam came over and stood on the 'B' to provoke a reaction from her sullen brother.

"Get off of there!" Ben said.

Pam took two steps back. Then her attention was caught by Ben's new friend, Jerry, poking his pink snout through the hog yard's iron gate, snorting for sweet pellets.

"That's Jerry. He eats right out of my hand."

"Really?" Pam asked.

"Wanna see?"

Pam followed Ben through the gate. They squatted at the barn entrance, petting Jerry's dry, bristly hide.

"He came right up to me yesterday and started to talk to me."

"Oh, sure! What did he say?" Pam challenged.

Ben grinned. "Jerry said, 'Feed me, oink, oink!'"

Pam stepped up into the barn behind Ben, with Jerry close behind.

"I cleaned out this whole barn full of pig poop," Ben told her.

The sows and bigger hogs were napping at the back of the cool barn in one huge mass of pork flesh. While they watched, a sow sauntered off outside to the water trough in the hog yard to slurp a gallon of water, then return.

Ben dipped his blistered hand into the sweet pellet bin and gave Pam half. He put a pellet into his mouth. "Mm, good!" he said, and crunched it to pulp, before spitting it out. Pam laughed at her nutty brother. Then he placed one pellet on his palm and they watched Jerry take it, sniffing the boy's clean hand for more.

The herd made Pam nervous. She pointed to a slatted, wooden ladder that led up to a dark, square hole.

"What's that?" she asked.

"The hayloft. I poked my head up there yesterday and there's this big mountain of hay. It's huge, Pam."

They gave Jerry pellets, one at a time, leading him out onto the hog yard's baked ground, worn to dust by tons of pork balanced on cloven hooves.

A couple dozen pigs Jerry's size, all his brothers and sisters and cousins, were lounging in a partially shaded mud hole behind the water trough. Ben charged the group, scattering them in all directions. Pam giggled at the sight of Ben chasing the swift, little pigs around and around the yard, kicking up dust in a squealing frenzy of comedy. Pam got into the chase. After the pigs huddled in a corner, she charged them as Ben blocked their escape down the barn alley.

Dutch heard the squealing pigs and rolled the creeper out from under the truck's belly. He listened to the continuing ruckus as he wiped his hands with the red, gas-damp rag hanging from his overall's back pocket. His green eyes squinted at the dust cloud in the hog yard. Incredulous, he swore, "Those damn kids can't be dumb enough to be chasin' them hogs on a hot day like this!"

In the midst of their first real fun together on the farm, Ben and Pam were caught off guard in mid-laughter, their legs as weak from laughing as from chasing the pigs and pulling on their curly-Q tails. Dutch came through the gate-a looming specter, veins bulging from his neck.

"You kids get outta there!"

His brown work boots were dull and all business stepping toward them; the dust they had stirred slitted his eyes to pinpoints of anger. His mouth seemed to barely open as he choked his words out. "Those hogs could die from runnin' on a day this hot. What's wrong with you kids? Get yer asses to the house!"

Pam scuttled past Dutch to the other side of the gate. Ben followed a few steps behind his sister, who was now limping heavily on her crippled leg compared to her movements only a few moments ago. Then it came, swift and powerful. Dutch kicked Ben hard on his buttocks, not knocking him forward to the ground, but rather, an upward kick that whiplashed his head back.

"Yer gonna learn not to chase those hogs," Dutch growled.

"I won't ever do it again," Ben promised.

Pam had turned to her brother, her face red, crying for him, as Duke circled them on their way to the back porch, herding them like cattle for his master. The feral cats scattered from the patio. Then another kick, one that punched

Ben's blistered palms to the ground. Pam dashed inside the back porch door.

Ben had never cried from fear of any person. His father had never struck him. His mother had washed his mouth out with soap, once. Ben had never struck his sisters.

When he scrambled to his feet, Dutch said, "Get in the cob house. Yer gettin' yer ass spanked."

Three years of pride from acting as the man of the house, his family's protector, disappeared in an instant. Ben's neck and face blushed blood-red. Inside the dark cob house, he realized his glasses were missing.

"No, Dad. Please. I won't chase the hogs."

The boy's pleading angered Dutch. Through gritted teeth, he ordered, "Pull down yer pants, Ben."

"No, Dad." He had chosen now to call Dutch his dad. And twice it fell on deaf ears.

Pam remained on the back porch listening to the sounds coming out of the cob house. Hearing her brother beg made her dry-heave, then vomit on her shoes and the porch's linoleum. Michelle and Debi were on the front porch cleaning windows, too far away to hear anything.

Dutch turned a five-gallon bucket upside down and zipped his overalls down to his waist. He drew the black belt with 'DUTCH' monogrammed in turquoise letters on its silver buckle from his jeans.

"Come over here, Ben."

Ben had pushed his pants down just below his white briefs. Incapable of escaping this nightmare, he went over to this man he hardly knew, close enough to see without his glasses that there was no mercy in his eyes-not a trace. Dutch bent the boy over his knee and folded the belt's leather down to a six inch long loop. Ben tried to cover his bare rump with his hand.

"Ben, move yer hand."

The belt lashed fast and hard several times.

84

Michelle thought she heard someone scream "Dad" far off. Then she heard Pam screaming in the front room. Michelle clutched Pam, alarmed to find her so hysterical.

"Pam, what's wrong?"

"Dutch is beating Ben for chasing the pigs!"

Michelle ran through the kitchen and out the porch door. Before she could reach her son it was over. Ben was buttoning his pants, still gasping from shock, coming out of the cob house.

"Go to yer room," Dutch said to Ben.

Ben passed his mother, crying harder because he was so angry at her for not protecting him. And he wanted her to know it.

"What happened?" Michelle asked Dutch, who was looping his belt on as he followed Ben out of the cob house.

"They were chasin' the hogs to death."

The look of disbelief his wife gave him angered him. "You know how much weight they ran off 'em? That costs money, Michelle."

Michelle was flabbergasted. "Couldn't you explain that to him? Did you have to spank him?"

"Those kids gotta learn." Dutch stalked inside the house. He wasn't finished. "Where's Pam?"

"Dutch, I'll ground her to her room. There's no need to spank her. They'll never chase those pigs again."

Dutch could see Pam standing next to Debi just inside the front room. She was scrubbing one hand over a swollen eye, still crying after Ben slammed his bedroom door behind him. Dutch grabbed a yardstick leaning against the kitchen wall and moved toward Pam and Debi.

"Mommy, don't let him spank me!" Pam cried.

Debi started screaming loud and high-pitched. Dutch carried the yardstick to his recliner and sat down as Michelle stepped between Dutch and the girls.

"Pam, come over here."

85

Pam cried. Debi's scream went higher.

"Dutch, don't do this," Michelle said, trying to remain calm.

"Michelle," Dutch warned.

Pam lost hope as her mother gave in, resigned to Dutch's need to discipline her daughter. Debi's crying became hysterical as her sister walked over to their stepfather.

"Debi! Hush!" Dutch barked.

Debi peed her pants, the urine running down the inside of her bare legs. Michelle snatched her into her arms, rocking her.

"Pull yer pants down," Dutch ordered Pam.

"No. Her pants stay on!" Michelle insisted.

Bent over Dutch's lap, Pam kicked her legs, screamed, and covered her rump with her hand.

"Move yer hand, Pam. Now!"

When she obeyed, he whacked away on her flabby bottom with the yardstick, until it cracked and splintered, and broke in two. Dutch let her up.

"Now, go to yer room."

Michelle followed Pam to the stairwell door, with Debi bawling into her chest. "Pam, I'll be up in a second," Michelle said.

Pam hobbled up the dark stairs without a thought of turning on the light. Michelle carried Debi into the bathroom to clean her up and quiet her.

Dutch took the broken yardstick outside, where he found Ben's glasses lying in the dirt. Back in the house, he handed the glasses to Michelle without a word, then strolled into his shop.

Michelle began to cry as she cleaned Ben's dusty lenses. She thought of Kenny, how he never spanked any of the kids. And of her new marriage. Now this.

Ben was lying on his side, curled on his bed, facing

the window to the back porch, its shade pulled all the way down. He was drowning in abject shame after suffering a child's spanking that hurt his pride ten times more than the leather belt that delivered it.

Ben had stood behind his closed bedroom door to hear Pam get hers, wishing he had the strength to rescue her. She was braver than he had been. He heard no pleading from her. No longer the man of the house, Ben Smith closed his red-rimmed eyes in the spinning bedroom, dizzy and nauseated, and afraid of the future.

Upstairs, Michelle and Debi sat on the end of the bed at Pam's feet. Michelle rubbed Pam's legs, explaining Dutch's side. Pam turned her swollen face up to her mother from her tearstained pillow. "He didn't have to kick Ben."

Michelle's hand shot to her mouth to stop the sounds that might come out. Michelle rose to her feet and told Debi to stay with her sister, assuring the girls, "Everything will be fine."

Moments later, Michelle placed Ben's glasses on his dresser. He turned his face away from her when she sat on his bed. She noticed his white socks had a dark ring around his ankles where sweat and dust joined just above his shoe tops.

"Ben," she called softly. "Benjamin Smith."

Michelle stroked a fingernail lightly on the back of his neck. He moved his head forward.

"You mad at me?" she said.

She started to cry. "I'm sorry for what happened. Dutch's animals are important to him in a way we don't understand now."

Ben's throat was choked tight; he was losing a part of himself, and that realization made him withdraw. He had to deal with his shame. Somewhere in the crushing fog of rage and fear, Ben wanted to hurt his mother for marrying Dutch; for taking him away from the comfortable places he knew, and planting him here-far away from sidewalks, paved streets, familiar faces, and their little apartment, where they had struggled and argued, and laughed, and he hadn't felt this shame.

"Ben, look at me, please!" Michelle cried.

He turned his perspiring face on his pillow just as Pam had done. When he opened his eyes and looked at her-she covered her mouth again. She had never seen this expression before in her children. This mix of anger and fear in her son's eyes battered at her heart until she felt it throbbing and erratic in her temples.

Uncertain, she said, "I love you Ben. You love me?"

He did not speak. He could see now that he had a chance to destroy her. All he had to do was keep still and close his eyes and she would die right there on his bed. He couldn't do it. He nodded yes a few seconds before her heart stopped.

She kissed him. "I love you more than anyone else in the whole world," she whispered, quietly exiting his room the way she entered.

Standing outside Ben's bedroom door, Michelle's eyes were on the pee-stained spot on the carpet where Debi had emptied her bladder, out of fear of the man she had married. Her children were terrified of him and hating her for bringing them into his house. She went into the master bedroom, removed her halter top and put on a red and white-checkered, short-sleeve shirt over her bare breasts, leaving the shirt tail out.

On the back porch she discovered, then quickly cleaned the vomit on Pam's shoes and the floor. Her Mexican sandals were lined in a row with her children's shoes on a piece of newspaper spread on the floor. She shoved her feet into the sandals and stalked outside to Dutch's shop.

"Come out from under that truck!" she demanded.

Michelle stood over him while he remained on his back on his creeper looking up at his furious wife.

"You listen to me! My kids are not farm kids. They were raised in the city. Everything's new to them here. I never spanked my kids. And you never will again!"

Dutch blinked, then stared at Michelle in disbelief. He rolled back under the truck's engine and picked up a wrench. His quiet voice rose to her from the truck's open hood. "I never meant to be mean to those kids. They could've gotten hurt real easy by those hogs, Michelle."

"You could have taught them that by explaining it to them. You don't kick them, or spank them. You're a strong man, Dutch. You don't know how strong you are."

Michelle left the shop with a pounding headache that sent her upstairs to nap between the girls. This has been a terrible day. With her eyes closed, she listened to the branches of the pines scraping the aluminum eaves outside the window.

She prayed for the four aspirin to work fast. And: "Please God, let me sleep and wake up to a happy family. Please God."

Hold Me

July, 1959.

On the 3rd of July, Ben bounced out of bed at 4:30 AM and helped Dutch with the chores for the second time. Then he helped load eight squealing hogs into the pickup, after Dutch installed sturdy wooden panels all around the truck's bed to keep the hogs from belly flopping onto Hwy. 20 on their four-hour drive to the Sioux City Stockyards.

Since there were no turns once the truck turned onto Hwy. 17, Dutch let Ben drive them the first hour to Webster City. He warned his stepson not to go over 45 mph with their two thousand-pound cargo. They stopped at a Webster City cafe to eat breakfast, before turning west onto Hwy. 20.

Last night at the supper table, Dutch had told Ben that, after they unloaded the hogs at the stockyards, they'd drive into South Dakota and buy fireworks.

"Firecrackies!" Debi had shouted.

"Yes, firecrackies!" Michelle laughed and rumpled Debi's flyaway hair.

Pam didn't have her usual appetite. Who cares about firecrackers? she thought cynically.

"Why South Dakota?" Ben asked Dutch.

"Cause they're legal in South Dakota. Can't buy 'em in Iowa, Nebraska or Minnesota. And I sure as hell don't think you want just sparklers and snakes on the Fourth of July."

After driving Dutch's truck, and with the exciting prospect of selecting and bringing home illegal fireworks, Ben was beginning to lose some of his enmity for his stepfather. As they ate their breakfast in the Pit Stop Cafe, Ben glowed with pride as Dutch introduced him to the cafe owner and a few patrons that knew him as "his boy" and "his son."

With Dutch behind the wheel again on Hwy. 20, Ben did something he hadn't done since the spanking. He called Dutch 'Dad.'

He asked, "Dad, how far is it to the stockyards?"

And, later, "Dad, can I drive some more on the way back?"

Twenty miles east of Sioux City, Ben's stomach butterflied at the top of each rolling Northwest Iowa hill, conscious of the shifting, thrusting-forward of their load as the truck descended hill after hill like a roller coaster. Ben noticed Dutch's smile-even a boyish laugh or two-as he seemed to say: This one's gonna be a big one.

At the world's largest stockyards, Ben was awed by the sheer number of hogs and cattle held in the wooden pens. The stench of animal dung and urine was so strong, Ben's eyes watered. No place on earth held more livestock at one time during this time of year.

Ben's thoughts were on Jerry. The pig was growing fast. Would he have to deliver him here one day? He put the thought out of his mind, thinking instead of the fun he was going to have with his fireworks, and the possibility that he might get to drive the truck again.

On July 4th, Ben was up by 5:30 AM, unraveling the bandoliers of Black Cats and red Ladyfingers on his bedroom floor, making fuse repairs to some. Snakes and sparklers for Pam and Debi were inside the bag on his dresser, along with two dozen bottle rockets he was saving

91

for the night. Dutch had bought huge Roman Candles and fountains, plus some ominous Cherry Bombs that he had stashed where the kids couldn't get at them.

Pam knew where. She and Debi had been playing upstairs after Dutch and her brother returned with the fire-crackies. Dutch carried a tall paper bag in one hand. Pam watched Dutch reach up to the door jam of the locked door of the room Dutch had said was his mother's sewing room. With a skeleton key he unlocked the door, placed the bag just inside, locked the door and returned the key to that high ledge.

By 8 AM, Ben had four dozen, two-inch tall, forest-green plastic army men lined up on the dusty ground around the light pole in the middle of the farmyard. Some were placed behind dirt clods, others behind the plastic army vehicles that had come with his troops. Dutch had told him to keep away from the propane tank, the gas tank, the shop, the house, the front yard, and Duke. Ben didn't have to be told to stay away from the hogs.

Ben was feeling great. Yesterday, after the yards, Dutch surprised Ben by stopping at a Sioux City farm implement store where he bought Ben a pair of buckled overshoes and work gloves-each a size too large, figuring the boy would grow into them. Dutch had passed on getting Ben a heavy coat on sale for $19.95.

To Ben's amazement, Dutch bought a six foot square, blue wading pool which rode back to the farm in the empty truck bed after Ben had swept out the manure, already solid from exposure to ninety degree sunlight. Dutch had assembled and filled the new pool when they got home that night, so it could warm a bit in the morning sun.

On his return from doing morning chores Dutch reminded Ben that he should stay away from the dry, yellow grass that bordered the feed house, barn, and chicken coop. Dutch grinned at the organized rows of Bob Cats and

Ladyfingers arranged single-file on two pages of newspaper. He told Ben to use the long-burning wicks instead of wasting a box of wooden matches. Dutch watched Ben light and toss a Ladyfinger at his plastic troops ten feet away: Pop! No casualties. Again: Pop! Another miss.

Dutch grinned. "Yer gettin' closer," he said, in a tone of voice that had gone back to his playful youth.

Dutch's joy came out young and free and contagious. Ben needed to play with a man-a father figure he could laugh with, and watch laugh without fear of reproach. Still, he felt a nagging uncertainty about his step-dad. Maybe it was that black belt around Dutch's waist, always there to remind him of the day he was brutally booted back to helpless childhood.

Ben held the burning wick as Dutch lit and tossed a more powerful Bob Cat at the army men. Pop!!

"Good shot, Dad! You got two."

"Ya gotta use the bigger ammo," Dutch laughed.

Ben threw a Bob Cat: Pop!! He hit the clod protecting one of the plastic soldiers. It flew into the air when the dirt burst out in all directions. Dutch stuck a Bob Cat in the dust under one of the jeeps, lit the fuse, and backed up a few steps: Pop!! Dutch laughed, but Ben thought the laugh seemed to catch somewhere in his stepfather's throat.

Without a word, Dutch headed for his shop, then vanished through the side door. Soon the wide shop door was hoisted up and the farmer lost himself in his play area, soothed by its perfect order, where wrench, ratchet, and bolt had its place-and better be there when needed.

Pam and Debi were dressing in their upstairs bedroom when Pam spotted a man walking down the long front drive. She stared at the man from behind the window curtains. Something about him seems odd, Pam thought, and she moved closer to the open window to get a better look at him through the dusty screen.

He had walked two and a half miles from his home near the northwest side of Ledges. He lived a quarter mile north of the Hutton Memorial, the steepest part of the sixteen miles of hiking trails in the park. He had taken the direct way to the Beal farm-the winding canyon road from the west to east through Ledges. No person alive knew Ledges better than Gene Rainbow. Every inch of dirt on every trail had felt his soft step a thousand times, day and night.

Gene had been the one to labor deep into the glacial ground, digging out the holes for the six public restrooms horseshoed east to southwest through the park. He had poured the concrete for the walkways at each restroom. Over the years, he'd picked up at least twenty tons of cans and bottles, plastic and paper-the garbage callously littered onto Iowa's oldest state park.

Pam couldn't see the man's eyes, shaded by a red baseball cap, or make out the white letters above the cap's bill that spelled "GENE." His pants were baggy; the pockets held things in lumps and bulges front and back.

Up close, the most noticeable things about Gene Rainbow, besides the constant palsied nod of his head, were his muscular arms hanging down nearly to his knees. Gene's head-wagging was set at the same speed as his heartbeat, troublesome when his heart pumped at a fast rate-when he'd just run up a flight of stairs, or seen something that scared the hell out of him. His darting blue eyes held a look of insecurity that made him very hard to be around.

In one big hand he held a grocery bag, its top rolled down for easy carrying, like a big lunch. Duke bounded from the back porch and greeted him chest-high on his six-foot tall, two-hundred-pound frame. Gene laid the brown bag down gently on the drive's white gravel near the T-bird's garage, going to one knee to let Duke lick his face and neck. Pam watched the man's long arms wrap around the dog in a loving embrace.

Pam hurried to meet this person-her first contact with the outside world in nearly three weeks.

Michelle answered the light knock on the back porch door. Ben paused in his play some forty yards away and turned to watch the stranger talking to his mother. Duke wagged about the visitor. Ben surmised he wasn't a stranger to Dutch.

"Hi." Michelle smiled, stepping outside to greet the man.

Gene's frenetic eyes shied from Michelle's, down to the brick patio. He removed two dozen fresh eggs in two cartons from the bag and handed them to the new Mrs. Beal, indicating with a finger pointing to himself and then to her, that the eggs were a gift.

"Thank you, Gene?" She read his cap.

Gene could in no way nod yes while nodding no. So he used his smile and a thumbs-up that meant yes, or that he understood or agreed. Michelle's beauty dashed his intentions to be outgoing and relaxed. Michelle showed no wariness of him. This Mrs. Beal appeared too nice for the Dutch Beal he knew.

Pam and Debi slipped out of the door and stood next to their mother. Debi, her thumb stuck in her mouth, looked wide-eyed at the man who seemed to be shaking his head no all the time.

Gene took out a handful of wrapped bubble gum/baseball cards from his sack and looked in Ben's direction.

"That's my son Ben. This is Pam. And my youngest is Debi."

Pam looked into the man's blue eyes, and thought she saw pain because of their ceaseless motion. Then it struck Pam: This was the guy Dutch had been talking about, the kid who fell off the bridge. The same weird guy who decorated the tree and played music in the cemetery.

Pam and Debi followed their mother and Gene over to Ben.

"Ben, this is Gene. He brought us some fresh eggs and something for you, I think."

Gene's work-stained hand opened, exposing the baseball cards, and offered them to the boy. He looked at his mother to see if he should take them. She nodded her approval, then walked back toward the house carrying both Debi and the eggs. Pam waited for Ben's reaction to the stranger.

Ben could see Pam thinking of the Christmas tree, the music, the railroad bridge-all reflected in her knowing smile. Ben handed Gene a Black Cat, pointed to his plastic army, and lit the fuse. Gene let fly the Cat too late; it exploded just a few feet from his hand. Gene laughed, high-pitched and ungoverned, the sort of laugh that Ben and Pam had never heard from an adult. It was a little boy's laugh. Another Black Cat and lit fuse. This time Gene's firecracker hit a jeep and blew it onto its side.

"Good shot!" Ben exclaimed.

Pam's smile faltered upon seeing Gene's tongue roll out of the corner of his mouth, leaving a spit drop hanging under his lower lip. And Gene's smile vanished.

Dutch was standing just inside the wide door of his shop, wiping his hands clean with his red oil rag. Dutch nodded Gene's way, saying, "Gene."

Dutch took off his green and yellow Dekalb hat, wiping the bare skin on his scalp with the sleeve of his worn purplish-blue t-shirt, and stepped toward Gene.

Gene Rainbow had an ulterior motive for visiting the Beal farm, and Dutch knew what it was.

"Gene, I hear you wanna be a bus driver."

Gene smiled, contradicting his nod, then spoke with extreme difficulty. "Test...Monday."

"Will you take a driving test, too?" Dutch asked.

A thumbs-up from Gene.

"Yer gonna have to get a phone if ya want to drive for the county," Dutch said.

By now, Pam had joined her brother, both kneeling near the light pole, rearranging the plastic soldiers, both listening to Dutch and Gene.

"The Christmas tree," Pam whispered to Ben.

"I figured that out for myself," he replied.

Gene began folding his empty bag nervously into a flat square that would fit inside his back pocket.

"You know the board may not approve you. You know that, don't ya, Gene?" Dutch's tone was not unkind.

Another thumbs-up.

"Okay. Well, good luck, Gene," Dutch said.

Gene walked swiftly away with Duke following after, leaping and wagging his tail.

Dutch was one of the nine school board members who would vote on Gene's application to drive a Boone County school bus next September. Gene Rainbow, with eggs and baseball cards had been lobbying for Dutch Beal's vote.

When Gene reached the top of the driveway, Ben called out to him. "Thanks for the baseball cards!"

Gene turned and waved with a smile, his long arms now swinging freely, no longer burdened.

Dutch stood behind his two stepchildren, who were still crouched in the July dust.

"I want you kids to quit usin' the toilet in the house durin' daylight hours. Use the outhouse."

Ben nodded yes, his eyes going to that damn belt, adding, "Okay, Dad."

Pam was horrified at the thought. Her words just came out. "But, Dad, there's wasps all over the outhouse."

Dutch watched her brown eyes drop to the black belt used on her brother. "They won't bother ya," he said.

Dutch went inside his shop.

"I have to pee, now," Pam said to Ben, her chubby thighs knocking together.

"Well, go!" Ben said.

"Will you stand by the door, Ben, please?"

Ben's face twisted in the exaggerated frown that other times had made Pam belly laugh. Still, he followed her over to the outhouse, the same one Dutch's parents had used. It was about ten feet from the cob house, but back a ways, twenty feet from the shop.

Pam creaked open the outhouse door wide enough to slip in, then stood frozen with fear. Ben put his hands on her back pretending to push her inside. She stepped back fast, bumping into him. She swung around. "You creep!"

Ben giggled at his sister's plight. "I'm leaving, now," he claimed.

"No!" Pam cried.

She stepped inside the windowless one-seater and gagged at the smell. The roll of toilet paper was damp and waffled from the morning dew. It stood on its end next to the dark hole. She peered up to the ceiling. The wasps were not there.

Ben closed the door all the way.

Pam imagined wasps crawling around inside, while her butt hung in midair above the crescent-shaped hole and its cool and creepy updraft-she never peed so fast.

Ben was holding his hand on the closed outhouse door when his sister burst through, pushing the door wide enough to escape.

"I'm telling Mom!" she shouted, heading for the back porch door.

Michelle stood at the kitchen stove boiling Gene's eggs to be used in her potato salad. Though Dutch didn't want her to light the stove on such a hot day, she had convinced him to let her bake two apple pies in the morning after breakfast. When Pam came into the kitchen from the back porch, Debi was eating cereal, already dressed in her bathing suit, excitedly kicking her skinny legs back and forth pretending to be in the wading pool.

"Mommy's going swimming with us," Debi said.

One look at her older daughter's face and Michele asked, "What's wrong, Pam?"

"Dutch made me use the outhouse. Ben held the door shut and I couldn't get out."

"That's an old gag," Michelle said. "Just ignore him."

"Why do we have to use that stinky old outhouse?" Pam whined.

"I'm sure your stepfather has his reasons."

Changing the subject, Michelle inquired, "How's your leg feel?"

"My foot hurts."

Michelle had Pam sit on a kitchen chair and stretch her leg as Edith had advised. Then she pressed on Pam's heel. "There?"

Pam nodded yes, wincing dramatically. Michelle took Pam's pudgy foot in both hands, extending her damaged leg before examining both legs together. "The left is still about an inch shorter. But the muscle's getting bigger since you quit wearing the brace. See that?" Pam only nodded, her eyes not showing nearly the same excitement as her mother's. Such sad eyes, Michelle thought.

"When can we go in the water, Mom?" Pam asked.

"I guess in about an hour it will be warm enough. Go put on your bathing suit."

"That ugly black thing?"

"Oh, Pam, it is not!"

"It's got a hole on the side," she pointed to a spot on her ribs. "Can't I get a new one?"

Her mother didn't answer, weighing it over. "We'll see," Michelle said.

Pam smiled. That meant yes.

At the top of the stairs, Pam decided to open the closed door to the storeroom. Dutch had put some of the things from their apartment in there, but those were of no interest. The furniture in the room was cluttered with boxes, some open, some taped; old clothes hung inside a moth-balled closet that gave the whole room its unique smell of old wood and dust and stale air. Nothing really caught Pam's eye. She went to a box, folded shut, and found a stack of boy's clothing. Why would Dutch save his old clothes, she wondered. Going through the little pants and knickers with matching shirts and socks gave Pam the notion that her stepfather was once a small boy, and must have once upon a time played with toys. But she found none. Maybe they're in the taped boxes, she thought.

Pam left the room as quietly as she entered, closing the door without a sound. She turned toward the locked sewing room, turned its doorknob, then looked up to the tall doorjamb, where she knew Dutch kept the key. She realized even if she stood on the little chair at her vanity she would-n't be able to reach it, and she doubted her brother could either.

She went into her bedroom and looked for something long she could use to retrieve the key, and found nothing. Her brain was searching for a better idea as she removed her one-piece swim suit from a dresser drawer. Dutch had told her mother that the vanity, dresser, and bed had belonged to his sister, now living in Wisconsin. How scary it must have been to be a girl and live up here alone with a bully like Dutch, Pam mused, while brushing her hair in front of the vanity mirror. Pam's chocolate-brown eyes dropped to the pink comb resting on the vanity's cluttered surface.

Quickly, she put on her swimsuit, then slipped on green rubber thongs. Now, she avoided the mirror. She knew she was fat, not chubby and cute. Pam picked up the pink comb and left her room with a plan.

Downstairs, Michelle asked Pam to show her the tear in her suit, still thinking about how to convince her husband to allow her to buy a new one.

"Mom?"

"What?"

"My comb slid under the door of that room that's locked."

"How'd that happen?"

"It slipped out of my hand and my foot kicked it under. Will you get it for me?"

"I'll have Dutch get it later. Use your brush."

"No," Pam whined. "Dutch might get mad at me."

Michelle knew her daughter had a point. "I don't have the key."

"It's above the door. You can reach it, Mom. Please?"

Soon Pam was leading her mother upstairs. Michelle tried to reach the key and was too short on her tiptoes. Pam brought the vanity chair out to the landing and placed it in front of the locked door. "Mom, stand on this chair."

Michelle unlocked the door and opened it. Their eyes went to the ceiling where a dozen strings suspended vintage 1930 and 1940-era model bombers and fighters. The tiny room had no windows. It was stifling hot in July. The wallpaper had aged to a colorless beige; it had peeled and curled in many places from extremes of temperature. A few other airplanes were clumped together on the floor as if they'd crashed and never been repaired. Michelle saw no signs that the room had ever held a sewing machine.

"Dutch must like airplanes," Pam said.

"Maybe so," Michelle replied. She picked up the comb and blew the dust balls from it, planning to wash it in the bathroom sink later. She stuck the comb in her back pocket, then closed the door, locked it, and returned the key to the ledge. When Michelle carried the chair to the girls' room, she noticed their unmade bed and started to straighten it, saying, "C'mon, help me make the bed before Grampa Hutch gets here."

"Mom, why does he have to come here?" Pam's voice rose to a whine.

"He hasn't met Dutch, so we invited him to the farm."

"He can't see it anyway," Pam retorted, and jerked the blanket toward the head of the bed, leaving it crooked.

"Pam, if you won't help, then move out of my way."

Michelle quickly went around the bed and made it, while Pam pouted about Hutch's visit.

Gene had taken the long way home, adding a mile-and-a-half by walking the south prairie of Ledges, then picking up a hiking trail past Lost Lake to the gravel road that ran along the Des Moines River. Stands of pussy willow hid doves still cooing morning greetings. He knelt at a healthy bunch of violet-blue Veronica, and splayed back the toothed, yellowish green leaves to better see the delicate spikes.

He plucked several, holding them way too tight, the stems crushed in his powerful hand in response to a sudden worry. What if Dutch voted against him, and he lost his long dream of driving a school bus? Why should that man control my world so?

Gene pulled his thoughts out of their negative swirl. If he allowed himself to dwell on failure, he would give himself a pounding headache that would persist until he slept.

His tongue spoke certain things more clearly than his own name, for he had taught himself four important words gleaned from the Bible his mother had left him.

"Love," he said.

Gene gazed at the Veronicas in his hand.

"Laughter," he said, as he remembered the day in the hospital bed fifteen years ago, when he dreamt that his best friend had told him to cheer up about his head-nod, and to think of how much easier it would be to brush his teeth. This thought brought the same joyous laughter he so desperately needed then, and needed again now.

"Forgiveness," he pronounced. It was the one word of the four that always made him cry, relieving the pinched pain behind his eyes that signaled accumulated worry.

At the narrow entrance to the cemetery, Gene paused. Then he stepped around the old markers, headed for his family's plot. He could hear the music playing from the radio. It was a miracle.

The tears that had misted his eyes a moment before, now fell in streams, salty and warm on his cheeks. He repeated "forgiveness" again and again, as he moved toward the Christmas tree that had been torched sometime during the night. It stood black and barren, a quarter of its former size. Gene could smell the reek of gasoline rising from the charred tree. The train set had melted into a chain of black and red globs. He found the silver star next to the radio, its heat-deformed case vibrating to Patsy Cline's voice coming out of the tiny speaker holes.

"Patience," Gene said.

He braced his shoe against the tree and pushed it down to the ground, breaking the trunk off just above the stand. He heaved the blackened tree over the back fence into a thicket of ragweed, then yanked out the tree stand anchored in cement and soil. Perhaps it was just as well that the tree disappear before it was seen by anyone who could hurt his chances of being hired by the school board.

Gene drew the empty bag from his back pocket and filled it with the remains of the charred train set and other leftovers in the ashes. He put the radio in his pocket since it still worked. He carried the tree stand and full sack of debris to a trash can beside a Ledges restroom.

The park was crowded with hikers, vehicles, and picnickers escaping the holiday heat. Summer students and faculty from Ames made up most of the hikers. Gene couldn't escape them on the narrow trails, or avoid them by stopping under the arched stone bridges, where they clustered to chat about people they knew in common. Rock-and-roll was in-and so was making fun of people like Gene Rainbow. He despised the herd mentality that caused them to stop, point, and stare at the strange man known as Mr. No.

Families from the closest towns filled the large timber and stone picnic shelters. Those from farther away held down blankets and gathered around open picnic tables covered with potato salad, baked beans, bags of chips, burgers and hot dogs, and jammed coolers of beer and soda. Folks came from all over: Boone, Fort Dodge, Marshalltown and Des Moines, Dayton, Rockwell City, Buckeye, Jewell, Eagle Grove and Clarion. This was their oasis of escape; it was Gene's year 'round. He said his four words over and over, until he found himself within sight of his one-bedroom trailer on a gravel road just off Route 23.

If he got the job, this would be a stop on his bus route. His brother's family lived in the ramshackle one-story shack in front of his place. He decided to check on his niece, Darlene, before shutting himself inside his little trailer.

Ray and Charlotte Rainbow drove eighty-three miles to Denison to work 12-hour shifts at Iowa Meat Packers. They were there today, earning holiday pay at the plant. Since infancy Darlene had been left alone to raise herself.

The Rainbows housed some four-dozen chickens in a coop too close to their house. The stink of chicken shit permeated even the clothes the Rainbows wore. Fifteen-year-old Darlene always smelled musty, as if she never bathed. Gene would have moved his trailer if not for the breeze that most-times whiffed the odors of his brother's homestead away from his windows.

Gene recognized Scott Lee's peach and white '56 Ford parked near the front porch. Gene wasn't sure how old the boy was, but knew he wasn't out of high school yet.

The screen door's mesh was too dirty to see inside the front room. And the front room was too filthy to enter without wearing shoes. Gene pushed open the door. Large glass ashtrays, green and rose-colored, sat on the tables and the floor, stuffed to their rims with Pall Mall butts, some with Charlotte's pink and red lipstick stains. A low sofa and matching dark-brown armchair displayed food crumbs, hairpins, and a scattered deck of cards. A wobbly-legged coffee table was angled far out from the sofa. Discarded clothes lay on the floor in every direction. The kitchen was stacked with dirty dishes; a swarm of buzzing houseflies attacked the scraps of meat left on plates on the kitchen table. Gene could hear Darlene's bed creaking. Down the short hallway, her door was open.

Gene had stood in Darlene's doorway often in the last two years. He'd even chased Scott Lee away a time or two. Just for a moment he pictured his niece as a happy toddler, not the harlot who demanded a pack of smokes, or a large bottle of RC Cola from her eager male visitors.

Lee's shiny, lily-white buttocks were in midair over Darlene's curvaceous body when Gene's foot kicked him off the bed.

"Uncle Gene." Darlene laughed up into her protector's eyes.

"For cripes sake!" Lee complained, scrambling to his feet and rubbing his bruised butt. "You said that crazy retard wasn't around."

Gene stood over Darlene nodding no, no, no, as she howled with laughter, holding one hand over her center, the other hand and forearm across her breasts. Her frizzy short-brown hair was wild and messy above a forehead gouged and scarred from a tomboy life. Gene reached for the thin

105

bedspread on the floor and covered her.

"No smokes today, Darlene!" Lee shouted, grabbing the unopened pack of Pall Malls he'd given her to pay for his pleasure. The screen door banged as Lee hurried to his car. Gene caught up with Darlene's naked body just off the porch, where he wrapped the bedspread over her shoulders again. Darlene waved her middle finger angrily at Lee's dust cloud.

"Scott Lee. You ain't gettin' no more from me, never!"

Gene started for his trailer.

"Uncle Gene."

He didn't turn back. Fifteen-year-old girls shouldn't be doin' that, he stewed. From Boone to Madrid she was known as the ugly girl with a woman's body, who would go to bed with any man or boy with a heartbeat. When word got out about this latest encounter, and Gene knew Lee would blab to his buddies within the next hour, it could ruin his chances with the school board.

Barefoot, with the bedspread wrapped around her toned and tan body, Darlene tiptoed around the sharpest rocks as she followed Gene to his trailer. A battered silver bicycle leaned against its side.

"Uncle Gene. Wait!"

He knew she would beg him for cigarette money, doing 'that thing' that so confused him, and yet gave him more solace than a year's worth of Bible reading.

Gene's trailer sat in a weed-choked break in the corn-field behind his brother's house. Darlene snagged her wrap on the milk crate step on her way through the trailer's only door. Irritated, she tugged it loose and demanded, "How in the hell are ya gonna drive a bus when ya only have a bicy-cle, for Christ's sake?"

Gene pointed a floor fan toward his armchair, turned it on high, and sat down. Darlene hiked the bedspread up high on her long, muscular thighs and let the breeze from

106

the fan dry her sweaty skin.

Gene took off his red cap and tilted his head over the back of the chair. He closed his eyes and the pitiful shaking of his white-blond head transformed into a slow roll from side-to-side.

Darlene went to the kitchen sink and wet a dishrag, patting it on her uncle's neck and forehead. The eleven years between their ages seemed unimportant as she knotted the bedspread over her breasts and sat across Gene's lap. She laced her fingers behind his neck, extending her thumbs to each side of his jaw, slowing the motion of his head to a tremor. He looked into Darlene's clear blue eyes. His eyes would soon be as clear as hers, and show a sparkle of gold in the irises, if he did what his niece wanted.

"Hold me," she said to the man who had diapered her and fed her, and had been more like a father to her than her own.

Gene swallowed hard as her hands pulled his face to the copper skin above her breasts. His arms closed around her bare shoulders, pulling her against him.

"Hold me tighter, Uncle Gene."

It stopped. His head was still, not even a twitch of motion. As long as he remained in the pressure of Darlene's hard embrace, he could speak. The two had discovered this small miracle long ago when Darlene was a little girl.

"Stop selling your body to all those guys."

Darlene started to cry. So did Gene. She let him talk.

"I can do good driving a bus," he said. "I'll buy new clothes for you and a washing machine. People say bad things about you in Boone. It hurts me to hear it."

Her uncle's selflessness brought a wave of guilt. "If the doctors see what we do, maybe they can make it last," Darlene cried.

"No. When I was in the hospital my doctor said an operation might paralyze me. At least now I can walk. I went over to Dutch Beal's place today. He's got a new wife and three kids."

"Did he say anything about driving the bus?"

"He probably thinks I can't do it. Sometimes I practice at the garage when nobody's around."

"Uncle Gene? Can you buy me a pack of cigs?"

"Would you steal 'em if I didn't?"

"Yes," Darlene said, and laughed.

"Okay, then."

The water was ice-cold at first, but after a few minutes it was a welcome respite from the hot day-and only one o'clock. Michelle wore sunglasses; every bare inch of skin around her black one-piece bathing suit was covered with a mixture of baby oil and iodine. She sat on one of the four corners of the wading pool with her lower legs and feet submerged in the Iowa well water. Debi and Pam sat in the water up to their necks on each side of their mother.

Pam was the first to see Ernie's white cab make the turn onto their gravel drive. The cab stopped in front of the T-bird's garage. Hutch's dreaded arrival was now here. Pam's heart raced as if she had taken one of her mother's pep pills, the California prescription renewed by her Des Moines doctor when she complained of fatigue and feeling blue.

Michelle strolled toward the idling cab in the relentless heat. Only Duke trailed after her. All of the cab's windows were rolled down. Hutch occupied the back seat, his cigarette pouched out from the middle of his mouth as his long, skinny fingers felt for a twenty-dollar bill inside his wallet. Ernie's head was turned toward his passenger. He jerked around at the sound of Michelle's voice.

"Hi, Ernie!" Michelle smiled.

"Hi, Michelle."

Ernie's eyes slid away from Michelle's full figure as

Debi came over to greet the cabbie who had taken them to get ice cream.

"Ernie, you're welcome to eat with us," Michelle invited.

"He has plans in Boone," Hutch said, extending the twenty to his driver.

Ernie took the bill saying, "Pick you up at seven, Hutch?"

"Seven? You have to stay for the fireworks, Grampa Hutch!" Michelle insisted.

To the cab driver she said, "Ernie, you come back at seven and have some potato salad, a drink, and stay for the fireworks."

"Yeah, Ernie, see you at seven," Hutch agreed.

Michelle took a bag containing a fifth of bourbon from Hutch's raised hand. Hutch's fingers were wrapped around the handle of his cinnamon-colored cane as Michelle helped him out of the cab's back seat. The cab's wheels started to crunch over the white rock, then braked to a stop. Duke stood braced, growling, on the driveway a few feet from the cab's front bumper. Ernie rolled up his window fast and called out to Michelle, who was leading Hutch toward the back patio, "Michelle. There's a huge dog on my front bumper!"

Michelle said, "He'll move."

Ernie stretched over the back seat and rolled up the rear windows while the farm dog barked and circled the vehicle. As Ernie drove away, Duke chased the cab almost to the paved Hwy. 17.

"Poor Ernie, you should have seen the look on his face," Michelle told Hutch.

He smiled. "Don't worry about old Ernie. His appointment is at the nearest bar. He'll be drunk in an hour and won't even remember it."

When Hutch approached, Pam clambered out of the

wading pool, instinctively covering her bathing suit with a bath towel. The old man wore a short-sleeved, white shirt with dime-size gray dots, its straight cut untucked and cool below his big belly. His silver hair, slicked back with hair cream, matched Bermuda shorts that were baggy all the way down to his knobby, white knees. Pam cringed at the sight of blue, knotted veins protruding from his bleached parakeet legs. Hutch's feet were covered with silver-colored nylon socks pulled halfway up his shins, and gray, canvas slip-ons with tiny holes over and around the front where his toes raised up ever-so-slightly to ward off any protruding obstacle.

"Here's Pam," Michelle informed Hutch.

"Hello, Pammy!" Hutch barked, his arm extended, expecting Pam to come to him for a hug and kiss. But Pam ran inside the back door, leaving Michelle aghast and explaining, "She's upset because Dutch made her use the outhouse."

"Poor thing. You do have indoor plumbing?" Hutch asked with his sightless blue eyes looking at Michelle.

"Of course we do! Dutch probably wanted the kids to know what farm life was like when he was a kid."

Just then, Dutch came toward them from his shop, unzipping his overalls to let Michelle know he had finished tinkering and was ready to be a host. "Oh," Michelle said, "here he comes, now."

Dutch slung a possessive arm around his wife's shoulders. "You must be Hutch. How are ya?"

The blind man replied, "Just fine, Dutch. And you?"

"Oh, I'm doin' okay," Dutch grinned at his young wife, letting the tone of his voice tell the other man that he enjoyed a good sex life.

Hutch grinned at the farmer, wide-eyed and joshing. "You know what they say. If ya ain't Dutch...it ain't much!"

Dutch let loose a snort of laughter. "Yes sir, that's a

good one," he said. Then the farmer's face reddened and creased along one side of his mouth, as if to say he really needed a good laugh, but that was as far as he'd go.

Duke had returned from chasing Ernie's cab and came up stealthily behind the blind visitor and barked. Hutch jerked spasmodically and grabbed Michelle's arm.

"Duke! Go lay down!" Dutch ordered.

The dog cowered and slouched over to a patch of shaded grass, circled, and lay panting on his belly, all the while staring at his beloved master.

"Where's Ben?" Michelle asked, ignoring the incident.

"I don't know. He's 'round here somewhere," Dutch said.

Ben was crouched next to Jerry at the back of the hog yard. He had reasoned that once Hutch arrived, Dutch wouldn't be busy with his work. For the rest of the day, Ben's every move would be scrutinized by his stepfather.

Ben hopped the hog yard fence and headed for the one spot he had not yet explored-the place on the farm he most feared.

The fixed ladder steps leading up forty feet were secure enough. Fear of heights. Fear of letting go. Those two things Ben had avoided since his cowardice at the rope-swing in Wichita. After that, and after the ass-kicking and ass-whipping dealt by Dutch-Ben needed some kind of victory, a risk to face and master.

His skinny legs quivered as he climbed higher and higher, ascending to the corn crib's platform, not daring to look down. There was no one around to shout encouragement, or to put him down. Standing on the platform he breathed deeply. But the air was hazed with dust from a hundred metric tons of golden corn stored nearly level with his feet on both sides of the platform. This was Dutch's bank.

111

He walked over to the closed little window facing the farm laid out before him. Across the gravel road Ben could see Lester licking his salt block under the shade of a century-old oak tree. Behind the bull's pasture: Ledges. The vehicles coming and going through the park's entrance were kicking up a dusty rim above the trees. Ben recognized another challenge: making Ledges his territory. Standing here was not enough.

The heat was stultifying in the corn crib. His every breath seemed to sear his lungs. He pounded upward with the heel of his hand at the stuck window until a chunk of glass crashed to the wooden floor. His heart and mind convulsed with a new worry: What would Dutch do when he found out? His mind racing with a thousand things that might happen, Ben pushed the glass down into the sea of corn at the edge of the platform.

Back and forth he paced on the seventy-foot platform, consciously winding up before balancing on one of the platform's narrow support beams at the top of the corn. Ben's fear of Dutch was greater than testing this vast sea of corn; he stepped off the board feeling his foot and leg sink calf-deep. When he felt the corn's pull no longer, he brought in the other leg. He sank to his knees, then held. He was no closer to drowning here than in Debi's wading pool. Elation filled him.

Dutch might never see the broken window. And if he did, there was no way Dutch could connect the damage to Ben. He tugged his feet out of the corn and hoisted himself back onto the platform. Standing again on the worn wooden planks, he pulled the baseball cards Gene had given him from his back pocket and opened one, finding a picture of Warren Spahn in his Milwaukee Braves uniform. Ben stuck the pink rectangle of gum in his mouth and remembered sitting beside his mother, one summer night, while they watched the Wichita team play. With a satisfied smile curving his lips, he descended the ladder and slipped out into the farmyard.

Pam thought it was stupid for her mother to walk Hutch around the first floor of the farmhouse, telling him about the rooms, when he was blind as a bat. Now, Hutch sat at the kitchen table sipping his straight bourbon and side water listening to Michelle go on and on about their new life on the farm and how much she and the kids liked it- leaving out the spankings and Dutch's limited attempts at conversation.

While their stepfather prepared the grill on the shaded grass, Pam and Debi lit black snakes on the brick patio. Dutch gave Ben a job that would keep him busy for three days, even if he went nonstop. Dutch called it "pick up sticks." That meant every twig and tree branch blown to the ground had to be gathered and stacked in a pile. Looking at all the debris on the ground, Ben thought the pile eventually would reach ten feet high.

Later, Hutch was gabbing away in a lawn chair near the grill, smoking a menthol, his bird legs crossed at his bare knees. Michelle loved any conversation that included her husband. And Hutch had a way of holding a person's attention with his perspicacity, his quick wit ready for anything. Hutch impressed the farmer by reciting the latest head count and prices of cattle and hogs at all the major markets in Chicago, Kansas City, Omaha and Sioux City. Dutch left his private stock sizzling on the grill to sit on a lawn chair next to Hutch and explain his opinion on this or that index move while his wife listened intently, arranging covered platters of potato salad and baked beans sweetened with brown sugar on a card table.

"Go tell your brother it's time to eat," Michelle told Pam.

Pam sought out Ben in the front yard, where he was raking leaves and twigs off the grass. After she gave him the message, she told him about the creepy airplanes hanging in the locked room upstairs.

"How'd you get in there?" he asked.

"I talked mom into opening the door." She smirked.

"Well, it's not much of a mystery," he said. "Why don't you find out what's in all those taped-up boxes in the storeroom."

"I don't want another spanking, that's why! Dummy!" Pam exclaimed.

When Ben returned to receive his paper plate of food from his mother, she ignored her son's dirty hands, knowing Dutch wouldn't want soap and water wasted on such a trifling matter. Dutch's eccentricities had surfaced one by one, beginning on the first day of their marriage. She hadn't worn makeup since their honeymoon night, when Dutch told her it looked like the war paint worn by Vegas showgirls.

Michelle risked giving Hutch an extra serving, justifying her act as much the same as a weenie or burger dropped on the grass and gobbled by Duke, who lay in the shade sniffing the barbecued meat. The dog had received two such gifts from his master.

Flies, black and quick from parasitic living off Dutch's animals and their waste, took advantage of Hutch's determined chewing. Now and then, he brushed them from his face.

Spurts of dialogue separated large bites of food. "Excellent, Michelle!" "Perfect potato salad." "Best baked beans."

After his third double shot of bourbon with a water chaser, his comments had become uniformly flattering.

The kids sat together on a shaded blanket far from Hutch, never finding him charming or funny like their mother and stepfather. When Michelle finally sat down on a lawn chair, she experienced the secure feeling of family

114

she'd been hoping for since she cooked their first breakfast together. As Dutch sipped his Grain Belt she acknowledged that her children were more disciplined now, and that they were certainly eating better. Dutch's tightness with a buck, and the money he saved, was better than postdating checks and the constant money worries of the past few years.

Pam enjoyed her meal until her mother's baked beans started to muffle onto the blanket beneath her and she knew the outhouse was due for a longer visit. Ben grinned at his sister's plight. Pointing to the old shit house, he whispered, "The wasps will be waiting for you."

Pam's fist came down on her brother's thigh, hurting him enough that he limped away to recover out of sight of Dutch's low tolerance for horseplay.

His meal done, Ben went back to lobbing firecrackers at his army men. Putting off the outhouse for as long as she could, Pam enjoyed seeing Hutch flinch at each exploding Bob Cat. But, then she had to go, and sulked over to the reeking privy.

She opened the door. Ben had been right. The black and gold wasps were aroused by her entry. Pam rushed out and headed to her mother.

"Mom, the wasps are in there!"

"They won't bother ya," Dutch said.

Ben followed his sister to the half-open outhouse door, looking back at Dutch's agreeing grin before lighting and tossing in a Bob Cat. Pop!! Dutch laughed when Pam came running outside pulling up her pants. Michelle's chuckle hurt Pam's feelings, but it was Hutch's roaring laughter after Dutch described what happened that turned Pam's face crimson with anger and humiliation. Michelle took Pam by the hand and led her into the house to use the bathroom.

"You got yer sister a good one, Ben! You better watch out, she'll getcha back!"

115

Dutch appeared to be proud of Ben for a change.

Ernie sat on the cab's warm hood smoking a cigarette and licking his chops, waiting for Michelle to bring him a paper plate of beans and grilled burgers warmed on the stove and a heaping portion of cold potato salad. On her way out with Ernie's plate, Hutch told her the cab driver didn't need any more beer, and to tell him he had said so.

The sun was finally starting to sink; in an hour or so they would all watch the fireworks Dutch was preparing in the front yard up by the gravel road.

Ben was sitting on his rump on the grass, slapping mosquitoes on his exposed flesh, fifteen yards from Dutch, who had welded a makeshift rocket launcher from a two-inch pipe and an iron bar bent to hold the rocket's base with fuse exposed above the ground. Dutch had rubbed kerosene on his neck, arms and face to keep the mosquitoes off. Finally, he'd seen Ben suffer enough.

"Ben, you know that glass container with the spout on the counter in the shop by the wrenches?"

"Yeah."

"Go put some on yerself so ya don't get eaten alive."

"Okay, Dad."

Ben ran past his mother, who was leaning against the cab's front bumper watching Ernie eat his first bites of her potato salad and beans. The dog lay panting on his belly, his brown eyes on Ernie. Ernie tried to offer Duke a piece of his burger, holding it out in the dog's direction. But Duke growled low and steady, making Ernie think his one hundred thirty-five pounds were no match for the seventy pound mixed breed.

Ben may have put on a bit more of the greasy kerosene than necessary, but it sure felt good to call Dutch "Dad." Ben thought, he's really strict, but he cares about me and protects me. Leaving the shop, Ben made sure he turned the light off above Dutch's sparkling wrenches, sockets, and ratchets, all organized by size, and cleaned by the same kerosene that kept Ben sniffing at his forearms.

Dutch was busy way out in the front yard. Ben's eyes went to the scraggly little rat catchers, the nice kitties that would not let his sisters come close to petting them. They had scattered into and under the cob house as he approached them.

He took a wooden match from his back pocket and lit a Lady Finger, tossing it into the cob house. It tickled the kerosene covered hairs on the back of his neck to hear the cats panic inside the place of his shame.

By 9 PM Ernie had dropped 10 cigarette butts onto the white gravel near his front wheel. Dutch leaned against the cab's fender and swapped army stories with the little man. Duke came over and nuzzled his master's thigh, wanting the pat he got, and returned to his spot near the patio as the lime glow of lightning bugs were growing brighter with the darkness.

Hutch and Michelle sat in lawn chairs some twenty feet in front of Ernie, still lounging on his cab's hood. Hutch had another bourbon and chaser on a folding stand, his hand touching the bourbon glass to gauge its location next to an ashtray. Debi and Pam sat on a blanket next to Michelle, covering their legs with the blanket ends to keep from being bitten by mosquitoes. Ben crouched near the bag of fireworks that Dutch had placed 30 feet away from the launching site.

Exploding fireworks could be heard to the north in Ledges, now invisible in the darkness. Dutch told Ben to light the bottle rocket standing ready on his launching ramp. Debi applauded the POP! and the orange sparks the slim rocket made fifty feet straight up. Pam was still sulking because Hutch had laughed at her dash from the outhouse. Then Dutch's Roman Candle made a powerful

WHOOSH! before exploding into umbrellas of pinkish purple, red and green-again and again and again-it thrilled
Pam. Debi gave a thumb-sucking gasp and clutched her
mother's calf with her other hand.

"Mom, can we light the sparklers now?" Pam asked.

"Dutch, can the girls light the sparklers now?"
Michelle called to him.

Dutch pulled sparklers from the bag of fireworks near
Ben and told him to light them with his butane lighter, and
to twirl them away from his body once lit.

"Not on the blankets. Stay on the grass!" Dutch
ordered.

Debi and Pam excitedly waved their silver sparklers,
pausing when Dutch sent up another WHOOSH! from a
Roman Candle, or when a conical fountain showered the
Beal front yard with vivid colors, illuminating the smiles of
Dutch and Michelle, the awestruck faces of Ernie and the
children, and the blank-blue stare of Hutch's that Pam
despised with a passion.

When Pam's sparkler sputtered out, Dutch warned her
that it was still hot, and to put it on the driveway. Michelle
took Debi inside with her to get Hutch one for the road.
Dutch was busy correcting the angle of his rocket launcher
after the last blast tipped it sideways.

Pam took a long look at Hutch, then said, "Ben, light
me another sparkler."

When Ben came over to her with the lighted sparkler,
she whispered, "Now, give me a firecracker."

"No."

Then a miracle happened. Michelle called out to
Dutch from the front porch that he had a phone call. Dutch
hustled across the yard holding his shirt pocket to keep
things from falling out. Hutch crossed his legs and lit up a
cigarette with his silver lighter. Ben shoved his sister aside
before she could reach into the bag of fireworks while still

118

holding her lit sparkler.

"Wanna blow yourself up, dummy?" he asked.

"Not me. But if you don't give me one, I'll tell Dutch you broke his clock."

She had him. Last Saturday morning, when Dutch and Michelle were in Boone grocery shopping, Ben had knocked the gold-colored, plastic, star-shaped clock off the wall, breaking one of the 18-inch points in half. He had used Elmer's Glue to put it together. Dutch had saved over two thousand S & H Green Stamps to get the battery operated clock.

"There's only Cherry Bombs in there," Ben said.

"Give me one right now-or else!"

Ben swallowed hard and handed Pam one of the infamous firecrackers, illegal in forty states.

In the kitchen, Dutch was on the phone with Buzz LaFleur, who farmed 3 miles southwest of the Beal place, a lifelong friend. Buzz was inviting Dutch and his new family over for a chicken dinner on Sunday when the Cherry Bomb went off. The explosion rattled the kitchen windows and Debi, who screamed. Even Buzz's wife standing at her kitchen sink heard its blast over the phone.

"I better go see what's goin' on," Dutch told Buzz, then slammed down the phone.

Praying that Pam and Ben were not hurt, Michelle dashed out the back door behind Dutch, dragging Debi.

They encountered Ernie leading Hutch to his cab. When Michelle and Dutch got closer, they could see the grimace on Hutch's face and his tousled hair.

"What happened?" Michelle said.

Ernie was inclined to protect the kids, but he couldn't think of a good story, or beat Hutch's reply. "Those brats tried to blow me up!"

Dutch opened the cab's back door and helped Ernie get Hutch inside.

"My ass and legs are numb. My ears are ringing. Bring me a drink, Michelle!"

"I'll go get it," she said.

"Make it a double!" Hutch barked.

After inspecting Hutch's legs and finding no open wounds, Dutch was now ready to focus on his step-kids. He stalked over to the bag of fireworks and called out to the kids, "Get yer butts over here!" No answer.

Michelle's blood pressure was skyrocketing and her skin crawled with fear when Dutch shouted for the kids a second time. She raced outside with Hutch's double and handed it to Ernie to deliver to Hutch who lay prostrate on the back seat. Hutch seemed more stunned than hurt as he gulped down his bourbon without a chaser.

From a distance Michelle could see the silver flash of her husband's belt buckle at his waist. Her concern for Hutch diminished with each period of silence after Dutch's unanswered calls. Then he said, low and firm, "Duke, go get 'em."

To Michelle's horror, her husband had sicked his dog on her children.

Three hundred yards down the dark gravel road that ran along the east side of Lester's pasture, Ben and Pam stopped running to talk it over. Pam's leg really hurt and she was gasping for breath.

"We have to go back," Ben said.

"Easy for you to say. You aren't the one who did it," Pam replied.

"I gave it to you. That's enough to get me into the cob house," Ben said.

"What about me? I'm the one who ran over to Hutch and dropped it under his chair. Did you see his face?" Pam asked.

Pam's description of Hutch's expression, and Ben's memory of Hutch's bird legs flying heels over head into the side table, toppling glasses and the overflowing ashtray, produced hysterical laughter, until they heard Duke's paws throwing gravel, closing in on them.

"It's Duke! We've got to go back," Ben said.

Pam followed her brother toward the farm.

"We have to say it was an accident," Pam said.

"Ernie saw what happened."

"So what. It's our word against his. We'll say I got scared and threw it away from the bag of fireworks," Pam said.

"Dutch knows I wouldn't light it near the bag," Ben said.

"I'll say it was me...I lit it...and got it myself. Don't worry," Pam said.

Duke came up to them, wagging his tail, circling them, finding them as Dutch had ordered.

As they neared the turn in the road that meant they were close to the farm, Pam went into a tearful act of contrition that made Ben look guilty as sin. Dutch's truck roared toward them, on his way to find them. Ben stepped into the path of Dutch's oncoming headlights, fearing more trouble from his stepfather the longer he searched and found nothing. Lucky for Ben and Pam, Michelle was in the truck, too, with Debi.

"It was an accident, Dad," Ben swore.

Dutch said, "Get back to the house!"

Michelle noticed he used the same tone he had used when he commanded Duke to "get 'em." Ben and Pam ran toward the house, and Duke galloped with them, barking and leaping. Dutch threw the pickup into reverse and backed at high speed all the way to the barn.

Michelle and Ernie were their saviors. It only cost Michelle a migraine and a lost night of sleep listening to Dutch go on and on about how sending the kids to bed early was no kind of punishment. But it had been Ernie, who agreed that it looked to him like the girl got scared when the firecracker was lit, then tossed it over her head to get rid of it, who convinced Dutch.

"It was an accident," Michelle repeated several times to the victim. All the while, Hutch suspected who planned it and why.

"That Pam has the same goddamn temper as Edith," Hutch barked, as Ernie drove the cab onto Hwy. 17 going south.

It only took one August day for Ben to know it was his worst month. Dutch drove him out into the bean fields at 7 AM to hoe beans, leaving him there with a thermos of ice water and a machete with a wooden handle and sixteen inch blade. For two weeks, his body had been saturated with ragweed; every breath outdoors brought in new pollen to attack his nose and lungs. Now, he found himself planted amongst vast numbers of the weed, knowing that even if he killed every one in Dutch's bean field, their venom, floating in the milky haze, would remain untouchable for five hundred miles in every direction.

Dutch had taken Ben into this field at sundown the day before, demonstrating with the blade how to chop the weed low to the ground.

"Get 'em low," he had directed. "And don't hit the beans. Like this."

Chop! Chop! Down went the juicy stalks of ragweed that were robbing the beans of precious nitrogen.

"See?"

Ben nodded yes.

Those two swift, powerful cuts that Dutch wielded with such ease haunted Ben's early morning dreams. The ragweed-all green. Its juice when cut ran blood-red. A dichromatic vision, opaque and draining. Once he stepped onto this lonely bean field, his limbs were already sapped of

122

any strength.

Row one went the fastest. But soon, it was beginning to take twice as many chops to make a kill. It was harder to breathe and hotter than any morning in July. Ben sneezed, blowing snot and his glasses off his face, temporarily dispersing the cloud of mosquitoes that hovered around his exposed flesh. Each convulsive sneeze drained more energy from his sweaty body.

More and more often he headed for the thermos, his long jeans wet and slick around his waist. He took off his soaked t-shirt and stuffed one end of it into his back pocket. Under his left glove: blisters, red and puffy, already filled with fluid, forced him to switch the machete to his right hand. Four chops. And a bean plant or two, which he hastily replanted. For a few minutes, fear of Dutch took his mind off fatigue.

Around 11 AM, Ben saw his mother steering Dutch's truck toward him down the narrow two-tire pathway that ran along the far side of Lester's pasture. By now, if Ben didn't hold his head up and back, his glasses slid right off his ears and nose. He was so haggard and whipped by sun and ragweed he didn't notice his mother's and sisters' shocked expressions until they parked beside him.

Michelle gasped, holding her hand over her mouth when she saw his sunburned shoulders. Her son's eyes were so itchy, red and pollen-soaked, he seemed to wince whenever he blinked. Debi and Pam were so devastated by Ben's appearance they both wept the entire time their brother sat next to them in the truck and ate his lunch. He complained between bites of his tuna sandwich.

"Look at my hands!" Ben cried, his tears unnoticed in his sweat. He blew his runny nose into his t-shirt bunched on his lap.

"I'm so tired, Mom."

Michelle lost her composure after Ben turned to the

123

passenger window and she could see the circle of mosquito bites behind his left ear. She knew if she returned to the farm with her son it would not be good for any of them. Michelle decided to stretch Ben's lunch break to an hour. She rubbed insect repellent all over his exposed skin while he hung his head back against the truck's seat. Pam and Debi sang a few lines of "Yes, Jesus Loves Me" until their brother yelled, "Shut up!"

The girls' singing marked a moment of insight for Michelle concerning her marriage. It had been the same way with Kenny. They had no common faith. Something greater than themselves that could bind them everlastingly.

In his sweltering trailer, with a fan blowing on his perspiring head, Gene lay on his bed reliving the day of his driving test. It had taken all of the time allotted for him to answer the questions on his Iowa School Bus Driver Test in the Boone Courthouse on State Street. The examiner went over Gene's test and was astounded when he found no errors. "A perfect score," he mumbled to the applicant. Gene smiled, his head shaking faster than usual from nervousness.

He passed his vision test and went outside to wait for the same examiner to drive him over to the Boone City Garage for the behind-the-wheel part of the test. The world seemed more friendly and open to possibilities as he stood near the top step just outside the courthouse doors. He'd been thinking, God, don't let the county's insurance carrier find me a risk and give the school board a reason to say no.

The route began on Park Avenue north on Story Street. Across railroad tracks between 8th and 11th Streets. A twenty-two mile test of shifting, braking, turning and parking. The examiner had been greatly concerned with Gene's vision-whether his reaction time was compromised by his head movement. It made Gene nervous at first to have the man sitting across the aisle in the front seat next to the door, checking things off and writing things on his clipboard.

Midway through the test, it was obvious to the examiner that Gene's long arms were strong enough to handle the wheel easily and that his spatial skills and reaction time were as good as any he'd tested.

After Gene parked at the garage and turned off the engine, the examiner kept writing for what had seemed an eternity. Gene wished he could speak out, loud and clear: How'd I do? Did I pass?

Finally, after an interminable delay, the examiner rose from his seat, smacked the clipboard against his pant leg and said, "You did just fine, Gene. Just fine."

A Terrible Fall...Then Winter

September, 1959.

"Here it comes," Ben said.

"Here it comes," Debi repeated, jumping excitedly as her mother held her by the hand. They stood on the side of the road across from the Beal front yard.

Blue Bird bus #73 turned its new, yellow frame toward them, leaving Hwy. 17 on this first day of the new school year. Pam and Ben Smith were by far the best-dressed kids bussed in from rural Boone County. Pam's red, knee-high socks ended just at the hem of her red corduroy dress. Ben was ten pounds heavier than when he moved to the farm—mostly muscle from hoeing beans for eighteen ten-hour days in August. Michelle had made Dutch pay Ben a buck an hour, which gave the boy incentive to get out of bed and slash through another acre of ragweed, the pollen still thick in the air and causing Ben's nose to run and his eyes to burn.

Michelle was proud of Ben in his gold slacks and black, short-sleeved rayon shirt. His dull-black slip-ons were new, too. Michelle had told him he looked snazzy as he walked down the white-gravel drive with his tin lunch box in-hand. She thought he used too much pink butch wax to raise his hair two inches above his forehead, but she kept it to herself.

The Beal family looked tanned and beautiful to Gene, as he geared down to second, then first. He thought, if ever there was a parent who worried about her kids' welfare,

126

Mrs. Beal would be the one to ride along to see if the new driver, just beginning a probation period, could deliver them safely. She greeted him with a respect few displayed toward him.

"Good morning, Mr. Rainbow."

Gene smiled, waving his ten fingers at once from the top of his steering wheel, his red cap's bill curved down and touched his sunglasses. Michelle saw that his drab-olive baggy pants were clean, and so was his faded red and white-checkered, short-sleeve shirt. She noticed that he wore a Timex watch around his right wrist.

"Mind if we come in and look a second?" Michelle asked.

Gene waved Michelle and Debi into the bus. The three pairs of kids already on the bus watched Ben and Pam take their seats right behind Gene. They were all wide-eyed and gaping at Mrs. Beal, thinking, surely this was the most beautiful woman ever to live in the whole county. Gene was churning with anxiety at the thought of being in the bus with such a superior looking being, until she spoke to her daughter.

"See, Debi. This is what it looks like inside a school bus. One day you can ride to school on it, okay?"

Debi nodded yes.

"Wave goodbye to Ben and Pam!"

"Bye bye, Ben! Bye bye, Pam!" Debi blew kisses to her brother and sister.

Little Debi's cuteness shot straight into Gene's heart. His laugh startled Ben and Pam. It came out of his throat, sharp and high.

Gene felt good that Mrs. Beal trusted her children to his care to and from school. He waited to pull in the stop sign outside his window until mother and child stepped back to wave goodbye to his bus.

Pam turned toward the window and saw her mother

127

and sister still waving through a thin veil of brown dust churned up by the bus's tires.

"I hope she doesn't do this every day," Pam quipped to Ben.

Pam caught Gene's smile in his big overhead mirror. *He hears good,* she thought. Just then, Pam farted on the forest-green vinyl seat.

Ben elbowed Pam's side, adding in a whisper, "Don't. He thinks I did it."

Pam started belly laughing. That, combined with the bus's bouncing, her first-day-at-school jitters, not to mention the four poached eggs on toast she had eaten for breakfast, produced more sounds from the vinyl.

The other passengers, quiet, well-behaved country kids, couldn't hear what the new kids in the fancy city clothes were laughing and snickering at, and supposed it was aimed at them. They had been prepared to dislike the newcomers. They all knew these were Dutch Beal's stepkids. Their mothers had condemned Michelle as a city divorcee half Dutch's age, who obviously married him for his money. To a man, their husbands had responded, "Good luck gettin' any of it from Dutch."

On Gene's route, a stop came about every quarter mile, sometimes two or three miles, depending on where kids lived, marked in red ink on the three-page map on the clipboard kept under his seat.

At the fourth stop, Gene picked up his niece, Darlene. She wore green knee-high socks and a white canvas dress with shoulder straps. Darlene sat up front, her back against the window across the aisle from Ben, snapping her bubble gum loudly above the rattles of three-dozen closed windows vibrating on metal frames. The Smiths could smell some kind of stale odor coming from her clothes.

Pam's nostrils flared in Darlene's direction, partly because of Darlene's lack of hygiene, but mostly, it was

Darlene's body language-so open and bold without Pam's self-conscious stiffness and lack of self-confidence in public.

Darlene waved at Ben with a wad of her bubble gum on the tip of her finger, stretching a line of gum out from her yellow-stained teeth. Ben's face reddened as the older girl kept looking at his profile long after his eyes darted from behind his thick glasses to the back of Gene's moving skull. Pam was glad she didn't sit where Ben did. She wanted no part of Darlene Rainbow.

Gene was right on schedule as he parked in line with two other buses at Boone Grade School. After Gene opened the door and stood up near his seat, Ben noticed something amazing. He wanted his sister to see it.

The younger kids piled off the bus, then Gene drove on to the combination junior/senior high school.

Darlene rose and hopped off the bus first, calling, "See ya later, Uncle Gene!"

The other kids exited before Pam and Ben. Pam wanted to get a look at what Ben had been whispering about in her ear. Just then, as Gene turned toward them, Pam saw it, too.

This was no time to comment. They hurried off the bus.

Ben purposely walked slowly toward the school building so Pam's limp would not be so obvious to those innocent-cruel eyes of children who looked for handicaps and shortcomings in order to bolster their own need to fit in and be normal.

Ben escorted Pam to her classroom after finding Pam's name under a 7th grade listing on a bulletin board in the main lobby.

"I'll see ya at lunch," he told her as she entered the classroom.

Ben's room was a good ways from Pam's. He didn't

even look for his teacher's name on the 7th grade listings. He was just glad he wasn't in the same classroom with his sister. The teacher's name, Mrs. Jorgenson, was printed on the chalkboard. Ben could easily read it as he took a desk at the back of the room.

Betty Jorgenson had graduated from high school with Irving Beal, and even had a couple of movie dates with him their senior year. She couldn't take her eyes off of Ben, partly because he was now Dutch's stepson, partly because he seemed remote. She felt his aloofness and controlled fear. It touched her all the way from the back of the room. She had seen the same sort of anxiety in another student back when she first began teaching.

Mrs. Jorgenson looked away from Ben when he noticed her staring at him. The desks were filled with thirty eager faces she had all but ignored until she called the roll, asking each student to raise his or her hand. Ben's ears reddened when she called out Benjamin Smith. He hated that name. Like Benjamin Franklin.

Pam and Ben did not have lunch at the same time, or the same recess schedule. At 3:15 when it was time to board Gene's bus, Ben again escorted Pam.

"Look at his belt," Ben whispered. "Is it the same as Dutch's."

Yes, there it was, the silver background and the raised turquoise letters: D. J.

"The belt is brown," Pam whispered, once seated in their same spot behind the driver.

"Not the belt. The buckle," Ben hissed.

"You're right. It looks just like Dutch's," Pam whispered.

Pam and Ben rolled their eyes at each other. Neither said a word until they could see Debi and their mother waiting at their stop.

Debi started jumping for joy when Michelle pointed

130

out Gene's bus skirting the south border of Ledges, heading for the farm.

The dust on the road nearly choked the two as the bus rolled to a stop.

"See ya tomorrow!" Debi exclaimed, repeating her mother's words and waving goodbye to Gene as he closed the door behind Ben and Pam.

On the way to the house, Pam whispered to Ben, "What do you think about Gene's belt?"

"The buckle is just like Dutch's."

"Who do you think D. J. is?"

"How would I know?"

Michelle was much more animated about their first day in school than Ben and Pam were. She made a pitcher of Kool-Aid and sat with them at the kitchen table as they read their homework assignments out loud to her. After a few lines from Ben, he asked his mother if he could buy a BB rifle with his bean money.

"If Dutch says it's okay," Michelle replied.

"Will you ask him for me?"

Michelle, thinking it over, proved to her son once again that a few moment's thought produced a yes. When she got up the courage to follow through, Dutch had told Michelle, "We'll see."

Friday night, Dutch was working on his books at his roll-top desk in the master bedroom. The scent of his pipe tobacco hung in the air, though the pipe he drew on was out. Only the faint sound of his lip suctioning off the pipe could be heard.

Ben's feet moved silently over the carpet. The veins in Dutch's temples bulged blue-green and alive as he went over every little notation in his ledgers. Ben had entered the sacred place where Dutch made his money appear on paper, where every detail of farming was logged and noted with satisfaction in the knowledge that he'd never lost money in the long run. Ben stood nearby and didn't speak, until Dutch raised his head in his direction.

"Dad, could you take me to Boone tomorrow so I can buy a BB rifle with my money?"

"That'll take pretty near all the cash ya got. Yer sure?"

"I'm sure."

"Don't come complainin' to me that you want something else and haven't got any money."

Ben nodded his agreement.

"I s'pose we can go tomorrow. Next week I start combinin' and there won't be time for nothin' else."

"Thanks, Dad."

Ben left quietly. Dutch went back to contemplating his corn crop, now ready to husk. The corn looked real good, the shanks weren't too long for the ears, or high up on the stalk where they'd be more likely to be pulled down by wind, besides being inconvenient to husk. If the price stayed about the same, he would have another good year.

By noon Saturday, Ben was sighting his army men and picking them off pretty good. Dutch had fired the first twenty rounds with him, showing Ben how to hold the pump-action rifle against his shoulder and how to sight. Since Ben was left-handed he sighted with his right eye instead of his left.

"If you're smart," Dutch told him, "you'll use the feed house for a backstop so you can reuse yer BBs. And you won't put out the windows in the chicken coop."

Ben heard the threat. "I'll be extra careful," he promised.

Later, Dutch came over to Ben, giving the boy a start as he rubbed his pollen-soaked eyes.

"Give me that," Dutch said, taking the new rifle from Ben and heading into the machinery shed, where he started shooting at sparrows in the rafters.

"They shit on my machinery. This'll persuade 'em to build their nests somewhere else."

After a few shots Dutch nailed one and it dropped dead to the dirt floor.

"There's more in the barn, Dad. Can I shoot them?"

"Not with the hogs around. You can go up in the loft and pick 'em off."

After thirty minutes in the dark hayloft, Ben was gasping for breath, suffocating from hay and heated dust. Outside again, sitting in the shade of a tree, Ben began to breathe easier. Concealed at the edge of the farmyard, he spotted Pam leaning over the hog pen fence, feeding pellets to Jerry. As he watched the pig gobbling the treats from her hand, it occurred to him that his sister had devised the ruckus in the farmyard three weeks earlier.

He had just finished his tenth day in a row hoeing beans. Ben had dragged his tired body over to the truck's open tailgate and lay prostrate as his mother drove him home where each evening he fell into the wading pool. His eyes, swollen from pollen, were mere slits as he imagined diving face-first into the water-shoes and all. Dutch hadn't returned yet from Boone, where he had gone to buy parts for his combine. Michelle made the turn into the farmyard and screamed, "Ben!"

He shot up like a squirrel.

"The pigs are in the pool," Michelle yelled.

Ben's oasis had turned into a muddy swill. Four hogs were standing inside the pool, snouts dripping, beady eyes focused on the outraged woman. Twenty other hogs were rooting near the house, grunting over their new territory.

"Where's Duke?" Ben hollered to his mother.

"He's with Dutch."

For an hour Michelle and her son chased, yelled at, cursed, and cornered. Pam and Debi stood in the safety of the back porch shouting directions and laughing until their sides hurt, and the wily pigs were all back in the hog yard.

Dutch was really mad; however, he blamed himself for somehow leaving the gate unlatched and for taking Duke away from his job. The worst of it was the loss of Ben's daily soaking after long hours in the bean field; the hogs hooves had ripped the bottom out of the plastic pool.

Now, Ben watched his sister and Jerry with mixed feelings: annoyance and grudging admiration.

That night, Bonnie LaFleur baby-sat the Beal kids while Michelle and Dutch went out to the bar in Des Moines where they first met. Dutch wore his bronze-colored suit with string tie and pointed cowboy boots. Bonnie, 17, and fifty pounds away from fitting into any of last year's clothes, had never seen a woman wearing a mink stole in person. Dutch had let Michelle go to her old hair dresser to get her natural brunette color back. Michelle's hair, wound up to a beehive, combined with her two-inch heels, gave Bonnie a towering first impression of Mrs. Beal.

Pam and Debi watched their mother and Dutch drive away in the T-bird from their front porch windows. Bonnie fixed them a meal of pork chops with mashed potatoes and gravy, and sweet corn that Ben had cleaned. Dutch was paying Bonnie fifty cents an hour. At that rate, for three kids, she left the supper dishes stacked on the counter and spent the evening watching TV from Dutch's recliner.

Bonnie snored. At bedtime, the girls were sitting on the floor in front of the recliner watching their baby-sitter snort like one of Dutch's hogs. The TV news played behind them. Rather than wake Bonnie, Ben whispered to his sisters that if they got ready for bed quietly, he'd stay with them in their room tonight after he did the dishes.

A half-hour later when Ben had dried and put away the last of the silverware and neatly folded the damp dish-towel over the oven door handle, he went into the front room, still filled with Bonnie's snoring, and turned off the television. This was an unexpected opportunity to satisfy his curiosity.

The walnut double doors to the master bedroom were closed, pulled together as if Dutch wanted no snoopers in his office. Ben slipped inside, shutting the doors quietly behind him. He turned on the desk lamp and eased up the roll top. The bank savings book was inside the front drawer. He opened the book, looked at the last entry, and counted five zeros after the number. His stepfather had saved more money than Ben ever imagined.

He wanted to tell Pam what he had found, but he couldn't trust Debi. His little sister could easily blab about it and get Ben killed for spying on Dutch.

Once Debi was snoring between them, Ben whispered, "Dutch is rich. I looked in his bank book."

Pam whispered back, "Don't expect him to spend any of it on us. He wouldn't even buy me a new bathing suit."

"He already warned me he wouldn't," Ben replied.

"When do you think we'll hear from Dad?" Pam asked.

"Korea's a long way off, maybe never."

Ben went to sleep thinking of his father, remembering the very few times they were together. Pam dreamt she was dancing with Prince Charming dressed in a white sailor suit. Her legs were symmetrical and without pain. Ben's presence allowed her mind to rest safely on this pleasant fantasy, avoiding thoughts of another day without her daddy.

By the first Sunday in October, when Dutch's corn had been in for nearly two weeks, at 4:30 in the morning came Ben's greatest gift from God: the first freeze. Twenty-nine degrees and all the sniffing, itchy eyes, sneezing, and miserable suffering was over.

By 7 AM, while the October light in the eastern sky

shone purple and orange, Gene Rainbow and Ben Smith were crouched behind six bales of hay stacked side-by-side two-high in Lester's pasture. Dutch and three farmer friends waited with their shotguns for Gene's raised hand to signal that Dutch's disc-throwing contraption was loaded and ready to toss the first clay pigeon a hundred yards into the eastern sunrise.

One of the marksmen yelled, "Pull!"

Ben was thrilled watching the saucer reach the apex of its flight, then shatter to pieces when a shotgun went off twenty feet behind him. The smashed clay pigeons fell to the ground like dark hail.

Bending low behind the hay fortress, Ben wondered how Lester had been convinced to move across the road into another pasture.

Ben knew his step-dad's voice would call out next. "Pull!"

Ben stopped breathing until Dutch hit his mark. Boom!! Then Gene was pulling him down at the shoulder, because Ben rose up above the protective hay to exclaim, "Good shot, Dad!"

Gene's stern, moving eyes softened when Ben blushed at the stupid thing he had just done. It was far better to be pulled down quietly by Gene, than to be booted by Dutch in front of the other men.

"Move it out ta seventy," Dutch called.

Gene changed the distance by moving a tiny piece of protruding metal below the machine's arm. Misses would be more frequent, and so would the cuss words.

Gene had been their disc thrower for some ten years. As payment he got a free lunch at the Madrid Cafe eleven miles south. These men had helped him get maintenance work at Ledges State Park, and the job as bus driver for the county. All wrote letters of recommendation supporting Gene's employment and character. Dutch was the only one

Gene worried about. Ben reminded him why.

Five rounds later, Ben took Gene by surprise, pointing to his waist where his jacket had hiked up, and asking, "What's the D. J. stand for?"

"Pull!" Dutch barked.

Gene's strong fingers trembled noticeably on the release button. The boy's question hung in the air for three or four seconds. Until the shotgun's blast startled them both. Gene turned to load the next clay pigeon, leaving the question unanswered.

The two farmers with the lowest scores had to buy lunch for all. On Sundays, the Madrid Cafe was only open for lunch. At 10:30, they were the first customers to arrive. Gene and Ben sat at a booth next to the one occupied by the other men, Ben's back to his step-dad's. Dutch was in a good mood since he wasn't buying lunch.

Ben wondered how Gene could place an order if he couldn't talk. After Ben ordered a Coke with a cheeseburger and chips from the waitress, Gene pointed to the meat loaf special paperclipped to the inside of the menu. Before she could ask, he pointed to green beans, mashed potatoes and coffee, smiling after she repeated his selections.

Dutch and his party were distracted, joking with the waitress, when Gene pulled a napkin from the dispenser on their table, and drew a stub of pencil from his shirt pocket. He wrote something on the napkin. Ben thought he was going to show the note to him. Instead, Gene put the napkin and the pencil back into his pocket.

Gene ate his meal without savoring a bite, his forehead six inches from his plate. Ben was amazed how his companion was able to jab a fork so fast into his constantly moving mouth without poking himself. Before Ben could finish his cheeseburger, Gene was swirling his second slice of Old Home white bread, soaking up the meat loaf gravy and leaving his plate as dry and clean as if pulled from a cupboard.

For an awkward few minutes, while the men behind him gabbed and worked toothpicks, Ben thought of the Christmas tree and the radio in the cemetery. There was no point in asking Gene about it. His speech was too garbled. Pam would know who to ask. She was brave about things like that. Ben kept his eyes averted, watching the cafe beginning to fill with locals coming in for their Sunday dinner. Dutch and his group knew and greeted everyone. Some strolled over to Dutch and shook his hand. All mentioned that Dutch had his corn in before the price dropped a quarter a bushel, joking that he had arcane or covert connections.

"Yeah, and I seen ole Wilfred Biggsdorf lyin' in Beal's southeast ditch. And when he seen Beal's combine headin' toward 'im, he went out and got his."

During the laughter that followed, Ben was paying more attention to Gene, who had left their table to buy something from inside the glass candy case near the register.

Dutch drove his truck into Ledges, a shortcut that led to the gravel road where the Rainbows lived with their chickens and dirt. Gene handed Ben a package of baseball cards. When Ben looked up at Gene, the bus driver hushed the boy with an index finger to his lips. After Gene hopped out of the truck bed he waved goodbye to Dutch and ambled toward his trailer. Ben was surprised to see that Gene lived so close to Darlene, and in such cramped quarters.

The package of baseball cards in Ben's hand had already been opened. Ben's first thought was that the gum was gone. He was wrong. The motion from Gene to be quiet was both clear and even more confusing, as Ben unfolded the napkin from the cafe and found two words printed in pencil: Dutch Junior. What did that mean? "Junior" usually meant somebody's son. Could Dutch have a son? Pam would find out, Ben assured himself, while his anxious mind warned him to be even more alert when around his stepfather.

Gene fell onto his twin-bed in his tiny bedroom, staring at a point midway on the arc his ever-moving eyes drew on his whitewashed ceiling. He was worried. Should he have done that? He reached under his pillow and slid out his Bible, placing its hard cover under his head. Gene hadn't really been conscious of the day's date when he gave Ben the information he requested. Now, it came to him suddenly.

He turned his attention to the face of the belt buckle at his waist. He only wore it when he was sure Dutch wouldn't see it. Today he'd made a bad mistake and Ben had called it to his attention. Thank God, Dutch had been so busy trying to impress his friends, he hadn't noticed the buckle. But the situation on the Beal farm troubled Gene.

He rubbed the raised turquoise letters, tracing the D and the J with the same finger he used to hush Ben. His eyes went back to the ceiling. Memory turned the white surface into a movie screen-a private show he hadn't allowed himself to see since he was about Ben's age, during the first week in October.

Indian summer. Seventy degrees by ten in the morning. They had agreed to skip school that Friday and meet in Ledges at the top of the sandstone steps, part of the Reindeer Ridge Trail they called Long Drop. Here the sandstone cliffs stood seventy-five feet high. Below lay the western center of Ledges, where two streams joined and ran together for a hundred yards. Irving Beal, Jr., and Eugene Rainbow, both eleven years old, were best friends. Gene's head was still then. Gene was the one who had given his friend the nickname D. J., because Irv or Irving didn't fit his personality.

For them, Long Drop was a place to name things:
They decided Gene would never again be called Eugene.
The two creeks in Ledges they named White Creek and
Green Creek for their colors. And at least seven Oak trees
within Ledges were named. The oldest and tallest was
named George after George Washington. Seated above
Long Drop, D. J. and Gene talked about things they dared
not talk of to others.

Ledges was a bastion of solace for D. J. This was a
place he could go to escape his father's compulsive talk of
money and losing the farm by drought, flood, locust, or
banker's pen.

Both boys had close-cut, white-blonde hair. D. J.'s
pointed nose was like his mother's and like Gene's who
took after his own mother. Both were about the same height
and weight, their eyes about the same shade of blue. They
looked like brothers.

Gene had waited for an hour before moving down to
a place where White Creek curved away from the river,
where he would have an open view of D. J. coming down
the road. Gene's boots tramped on the damp fallen leaves
scattered by a cold September near the stream's edge. The
whispering orange and gold leaves overhead shaded him
while he watched D. J. approach.

"How cold you s'pose the water is at High Bridge?"
D. J. asked.

"Real cold, I guess. Why?"

"Think we can make it across without fallin' in?"

Gene smiled at his friend as they walked northwest
toward High Bridge. Built in 1901, the bridge spanned the
Des Moines River. Massive wood timbers supported steel
girders which, in turn, supported two sets of shining steel
railroad tracks. The boys had been there before.

D. J. wore the turquoise belt buckle that Gene had

saved for all year and given him last Christmas. His friend had attached the shiny buckle to his old brown leather belt.

They were close enough to the river to hear its gurgling, slow-churning currents moving south. Their objective was to avoid being spotted by any human 'til their return to Ledges after school let out. Gene's parents would punish their son for playing hooky with silence and guilt. D. J., if caught, would surely get the beating of his life with the very leather belt around his waist.

On the two-hour walk to High Bridge, the boys talked about how Mrs. Jorgenson was their favorite teacher, and since she really liked both of them immensely, by Monday she'd give them a knowing smile and forget all about Friday's truancy, not even asking for a parental note explaining the absence.

It was close to noon by the time they reached the bluff 185 feet above the river, site of the highest and longest double-track railroad bridge in the country. A half mile long, at the other end of the bridge was a freshwater tank where they could quench their thirst from the long trek without being seen by anyone except grazing cattle.

Under the tracks, massive crisscrossed timbers held the weight of the rails balanced on parallel girders-narrow steel ledges facing each other across twenty feet of terrorizing empty space. The lip of the steel protruding from the top of a girder was just wide enough for a boy's foot to find purchase.

"You take that side," D. J. said, pointing across the void.

"No, we go on the same side, or I'm not going," Gene said.

"Alright then."

Gene was the strongest of the two, but D. J. was the risk taker; D. J. always went first.

"Keep talkin'. It keeps my mind from thinkin' about

it," Gene said.

The boys laughed to keep from crying. Their backs scraped against the metal bolts anchored deep into the timbers while they side-walked, right foot then left foot, for fifty feet until encountering a cross beam they had to straddle and hug with arms wide, feeling for the ledge on the other side with the toes of one foot. Climbing around one of these cross beams, Gene looked down to the muddy Des Moines, his legs trembling at the thought of the terrible fall.

"If somebody sees us, I'm tellin' my dad we were goin' fishin'," D. J. said.

"Without a pole?"

"You think of somethin' then!" D. J. shot back.

"I can't think here," Gene said.

"Yer dad ever give you a whippin'?" D. J. asked.

"No. He just looks at me with his sad eyes and I feel real bad. That's worse than a whipping."

"No way! I'd rather jump off this bridge," D. J. said.

"Well, we ain't gonna get caught, so quit talkin' about it," Gene said.

Gene knew Dutch Beal was quick to punish his friend and that the beatings were severe. Dutch was well-known to be one of the strongest men around.

Once, when he was visiting D. J., Gene saw Dutch lift a 55-gallon barrel filled with garbage to his shoulder and toss it easily into his truck. Gene always remembered that feat of strength when around his friend's father.

D. J. needed the challenge of crossing High Bridge more than Gene did. Ellen Beal, D. J.'s mother, had been locked up in Cherokee State Institute for fifteen months. Her family history of chronic depression was well-known in Boone County. Dutch and D. J. both feared what she might do in one of her black moods. After Dutch found her in their bed, bleeding to death from razor cuts, the hospital offered the only answer. Dutch had made the one hundred forty

142

mile drive only twice in 15 months to visit his wife of 10 years. After his first visit, D. J. refused to go again. He planned to go alone, one day, and get his mother out of there when he was old enough to drive, if she wasn't out by then.

The High Bridge represented the ultimate boyhood conquest, with each a witness for the other. Right foot slide, left foot slide-it would take nearly three thousand of these hesitant steps to reach the other side.

Gene was the only person on earth who made D. J. feel real and important. Each understood the other. Their bond was deeper than friendship. And it would be tested and proven beyond any doubt under this bridge in Central Iowa, when October began so unseasonably dry and warm, and the wind was still between them and the river.

"I have to go pee," Gene announced.

"So pee!"

"Wait for me," Gene said.

D. J. waited while Gene peed, his urine arching out and down into the river. They laughed when D. J. admitted that now he had to pee. At that height above the churning river, it wasn't easy to release the bladder, perched like two fledglings afraid to fly.

A few steps further and they'd be a quarter of the way across. Then they heard it far off. This had never happened before in the three times they had attempted the crossing, only to fail and return cautiously to where they began.

"A train!" D. J. cried.

"What do we do?" Gene asked, his eyes wide with fear. "We can't go back before it gets here."

"We gotta find a place to hang on," D. J. answered.

The boys moved forward, stepping more quickly than before toward one of the huge wooden cross beams, but they didn't make it. A half-mile away, one hundred thirty-seven cars pulled by four Burlington Northern engines were closing in on the bridge, coming toward them from the side of the river-cut gorge they were trying to reach.

As the very earth that connected with High Bridge rumbled portentously and the bridge began to shake, it was clear to D. J. there was nothing stable to hold onto except each other.

"Quick, sit down and grab something!" D. J. said, easing down to straddle the girder they stood on. Gene wrapped his right arm around D. J., holding with his stronger left hand onto the vibrating bridge. A sick feeling filled his stomach.

The train was moving at thirty-two mph when the first engine rolled onto High Bridge, much faster than the posted speed limit of twenty-five mph.

The strength with which the boys squeezed each other and the beam beneath them didn't matter; their bodies bounced on the trembling girder, creeping slowly forward toward the onrushing train. The unbearable power and noise above them reached the apex of sound and motion as the four engines roared overhead, drowning out Gene's warning.

"I can't hold on!"

Gene's hand quivered from the stress of his grip on a rivet; not nearly enough leverage to keep D. J. from swaying toward the edge of the girder. If Gene was to keep D. J. from sliding any farther, he'd have to pull him backward, but he couldn't reach anything to anchor himself.

"Push back toward me," Gene yelled close to D. J.'s ear.

"I can't!"

"Push!"

At that instant, in slow-motion, with the long string of boxcars not even halfway past them, D. J. turned his head over his shoulder and the two friends locked eye to eye. D. J. believed he was going to die. Gene saw it and his mind filled with life-flashing moments. Their friendship made life worth living. The grim things that happened in their world could be handled when they went up to Long Drop and faced them together and laughed them away-and the world was sweet again. Eugene and Irving: no more. Gene and D. J.-best friends.

Then, D. J.'s hand slipped off the girder, throwing his weight into space. Gene tightened his right hand in time to catch D. J.'s forearm. The added weight pulled Gene's left hand away from the rivet he had been clinging to. Now, Gene's powerful left hand gripped the girder's edge.

"Gene, don't let me fall!" D. J.'s scream was muffled beneath the racket of steel wheels rolling on the steel track above their heads.

"I won't," Gene mouthed back, his eyes making the promise.

Now Gene was positioned to use the muscles of his stronger left arm to anchor and pull against his friend's weight.

D. J. managed to get his left hand around Gene's wrist. But even if the speeding train had not been overhead, it was too late.

"I can't pull ya up," Gene yelled. "Climb up my arm!"

D. J.'s hand was slipping, losing strength in his terror of falling. "I can't," he cried.

"I'll swing you out toward the middle of the river. On the third swing, let go," Gene shouted.

D. J. looked down the narrow chute of darkness nearly twenty stories to the river. "Don't let go, Gene, please!" D. J. begged.

"Listen to me. I'm jumping right after you. Okay?" Gene shouted.

D. J.'s eyes lost their fear. That was something Gene would always remember: that moment of total trust in D. J.'s eyes.

"Okay," D. J. called, nodding.

Gene counted, swinging D. J., shouting above the train's roar.

"One." He swung D. J. out, then back.

"Two." Then a much bigger swing.

"Three!"

Gene gave it his all, and felt his biceps muscle pop, giving his friend a clear flight past the towering support beams. He watched D. J.'s long, terrible fall feet-first, then a splash into the shadowy blackness.

Suddenly the shaking ceased. The train had crossed the bridge. Gene was exhausted, but had no time to recover. He thought, what if D. J. is down there holding on to one of the wooden beams, waiting for me? Before thinking any-more, or looking down, he threw himself out into the same black void.

The last thing Gene recalled was the sensation of all the air rushing out of his lungs as he fell.

Gene raised his quaking head from his Bible and stared at D. J.'s buckle at his waist. Then his eyes traveled to his closet, where he kept a stack of games and toys that once belonged to D. J. Dutch had filled two gunny sacks with his son's toys and had thrown them out. Much later, Gene dug the sacks secretly and silently from the Beal farm refuse heap.

The town gossips had buzzed: "Both those boys tried to kill themselves!" "Two accidents in one day, what a hor-rible coincidence!" "His mother's in Cherokee, ya know. What a shame."

Gene knew there was more to D. J.'s death. He had the proof. Why else would D. J. leave it there?

For five months Gene had slept in a coma in a Des Moines hospital. The fall and his near-drowning had left him with severe neuropathy related to speech and head movement. He spent a year in a wheelchair, and two more years supported on crutches, learning to walk smoothly

146

despite the uncontrolled jerking of his head.

Dutch never approached Gene about that day. Gene never divulged anything about it to his parents. The buckle at his waist proved it for sure. "That's why I let Ben know. That's why I let Ben know," his mind repeated over and over to quiet the gossip that had haunted him for fifteen years, and drowned out the truth.

Pam and Debi were playing dolls upstairs when Ben came into their bedroom breathing hard after helping Dutch move the hay bales and skeet thrower out of Lester's pasture.

"I have something to show you," Ben said to Pam.

"I'll be right back," Pam told Debi, who was happy to be left alone with her dolls.

Ben took Pam out onto the upstairs landing and showed her the napkin Gene had given him.

"Dutch Junior," Pam read.

Ben hushed his sister to whisper. "After Gene gave it to me, he did this." Ben put his finger to Pam's lips, imitating Gene. "Pam, don't you see? Dutch has a son. Right?"

"You're kidding!"

"When we were loading the clay pigeons, I asked Gene what the D. J. stood for on his belt. He got all nervous. He wrote this down later at the cafe and hid it inside some baseball cards."

Pam's eyes opened wide, unblinking and brown. "A son?" she whispered. "Maybe he can write down some more stuff about it."

"I think we should tell Mom," Ben whispered.

"No. Not yet. What if he was making a joke like...it stood for Dutch Junior...ha ha...but it really didn't," Pam whispered.

"You should've been there. It wasn't like that."

Pam thought a few seconds. "Maybe Mom already

knows and it's no big deal. Don't say anything about it. It may be nothing."

On the bus Monday, there was a palpable tension between Gene and the Smith kids. Gene wasn't wearing the D. J. buckle on his belt. When they reached the school, Pam hastened after Darlene who was always the first student off the bus. Surprised by his sister's behavior, Ben hurried to catch up.

Just inside the high school's main entrance, Pam called out, "Darlene?"

Darlene let the younger girl catch up with her, though continuing to walk. "Do you know anything about a Dutch Junior?" Pam asked.

"D. J., he was my Uncle Gene's friend."

Not knowing what else to ask her, Pam said, "Oh."

Darlene disappeared into the maze of students. Ben and Pam said nothing to each other as Ben walked his sister to her classroom.

Winter arrived a week before Thanksgiving. The first snow lay in a thin sheet of tiny crystal balls that blew about the frozen school grounds, changing the white patterns over black soil and gold grass every time a swirling gust blew out of the north, stripping the last leaf from the forked branches of a million trees in the Midwest.

Gene stood listening to the other drivers discuss the weather, shaking his head as if he disagreed with every comment. He wore a faded-blue, hooded sweatshirt. His nose was dripping, freezing on his upper lip, while his hands stayed warm inside the pockets.

"It's seventeen degrees now. Gonna drop ta two-below tonight," one driver said.

"Wind chill's s'posed to be minus twenty I heard on the weather this morning," another driver said.

"Better park in the garage after this run."

"Yeah."

Ben didn't remember it getting this cold in the city. Walking from the school entrance to the bus with Pam, Ben could see the drivers grouped near Gene's bus. They looked cold, lifting each foot in turn slightly off the frozen cement and shivering.

He said, "Mrs. Jorgenson gave me a part in the Christmas play." He wasn't happy about it. "I have to greet the audience and give the introduction."

"What introduction?" Pam asked.

"Something she wrote."

"It'll be something stupid," Pam laughed while pointing her finger at Ben's reddening face.

"Shut up!"

Darlene, without a coat on, ran onto the bus and chased a boy out of her seat by jerking her thumb in the direction of the back of the bus, saying, "Outta my seat, Cracker!"

Darlene had turned sixteen last week. The day after her birthday, her Uncle Gene bought his first car, a forest-green, '49 Chevy. He took her for a drive. When they returned, he motioned for Darlene to grab hold of him there on the Chevy's front seat. With his head still, he told her if she didn't flunk any more grades and graduated from high school, he would give her the car for a graduation present.

Now, Pam noticed something different about Darlene: she was carrying school books home for the first time. But she still smoked. Pam could smell smoke on her and knew she had been sneaking cigarettes in the girls' bathroom. Ben and Pam were afraid of and envious of Darlene Rainbow's free spirit.

On this Friday, when Gene stopped in front of Darlene's house to let her off the warm bus, Darlene turned her head back to Ben and Pam as her uncle opened the door.

149

Darlene winked and said, "See ya tonight!"

Ben and Pam were confused. What was that all about?

They had to wait three hours for an answer. Dutch and Michelle were planning on going out for dinner and drinks in Des Moines, and their baby-sitter had come down with a bad cold. In a spot, Dutch had called two other prospects before calling Darlene late last night.

Pam eavesdropped on Dutch and Michelle's conversation behind the master bedroom's closed doors while they were getting ready to go out.

"How old is this girl?" Michelle asked.

"I dunno, but she's very mature for her age. And she won't eat half as much as Bonnie."

"How do you know her?"

"She's Gene Rainbow's niece."

Pam returned to dry the stacked dishes Ben had just washed. "Guess who's baby-sitting us?" Pam asked.

Ben shrugged his shoulders and pulled the sink stopper to drain the greasy dishwater.

"Darlene Rainbow."

"She smokes," Ben said, grimacing at the food scraps caught in the strainer he lifted from the drain to dump in the garbage can under the sink.

"Mom won't let her smoke in the house," he added.

Pam stopped drying dishes and started mocking Gene's head motion.

"Cut it out!" Ben snapped, tired of her sister's bizarre sense of humor.

"Don't you see?" Pam continued shaking her head no.

"What?"

"D. J.," Pam whispered.

"She doesn't know anything. Dry the dishes!"

"I hear Darlene goes out with guys who've graduated high school," Pam said.

"So?"

"So, she's only in eighth grade," Pam said.

"She should be in the tenth grade but she flunked twice."

"How do you know so much about Darlene Rainbow," Pam questioned her brother.

"Tom Beeson sits across from me in Mrs. Jorgenson's class. He lives down the same road she lives on, before the stop sign. He knows all the Rainbows."

Pam digested this bit of information, wondering if it would be useful in the future. Then, bored with her task, she thought of a way to get out of it.

"If you finish drying the dishes," Pam bargained, "I'll help you memorize your lines for the Christmas play."

Ben didn't have to think long about it. There were lots of dishes to dry, but he was terrified about being in front of an audience.

"Okay," Ben agreed.

By five o'clock it was dark out as Gene's Chevy rolled up to his brother's front porch and parked with the headlights on high beams. He didn't want to get out of his warm car. The temperature was below freezing and the wind had picked up. Mainly, Gene didn't like what he saw in his older brother's house. It was always a mess-adding up to a stinking pig pen in cold weather with the storm windows on and the furnace heat turned up high.

Darlene burst out her front door wearing a mid calf length coat made of rabbit fur. It was her mother's dress coat and Charlotte never put it on-Ray only took her out to eat chicken and get drunk on pitchers of beer at Crossway Tavern in Boone, not a place for rabbit unless it was breaded and fried.

Though her uncle's car was warm and toasty, Darlene kept her hands in her mother's coat all the way to the Beal Farm. She left her smokes at home. She'd heard Mrs. Beal was beautiful and Darlene didn't want to make a bad impression on her. Gene could smell some overly sweet perfume on his niece, the same scent she'd splash on her bedcovers and on her body when a boy was coming by for a quickie.

Darlene's hair was frizzed and curled from a home permanent she gave herself every three months, or so. Gene snuck a look her way. She wasn't the same terrified four-year-old girl left alone in her house all night, when her parents switched to the graveyard shift in Denison. He'd checked on her every night, after his folks died and he moved into Ray's trailer. Many times, little Darlene had fallen asleep, curled-up on a kitchen chair, her head resting on the table, with the radio blaring. But she'd always wake up in her bed, all tucked in, with her pajamas on. In the morning she'd find her young uncle sleeping without covers on the front room floor with his head always moving, while her parents snored the whole day through in their dark bedroom.

Passing Lester's pasture, Gene's thoughts about his niece vanished, pushed aside by memories of the High Bridge. His eyes glanced up at the house toward the room that had been D.J.'s.

When the Chevy rolled to a stop, Darlene opened the passenger door and stepped out. Gene smiled at her, then watched her walk fast to the back porch door where a light had been left on. He drove slower leaving, his mind on the summer night he slept over with D. J.

It had been the summer before the High Bridge fall. D. J.'s mother was locked up in Cherokee. The days had been so hot the animals were using three times their normal water. The relentless heat had taken a terrible toll on Dutch's relationship with his son. That night, the farmer had gone out to have a few drinks in a Des Moines air-conditioned bar. Dutch had said Gene could stay-over.

152

The boys agreed to meet at Long Drop. Gene remembered how hot it was walking through Ledges in the late afternoon. He recalled seeing carp swimming upstream to nibble on streamside grasses. Old-timers said it was a sign of a long drought ahead, which meant terrible losses for the corn yield if rain didn't come soon.

D. J. waited at the very top of Long Drop, where Sioux warriors once gathered to boast of their wars and adventures. He had been there for two hours and was not his usual chipper self when Gene arrived. D. J. sat stroking his brow, looking west, speaking to his friend without changing his gaze, as if he were alone.

"When I die," he said, "I wanna be buried in that cemetery by Lost Lake. Close to this place. It won't happen though. My dad's parents are buried in a church cemetery in Madrid. People walk by them every Sunday, I bet. Here is much better."

Gene sat down next to D. J., who turned to him, their eyes not two feet apart. D. J.'s face contorted and he began to cry, shaking convulsively. Gene put his arm around D. J.'s neck for fear he'd fall right off Long Drop.

"What's wrong?" Gene asked.

It took some time before D. J. could speak. There was so much pain in his throat he was stammering and hardly breathing at all, choking to get his words out.

"You miss yer mom?" Gene asked.

D. J. leaned into Gene's shoulder sobbing. Gene rocked him sideways, patting his arm, waiting for D. J. to say something.

D. J. began, "I was filling the water tank for the hogs when Dad called me over. He was standing by the chicken coop looking real angry. When I got close, he reached out and grabbed the back of my neck. He dragged me over to the chicken coop, yelling, 'You see what you did with that BB gun?' Then I saw that some of the windows were bro-

153

ken. Dad practically pushed my face through the glass, he was so mad."

"What happened?" Gene asked.

"He kept yelling, 'These windows have to be replaced. Every Goddamn one of 'em.' And I tried to tell him that I didn't mean to, that it was an accident, but he wouldn't listen."

"Did he take your rifle away? Is that why you're crying?"

"No. Dad whipped me real bad with my belt. Then he locked me in that little room upstairs where I used to hide from Mom when she got crazy. You know, where I strung up all my airplanes."

"Yeah, sure," Gene said, wishing he could take away all of his friend's pain.

"It was so hot, Gene. If I'd had my belt, I would've hung myself," he cried. Then he screamed, "He wouldn't let me out 'til the next morning!"

This telling of his ordeal seemed to quiet D. J., and soon they were walking over to the Beal farm, talking about the sandwiches they were going to fix for their supper.

Gene turned off his headlights and engine outside his trailer, then lay on his side on the seat with the crown of his head rubbing the passenger-side armrest. His special words moved his tongue but made no sound: love and laughter, forgiveness and patience.

"Could get a foot of snow," Dutch said, sitting across from Darlene at his kitchen table.
The rabbit coat was slung carelessly over the back of a kitchen chair, an offense to the sense of order in the Beal house. Darlene's linty wool slacks were a gaudy array of faded colors and labeled her dirt poor. She wore a rust-colored, cotton turtleneck that covered three red hickeys on the nape of her neck. Just under her left sleeve on the inside of

her wrist was the red and purple bubble gum tattoo she pressed-on three days earlier. Darlene's eyes were brownish-yellow and almond shaped, giving her countenance a sexy-sinister appeal to teenage boys looking for an easy score.

Dutch asked, "Your uncle like his new car?"

Darlene shrugged.

Trying again, he asked, "Your folks doin' okay at the packing house?"

"I guess," she replied.

Ben stayed in his room with his door closed shooting rubber bands at the baseball cards Gene had given him. The cards stood on-end against the baseboard, each player taking a shot that sent him flying up or down-face-down meant he was dead. Face-up and he'd stand again to take another shot launched from fifteen feet away, until all were dead. With each cardboard death, Ben mimicked a crowd's deafening approval, a sound like the howling wind.

Michelle was taking inventory of the contents of her purse for the evening out when she heard the cracking sound of baseball cards smacked down on the other side of her bedroom wall. She had hoped Ben would have made friends in school by now. Pam and Debi had each other; but her son-he was much too solitary for a boy his age. This bothered Michelle.

Two letters had come from Kenny in Korea. Pam read them both several times out loud to Debi. Ben had skimmed them once, then stalked outside to be alone. It was obvious to Michelle that Ben believed his father had deserted him, leaving him to the worst possible person-a hard farmer with a temper. Making a friend would help Ben adjust, she thought, as she dabbed White Shoulders behind each ear and on her wrists before wrapping her mink stole over her brown wool suit.

Michelle's skin, still golden from summer, made the

diamond ear rings given to her by her wealthy Wichita boyfriend sparkle below her brunette beehive. She was the most impressive woman Darlene Rainbow ever laid eyes on. She studied the way Mrs. Beal's two shades of lipstick outlined her lips. When Darlene put on lipstick, the effect was more like the exaggerated mouth of a circus clown. And when Mrs. Beal spoke, none of the lipstick had smeared on her brilliant white teeth, all perfectly straight, each row.

"You must be Darlene," Michelle greeted the girl, smiling as she entered the kitchen with such an abundance of beauty and friendliness in her hazel eyes that Darlene felt ashamed of herself for the first time she could remember.

"Hi," Darlene said, trying not to show her tobacco-stained, jagged teeth.

"Bedtime is ten. The kids usually take their baths around nine. Help yourself to anything if you get hungry," Michelle said.

Michelle could feel Darlene squirming in her presence and empathized. She had been the ugly duckling in her mother's house, constantly compared to her sister. Just then, Pam and Debi bounded down the stairs that opened to the kitchen. Pam gazed at the gum-snapping rough girl who smelled dirty and wore the same clothes most every day on the bus and saw humility and shame. Pam recognized it right off. She'd seen it a million times on the faces of girls and women caught off-guard by her mother's natural beauty.

Michelle introduced her baby to Darlene.

"Darlene?" Debi asked.

"Yes." Darlene smiled.

Debi smiled back. "Wanna see my dollhouse?"

"Sure."

Debi took the older girl's hand and started for the stairs, as Ben came into the kitchen quietly.

"A pillow and blankets are on the sofa for you,

156

Darlene," Michelle said.

"Okay, thanks."

Dutch opened the porch door for Michelle. She lingered a moment more. "Ben, why don't you show Darlene around?"

"Upstairs first," Debi insisted.

Ben led the way up the stairs knowing Pam wouldn't climb the stairs on her bad leg if she didn't have to. From the front room window, Pam watched the exhaust of Dutch's precious T-bird clouding around her mother's ankles while she waited in the cold in her two-inch heels for Dutch to back the car out of the garage. She watched her mother slip into the front passenger seat; the interior lights illuminated her mother's broad smile. Pam then moved to the west window near the TV, following the T-bird's headlights onto the pavement, turning right, passing across her breath fogging on the cool glass, speeding from left to right until the red taillights vanished, leaving her alone and angry.

Right off the bat Debi took to Darlene. As soon as Ben flipped on the ceiling light above the bedroom, Darlene attacked the paper dollhouse with the energy of a small child on Christmas morning. She sat right down on the wood floor with her legs spread wide, the dollhouse between her calves. Debi watched the baby-sitter's eyes peer into each room, studying all the furnishings.

"I always wanted one of these," Darlene said.

Ben stood in the doorway wanting to get on with the tour.

"The other bedroom is full of old junk," he pointed. "Debi can show you."

"My Uncle Gene has a bunch of old toys," Darlene said.

She rose from the floor with ease and flexibility, leading Debi out of the room. Ben turned off the light.

"Dutch doesn't want us to leave any lights on," Ben

157

informed her.

"We can't leave any lights on or we get spanked," Debi added, while Ben led them to the room next door.

Darlene's five foot five inch body towered over Ben as she stood beside him, arms akimbo, surveying the stored furniture and piled boxes.

"A record player. I should have brought some of my records with me!" she exclaimed while skimming through the albums standing in an open box. She picked up the portable record player and deposited it in the girls' bedroom. "I'll call my Uncle Gene. He'll bring 'em over."

Ben had to run back to turn off the storeroom light, momentarily forgotten following Darlene's energy down the stairs.

"Should I have my Uncle Gene bring over some of his toys?" she asked Ben, looking up at him from the bottom step. Ben nodded yes, thinking how different this baby-sitter was compared to the snoring Bonnie.

When Gene arrived at the Beal farm he was surprised Duke didn't greet him. Muffled barking told him that Dutch had locked the dog in the shop, probably so old Duke wouldn't take a chunk out of the new baby-sitter, he thought. Duke was a dog with more bite than bark, and Dutch liked it that way.

A half inch of wet snow had fallen since he dropped Darlene off. Gene didn't have to knock on the back door. Darlene, rarin' to play her music, ran to his car and grabbed the grocery sack that held her 45s. Gene carried in another bag for Ben.

Darlene and Debi hurried upstairs to the record player. Pam followed more slowly, while Ben watched Gene take a tattered box from the paper bag. Using the flattened bag to protect the table, Gene removed a tube of glue from his pants pocket. Ben opened the flat box and discovered the plastic pieces of a Spitfire fighter plane. Gene unfolded the assembly instructions and spread the printed sheet on the table. He leaned back in his chair and patiently watched the boy find and glue together piece after piece; sometimes Ben used too much glue here and there. Gene produced a rag for Ben to wipe off the excess, all the while smiling and shaking his head no...no...no.

Darlene played Elvis Presley's "Hound Dog" using a fat plastic adapter that fit on the stereo's spindle. Pam and Darlene laughed uproariously. They had forgotten to change speeds from thirty-three and a third to forty-five, and Elvis drawled like he was on a downer. Pam and Debi eyed each other knowing they had never played music so loud.

Uninhibited, Darlene began to dance, shaking her hips like Elvis and motioning for the girls to dance with her. Debi joined right in, hopping and skipping around Darlene. Pam unfolded her arms from her chest, clapped her hands, then dipped and rocked her shoulders as if warming up for bigger things. Darlene started "Hound Dog" again, her dancing feet making the floorboards creak to the music. Debi pranced and imitated her sitter's hip motions. Darlene whirled in a circle around Pam, then took both of her hands and danced face-to-face.

Darlene lost herself in the music; she couldn't care less about what other people thought. Before long, Pam's heart was singing from joy; someone finally had shown her how to be a gimp, the name snickered behind her back at school, and not care. Darlene shouted, "I love this song!" referring to Hank Ballard and the Midnighters' hit, "The Twist." The three of them twisted through the song five times. Pam felt Darlene's energy sizzle across their joined hands. Her leg hurt only if she stopped dancing.

All the ugly rumors Pam had heard about Darlene Rainbow could not change the fact that Darlene was fully alive, possessed of a life force that Pam wanted to suck into herself. Darlene wouldn't allow herself to be trapped in a life she never wanted or asked for.

When the girls finally tumbled downstairs, perspiring, breathing hard and laughing, Ben had most of the model airplane put together. His shoulders stiffened when Darlene squeezed them, her voice loud in his ear.

"Whatcha got there, Benny?"

Darlene leaned over Ben's shoulder and inspected the Spitfire. Red-faced, he glared at his sisters as they repeated "Benny" over and over, then clung to each other, quaking with laughter. Darlene moved behind Gene and slid her arms under her uncle's armpits, locking her hands, pulling him hard against the back of his chair. Gene's bobbing head slowed, then stopped moving. His eyes were anxious; he didn't want to startle the Smith kids if he spoke.

"I love you, Uncle Gene."

"I love you, too," Gene said in a breaking whisper.

Pam gasped. Ben stared at his companion in surprise. Debi jumped up and down, pointing her finger at Gene and shouting, "He can talk, he can talk!"

"Somethin' you wanna say? I can't hold ya all night," Darlene reminded him, kissing his neck and closing her eyes.

The kids watched Gene's eyelids flutter as he paused, choosing his words carefully. Pam moved around the table to get a direct look at her bus driver.

"I better get home before the snow picks up. I don't have snow tires," Gene said.

Pam and Ben watched Gene's head movement return when Darlene released him and he stood up.

"If you hold him tight as you can, he talks real good," Darlene informed Ben and Pam. "We don't know why it works that way, but it does."

She bent down to Debi. "It's a secret," she whispered. Wide-eyed, Debi nodded.

Gene put on his red cap and his coat, then waved

goodbye as he backed out the door to the porch, where he pulled on his overshoes.

Darlene ran outside in the slushy-white snow, calling out before her uncle reached his car. "Take me to the store tomorrow?"

He gave her a thumbs up. Darlene stood on the cold brick watching Gene drive away. She squatted and filled her cupped hands with snow, smearing the snow on her neck and rubbing it down inside her revealing, low-cut t-shirt.

The Smith kids were bathed and in bed by midnight. Darlene relished using Mrs. Beal's shampoo and soap, even shaving her legs; all luxuries far removed from the Rainbow's rusty well water and the coarse bars of Lava soap her mother brought home from the packinghouse.

Pam and Ben lay awake long after the sounds of Darlene's bath ceased. Each was thinking the same things: Gene could talk! Were those bruises on Darlene's neck?

Ben was just about to nod off when he heard the back porch door slam. From his window he saw Darlene scurry to the cob house, watched her strike a match on the rough wood of the door jam and light Dutch's pipe, sneaking a bowl of his walnut blend. Duke set up a racket loud enough to hear inside Ben's closed room.

When Dutch brought Michelle home at 2:15 AM, he stopped short at the sight of the Spitfire sitting on the kitchen table. Damn brats, he thought. They must have snooped in the locked room while I was out of the house. Then he smelled the acrid odor of fresh glue and realized his suspicion had been wrong. He picked up the flattened, water-spotted box and knew the source of the airplane. Leave it be, he told himself.

Michelle woke Darlene, asleep for only twenty minutes on the sofa. Dutch vowed that Darlene would never again bring Gene's things into his home, because she would never baby-sit for him again. He paid Darlene $3.50, then drove her home in his truck.

At nine the next morning Dutch tramped through a foot of heavy snow on his way to his chores. Michelle had been instructed to wake Ben. After breakfast he was to shovel the back patio and a path to the shop door. A heavy coat, thermal underwear, boots, gloves, a wool cap covering his ears, and a mother's compassion couldn't keep Ben's toes, fingers and ears, from stinging in the cold.

Ben was knee-deep in blue-white snow, following Dutch's foot holes, his heavy-handled snow shovel raised, searching for the patio's edge. It took him a while to figure where to begin and where to put the snow. If he was wrong, if he did the job badly, Dutch might make him shovel the long lane for the T-bird and more paths to the mailbox and the school bus stop. Ben cringed at the thought of such arduous labor.

About the time his torturous path to the shop was only half shoveled, Dutch did come over to Ben. "Shovel a path to the garage. Then do the driveway out to the road," he said.

Dutch stomped away through the snow. Under his breath, Ben said, "Thanks a lot, that'll take forever." His posture showed the strain of all the monotonous scoops, all the wrist-twistings to empty a full shovel higher and higher onto formidable snow banks. It was the kind of snow that made icy-hard snowballs with little effort; he wanted to plant one right between Dutch's eyes.

Ben had gotten proficient at killing army men, base-ball players and flies with a BB or a rubber band. The white baseball uniforms became Navy uniforms bearing the brunt of his anger toward his father. Now, he could feel his white-hot rage expanding with every scoop and lift of the shovel. How do you tell your mother you'd like to kill her for let-ting her new man shame you so deeply that it became a part of you, keeping you always fearful?

But then his mother's words crept in. This is probably all good for me somehow, Ben thought. I've been spoiled and Dutch will make a good man out of me.

In mid-December there was no end in sight to snow-fall. Ben had shoveled tons of the stuff off the same ground five times over. The Christmas play was five days away. His opening lines were few and he memorized them while shoveling, repeating the words over and over, until they had no feeling or meaning, just a straight line of sounds formed by his tongue. The glacial, crusty snow slid off the scoop and had to be shoveled twice while his resentment kept him all-the-while in an anxious state, a constant fear of doing wrong.

The night before the play, Michelle sensed her son's fear of forgetting his lines and invited Ben to lie next to her on the sofa while the family watched TV. The lights on the Christmas tree cast a multicolored glow in the darkened room. Days earlier Michelle joyously watched her kids hang the bulbs and splash on the silver tinsel. There were fewer presents wrapped under the tree, now, than last Christmas, when she had been strapped for money and raising her kids alone. But Dutch had popped for a gift to Ben from Santa that she never could have afforded. It buoyed her spirits to imagine that her thrifty, hardworking husband knew her boy so well. Ben was really going to be thrilled.

Now, with Ben snuggled close to his mother, Dutch sat in his recliner biting his pipe stem. Uncomfortable seeing his stepson cuddling with his wife, Dutch said, "Ben, move onto the floor with your sisters! You're too old to hang all over your mother."

Michelle was flabbergasted, caught off-guard and appalled by her husband's jealously toward one of her children.

163

Ben dropped to the floor, saying, "Gee, Mom, doesn't Dad know you're my mom?"

Dutch left the front room feeling suddenly exposed.

Later, when Michelle tucked Ben under his covers her words were soft and low. "Dad was raised differently than you kids. His mother wasn't a hugs and kisses mother like I am. He doesn't really mean it when he says things like that. I hope you can understand. I love you and the girls more than anyone else in the whole world. Okay?"

Ben nodded yes. His mother kissed him on his cheek. "Good night. I love you."

"I love you, too," Ben said.

The auditorium at Boone Junior-Senior School held two hundred folding chairs, all occupied by folks waiting for the Christmas pageant to begin. From behind the curtained wing Ben peered out and saw Dutch, his mother and sisters seated near the center of the room in the third row. The lighting was too dim to see all the way back to the last row where Gene and Darlene sat together.

Ben's fear of delivering his opening narration had become a monster that threatened to swallow him whole, licking clean his memory, and squeezing his breath out of him. Since moving to the farm he had become adept at hiding his fear before everyone but Pam.

On stage a single light focused on a short lectern. The curtain would not open and distract the audience until after Ben's recitation of 'A Christmas Night' written by his teacher, Mrs. Jorgenson. Pam could feel her brother's fear sweating her palms and ankles. Michelle thought he looked handsome in his red sweater and beige slacks, his thick glasses giving him a studious charm as he climbed the seven lonely steps of the podium, where he had to face a quieting crowd of rural families craving to be entertained after four gloomy weeks of winter.

"Good evening ladies and gentlemen. 'A Christmas Night' begins in a small town like ours."

Ben lost his next line, his face hot-red, struck deaf by the monster, unable to hear Mrs. Jorgenson's whispered help off to his right. His next sentence came out with a stammer. Ben tried to look at anything but Dutch staring right at him, but his eyes were locked on his stepfather's contented expression. Ben was showing his hidden shame to the whole town and he couldn't control it.

Michelle thought Ben's distress was merely stage fright. She smiled at the painfully-cute way his teacher's helping cues now could be heard all the way to the back row. Ben stammered each line as he heard it, disjointed and clipped of meaning.

Pam couldn't take it any more. She glared at an older boy in a Sunday shirt who sat across the aisle giggling at her brother's stuttering words.

Darlene had gone outside to have a smoke, and didn't see her uncle struggling with his memories, his mind moving back to that day at Long Drop when D. J. wept and talked about being beaten and locked in the sweltering upstairs room for breaking a few windows. Everything about Ben's physical bearing reminded Gene of D. J. When Ben finally walked away from the lectern and the curtain rose, Gene knew it wasn't over for Ben.

Humiliated and alone backstage, Ben's whole body felt chilled from drying perspiration. He wanted to be held by his mother. He wanted to hear her say that stage fright can happen to anybody. But Dutch was there gloating.

The other kids were doing well with their lines, not faltering much at all compared to his performance. Ben dashed outside without his coat, his mind hot with anger, his skin growing colder as his sweaty clothes began to freeze in fifteen degree air that was as windless as a butcher's freezer.

165

Turning the corner of the school building he heard a voice calling out to him from a car parked in the lot. "Benny! Over here."

Darlene was sitting behind the wheel of Gene's car, leaning her head out the window and flicking her cigarette's ash onto the blacktop. Ben was engulfed in her breath when she made a circle of her lips and exhaled a chain of smoke rings.

"I thought you were in the play?" Darlene said.

Ben stood two feet away from her, his hands and wrists ditched into his pockets, his upper body starting to shiver.

"I was. My part's over."

"Get in," she said.

Ben slid onto the front passenger seat, his glasses fogging in the car's warmth.

"Can you see anything with those?" she asked.

"Not very good." Ben removed his glasses and rubbed them back and forth against his chest.

"Didn't you see me?" he asked.

She shook her head no, blowing smoke out the window.

"Wanna go for a drive?" she asked.

"I better not."

"Ya don't look like ya wanna go back inside."

Ben didn't answer.

"Well, I'm goin' for a drive. You can ride along if ya want."

Anything was better than facing more shame.

Darlene started Gene's car. "You have a license?" Ben inquired.

"Who needs a license?"

She turned the heater's fan on too early, blowing cold air from below, making Ben's teeth chatter. She leaned forward and rubbed her fisted right hand on the foggy windshield. She flipped her cigarette in a glowing arc out the window, cranked it closed, and drove off in second gear.

"Put your lights on," Ben said.

"Oh." She laughed, pulling out the knob that turned on the Chevy's headlights.

They drove down Division Street, then north on Story, seeing very little traffic.

"Yer mom doesn't like me, does she?" Darlene said.

Ben didn't answer because he didn't know.

"How come I don't baby-sit you any more?"

"I don't know," he said, growing more and more anxious about Dutch catching him in the car with Darlene when he was supposed to be backstage.

After cruising a few more blocks, Darlene returned to the same parking spot and turned off the engine.

"I know where you can find out more about D. J.," she said.

"Where?"

Darlene lit up another cigarette, tilted her head back and blew the smoke straight up.

A half hour later, huddled on the T-bird's back seat, Ben thought about Darlene's words. At least she had gotten his mind off his lousy performance. Pam will have to help me, he thought.

Early in the morning on December 24th, Michelle let her kids open their gifts from their father. His last letter had said he would call them on Christmas Eve; she wanted them to be able to say a proper thank you. When Pam and Ben opened their presents, they each found silk pajamas which couldn't be worn until summer in Central Iowa. Debi received a tiny doll dressed in a kimono, a toy too delicate to touch. Michelle put the doll on a shelf in the living room.

Pam sat anxiously at the kitchen table from breakfast until just after lunch when the phone rang. She knew it had to be her father, because of her mother's sudden animation.

"Oh fine, just fine, we're all adjusting to country life. Pam's been waiting by the phone all day. I'll let you talk to her while I round up Ben and Debi. Okay, here she is."

Her father sounded far away, the telephone connection hollow and hissing when he first said "Merry Christmas." He asked her if she liked her new school and how she liked living on the farm.

"It's okay," she said, not saying at all how she really felt. All because he was too far away to rescue her, and she knew he didn't want to hear anything bad. No, nothing bad, whether here, or seven thousand miles away. His motto had always been: If you don't have anything good to say, don't say anything at all.

It wasn't until Debi came running in that Pam started to whine, crying, "I miss you so much, Dad." It was hard for Pam to relinquish the telephone. She felt like thumping skinny Debi's peanut head with the receiver.

Michelle ran into Dutch's shop, asking her husband if he'd seen Ben. He responded with a guttural, "No."

"Oh dear! Kenny's on the phone. I told Ben to stay in until he called."

From the platform above Dutch's stored corn, Ben watched his mother call out for him in the central farmyard. He had come to this highest place on the farm deliberately to get away from his father's call.

Very early Christmas morning, Debi woke her brother. "Ben, get up. You got a bike from Santa," Debi squealed.

Ben shot out of bed wearing cowlicks and slobber. He fumbled in the dark for his glasses on the dresser. Only the lights from the Christmas tree were on in the front room. Pam was already seated on the floor by the tree playing with a wooden, Victorian dollhouse. From his doorway he saw the red Super Chief parked on its kickstand, its whitewall tires and streamlined battery casing for the lone headlight drew his eyes, then his hands. The extravagant gift came as a total shock.

At that moment, while his sisters were squealing with delight as they unwrapped dolls to live in their new dollhouse, Ben felt guilty for avoiding his father's call, undeserving of the magnificent gift he knew had come from Dutch, not Santa. When he found a new lefty's baseball glove under the tree, he began to believe that his hard work and Dutch's discipline had manifested these things, paying off in ways he could finally see.

Dutch came out of his room wearing only white long johns. His long, knobby legs straddled the floor furnace grating. He clasped his powerful arms behind his back and watched the kids caper and dance over to the three stockings hanging from the west window sill.

"Merry Christmas," Michelle said, coming out of her room wearing a red robe and gray wool socks.

"Looks like Santa's been good to you kids," she continued, smiling on her way to the kitchen to make coffee.

Dutch watched Ben tinker with his new bike and push the switch that should turn on the headlight.

"Ain't it workin'?" Dutch asked.

Ben shook his head no. Dutch came over to the bike, turned the switch off and on, then opened the battery casing troubleshooting with his keen green eyes, before pushing the batteries back inside. He had the light and Ben's smile working again. But Dutch kept inspecting the bike, turning it upside down on its seat and turning a pedal, following the chain around to see if it needed oiling. Irving Beal oiled every moving part of every machine on his farm.

"You won't be able to ride it 'til the snow melts," Dutch said.

Ben fisted a hand around the bike's white handlebar grip. "Dad, when will that be?"

"At least three months, I s'pose. Maybe late March this year. You can wait."

Ben realized something just then. Dutch never looked him directly in the eye when he spoke kindly to him this way. That's strange, Ben thought. It's like he's afraid of something. Close up Ben could see that Dutch had sunspots and deep wrinkles that were magnified by the colored tree lights, something he hadn't really noticed until now.

"Well, I better get the chores done," Dutch said. He went into his room to get dressed.

When Dutch showed up in the kitchen ready for chores, Michelle had poured them each a cup of coffee.

"You're not working Christmas morning, Dutch?"

"The cattle have to eat on Christmas, too."

He flashed a quick grin at his wife, adding, "Unless you wanna feed 'em."

She went over and pecked him on his lips. "I'll have breakfast ready when you're done."

She went to the window and watched her husband in the darkness of early morning high-stepping in deep, unbroken snow with Duke excitedly bounding around him. She thought how generous her husband had been today. The glove, she could have managed. But never could she afford such a beautiful gift as that bike. She got back some of the love she had lost for her husband when he selected the bike so carefully, and wrote out a check for it just like that, without her even mentioning that Ben wanted a bike more than anything else.

Dutch's eyes were tearing when he rounded the corner of the feed house. Then cries of anguish only Duke and his cattle could hear filled the chill air. "Dammit all, damn it to hell!" Dutch was remembering another Christmas.

D. J. had slept with his new baseball glove under his mattress for a week to shape and loosen its webbing, as Dutch suggested to him. With the glove on one hand and a new ball in the other, D. J. practiced pitching at a small chalk circle on the side of the old outhouse. He was getting ready for the winter carnival at his school. The baseball coach, who never let him pitch when he was in the pee wee league, was going to be sitting above a giant tub of ice water. And anyone who could hit the bull's-eye with a baseball from sixty feet could soak the old geezer good.

Dutch paid D. J.'s nickel for five throws, then proudly watched his son throw five strikes in a row, dousing Coach Gibbs five times, until he refused to climb back onto the board balanced over the tub.

More snow fell in January than in December. Ben had heaped snow banks of shoveled snow all along the front drive, the back patio, and out to the shop. The sun might come out for a day, pale and chill as a freezer's light bulb. The added light gave him more energy to shovel and made it easier to imagine riding his red bike, now covered with clear plastic, leaning against a wall in the cob house. The once-dreaded storage room was now a museum of beauty preserving his most prized possession. Before and after shoveling, it had to be touched. Made real. If only he could imagine away all this damn snow.

Ben had his first ride on his Super Chief mapped out: all the way into Ledges. God, hurry up and melt this snow! This was his plea scoop after scoop, counting until losing count.

In the meantime, the bike remained cocooned in plastic. Dutch had explained that rust would set-in, that it would be nearly impossible to wipe dry every spoke and chain link. Not to mention that the bike had real chrome fenders. "If ya take real good care of it," Dutch had said, "one day it'll be worth more than Santa paid for it."

At four in the morning on the 3rd of January, Ben found himself blinking bleary-eyed into one of the pens in the barn. Wind chill was twenty degrees below zero. Why did I have to get up so early? Ben grumbled to himself. The sheer volume of noise convinced Ben Smith he would never be a farmer.

Jerry nudged Ben's rump as he held the barn light aloft for Dutch, who was talking softly to the massive sow lying on her side in the pen's corner under another covered bulb while her eleven babies were suckling.

"Easy," Dutch said, stroking the black ear of the five hundred pound mother who didn't appreciate having the light on at this hour.

Jim Vanderhaus climbed inside the pen with Dutch. He was there to return the favor for Dutch's help with his hogs a week earlier.

"Keep that light good and close to their hind legs," Dutch warned Ben.

When Jim gave a nod to Dutch indicating that he was ready, all hell broke loose. Dutch took a straight razor from his heavy overalls pocket and wiped the blade clean with a rag soaked in rubbing alcohol. Jim grabbed a squealing piglet by its hind legs and raised it in the air while Dutch sliced off its testicles. Ben's face twisted in disgust as the blue little balls covered in blood fell to the pen floor. The mother lumbered up to investigate.

"Ben, God-dammit, wake up!" Dutch barked. Ben flinched, stretching his right arm that held the light toward the men.

After Dutch castrated the first pig it stopped squealing. As her baby was being lowered into the empty pen next door, the sow gobbled up the bloody tidbits on the floor. Ben's stomach turned, and he fought off the urge to puke.

Dutch and Jim jumped back over the low wall of the pen when the sow decided to defend the remaining babies, thrusting her bulk hard against the fence where the men had been standing. Jim was quick to move behind the mother, where he grabbed a second piglet, hoisting it for Dutch to cut.

The din of squealing babies and their mother was unbearable to Ben's city ears as they continued for three hours, castrating all seven litters.

Walking out into the light of the rising sun, Ben's arms ached from hours of holding the light steady. Dutch and Jim talked in the central farmyard while Ben sat on the feed house step, his wrists hanging limp over his knees, his jaw slack with relief at being finished with the gruesome task. He watched Dutch blow snot from each nostril to the snow-covered ground, laughing with his helper after a brutal chore that was natural and easy for him. Ben wasn't sure if his butt was numb from the cold step under him, or from the image of Dutch kicking him good if he wasn't right on the spot with that light while seven insane mothers gobbled up each baby's straw-covered testicles, and scared even the man with the razor-the same man who fed and watered them faithfully for four seasons. His stepfather was but one of thousands who raised to kill. Not for pleasure, Ben realized...for the profit.

Ben was happy to arrive at the back porch without Dutch calling him back. After removing his boots on the lip of the porch steps he glanced toward his bike in cold storage in the cob house. His shoulders and neck had been tensed for hours, and now felt bruised and tender from the stress of seventy-six castrations.

Inside the back porch, to the right of the freezer was a cellar door he had never dared to open. He wondered what might be down there besides the cold potatoes Dutch carried up for supper in a white lard bucket. As long as there were doors like that one, and the locked one upstairs, this place could never be Ben's true home. He placed his work gloves on the window sill where Dutch always put his to thaw.

In the kitchen, Ben saw that a dryer-load of clothes lay

half folded on the table. The thought of Pam and Debi still warm and asleep seemed so unfair. Just because they were girls all they had to do was make their bed, then they were free to play with their dolls all day.

Ben skipped standing over the floor furnace to warm himself. He dove under his bedcovers in his white briefs, drawing his knees to his chin with palms together between his thighs, shivering. That thing Darlene wanted him to do plagued him, so disturbing it supplanted the horror of the piglets' repeated screams during the long night.

His thoughts were jumbled: I shouldn't have told Pam about it. I could have just kept it to myself. Who cares about D. J.? Dutch may have told Mom all about it, so it's nothing. But Pam, she's looking for a way out of here. She's not fooling me. If Dutch finds out, I'm dead. And for what?

Gene's speed along his route stayed the same, even on the iced, blue, snow-packed roads, because he had mounted Black Hawk Studs all-around during his Christmas break. He had wiped clean the interior of his bus from top-to-bottom, and all eight other county buses. The county didn't mind paying Gene Rainbow over Christmas break, simply because he did the work of three men-and gladly did each task better.

Pam was looking at the back of Gene's new black and green plaid shirt. A tiny metal fan rattled and blew hot air across Gene's left shoulder, wafting a breeze of stultification over Ben's whole being. They were thirty seconds away from the next stop.

Pam jabbed her brother's arm, rustling the paper bag against his side under his coat. He returned a frown that brought a smirk to Pam's lips, an expression which Gene caught in his overhead mirror, causing him to wonder about the source of Pam's amusement. Ben wanted to scream. If he could, he'd wrap his arms around Gene and squeeze out everything Pam wanted to know. Anything seemed better than completing this trade with Darlene.

Behind his dark lenses, Gene could see there was something going on between the Smith kids seated behind him. Darlene had been asking questions about D. J. lately. And these two, Gene surmised, were a part of it.

"How did D. J. die?" she had asked him.

That was as close as she came to the question that Gene always directed to the hardcover Bible under his pillow. The missing word: Why? He knew how D. J. died. What good would it do these kids to know what only he had known for fifteen years? They appeared to be in no danger, he reminded himself.

He pulled the silver metal handle that opened the door for his niece.

Darlene turned her legs sideways and faced Ben across the aisle. She smiled long at the boy.

"Ya got somethin' for me, Benny?" Darlene inquired.

Ben's guarded expression filled Gene's mirror. Darlene was up to something. That made it his business.

Ben waited until Gene was occupied turning at a four-way stop before handing the paper bag to Darlene. But stealth was useless; she noisily unrolled the top of the sack and peered inside, with every bus passenger suddenly curious about the contents.

"Thank you, Ben," Darlene said. "They look real nice."

She held the bag on her lap, wrapping both arms around it.

"Ben got me a Christmas present, Uncle Gene."

In the oblong mirror, Gene watched the boy's face suffuse with color. Why would Ben get her a Christmas present? he wondered.

Gene dismissed the thought; traffic was picking up on this part of his route.

Rumors & Cakewalks

In late January Michelle got a phone call from Edith. Michelle bristled as usual at her estranged mother's brusque words.

"Hutch needs his freezer defrosted. He says since Dutch never paid for the treatments on his leg. He wants you to clean his refrigerator."

It wasn't difficult for Michelle to persuade her husband to let her visit Hutch. "I'll defrost his refrigerator and that'll take care of his treatments for the fireworks accident," she told him.

A week into February, Dutch drove them into Des Moines. He had decided to let Edith work on his sore shoulder again, while Michelle went over to Hutch's hotel.

Driving through Des Moines with her husband and youngest daughter, Michelle realized she missed the activity of the city. She thought about her isolation on the farm without any friends just to chat with on occasion. Dutch and the kids were now her life. Still, she was not looking forward to seeing Hutch.

In Edith's basement, Dutch lay bare-chested on his back on the massage table. Every year about this time Dutch's right arm and shoulder gave him trouble. He lost sleep. Welding and machinery repairs in his shop sometimes became impossible.

With a pair of metal tongs, Edith lifted a clean white towel from a steaming pot. She cranked the towel through an old-fashioned washing machine roller to dry it, and wrapped Dutch's arm from wrist to shoulder.

"Hot," Edith said.

"Yes it is," Dutch agreed.

Edith had canny eyes. When she saw something she was sure of, she announced it no matter the consequences. "You like pain, don't you, Dutch?"

Michelle dropped Debi off at Dick and Merle's house so she could see Hutch alone. Driving the pickup along familiar Des Moines streets, Michelle thought about her early morning phone conversation with Hutch.

"Good morning, Princess," Hutch had said.

"Hello, Hutch."

"You comin' to visit me?"

"Yes, today, like Edith told you."

"I'm looking forward to seeing you...after getting my ass blown up."

"How are you doing with that?" Michelle asked, eyeing Dutch, who was listening to every word.

"There is this matter of who should pay to cover my burn treatments."

"You know I've agreed to do some cleaning for you," Michelle said.

"Make sure you show up. My freezer needs a good defrosting. Then we can discuss a rumor I think you will find interesting."

"About what?" Michelle asked.

"Your other half."

"Okay." Michelle had drawn out the O and K to indicate to Hutch's alert ears that she couldn't speak freely.

Shifting the truck into third gear she noticed her hands were rough now. Dutch had allowed her to get her hair done only once, to dye her blond hair to match her brunette roots, so she no longer would need to spend money on beauty salons. Dutch would never allow her to get a manicure.

"Yer the best lookin' woman in the county on yer worst day," he had told her. That was about as tender as her husband could be, she thought, while driving down a street lined with Elm trees and dirty snow banks.

She had lied to Dutch by not telling him she was dropping Debi off at her dad's place. Her stepfather's conspiratorial tone had warned her to come alone to the Hill Hotel.

Worrying that Hutch's rumor would be something bad about her husband, she ran a red light in heavy traffic. Her hands slid, slick with panic-sweat on the steering wheel, as she swerved around a car just entering the intersection on her right. A blast on a car horn to her left made her floor the accelerator.

After parking in front of the hotel, Michelle sat for a few minutes while she calmed herself. She looked down at her beige trousers and brown wool socks. How tacky, she thought, and consoled herself that Hutch was blind.

Climbing the hotel's two flights of steep stairs, the smell of pine disinfectant on the floor became so strong she nearly gagged in the unvented hallway.

Nels waved at her from his doorway when he heard her walking up the stairs, and again thought of the money she'd bring in, if she were one of his girls.

Michelle nodded at the pimp and continued on, walking fast, her penny loafers raising a cloud of dust from the hall runner.

As she approached Hutch's open door, she could hear the weather report blaring from his bedside radio.

"Hello!" she called to him from the hallway.

"Hello, Princess," Hutch hollered. He slugged back his shot of Jack Daniels and turned off the radio.

"Aren't you starting early?" Michelle commented.

"No such thing as too early for a sip of ol' Jack."

Hutch was sitting Indian-fashion at the head of his bed wearing boxers, a sleeveless white t-shirt and black

178

nylon socks; his silver hair was combed straight back, slick and perfect.

Michelle opened the small refrigerator's door and turned the temperature control to "off." She began to hack at the frost on the freezer's surface with a butcher knife.

Hutch lit a menthol with a snap of his lighter.

"You shouldn't smoke in bed," Michelle warned.

"I shouldn't do a lot of things in bed," he laughed, but his cornflower-blue eyes, sightless though clear, never changed expression.

Michelle found a bucket beneath the sink and held it under the front edge of the freezer. With the blade of the knife she scraped the loosened ice forward so it fell into the bucket.

"What's this thing that you heard about Dutch?"

"You knew he was married?"

"Yes."

"And he had a son?"

Hutch recognized at once from her gasp, that Michelle hadn't known any such thing.

"Who told you that?" she demanded, stabbing at the ice.

"I was playing cribbage with the attorney who handled his divorce."

Hutch didn't want to upset Michelle, at least not before she finished the defrosting job. He continued with uncharacteristic tact.

"It seems the first Mrs. Beal was crazy as a bedbug. Dutch made her sign contracts drawn up by this shyster. Their divorce papers gave him sole custody of the boy."

Michelle stopped chipping the ice and walked over to stand at the foot of his bed. "I'm not sure I believe you," she said. "Why would Dutch's lawyer tell you all this?"

Hutch replied, "He's a real good buddy of my ol' friend, Jack Daniels."

"Oh, I see."

"I hope you do. The ex-wife was still living on the farm a year after the divorce was final, without a clue, she was that far gone mentally."

Hutch calmly took a long drag from his menthol. "You better sit down, Michelle," he advised.

"No, go on," she said.

"Dutch worked out a scheme to get her off his hands. As part of the divorce she had taken back her maiden name, on paper. That's when Dutch got some quack to commit her to Cherokee as a ward of the state, at no cost to himself."

Michelle felt the blood drain from her face. Lightheaded, she took hold of the footboard of Hutch's bed. "What about the boy?"

"That's the real kicker. After his mother was committed, maybe he killed himself."

Michelle took a deep breath, then expelled it in a rush. "How?" she asked.

"The lawyer didn't tell me."

Michelle sat down on the foot of the bed, running Hutch's words over and over in her mind.

"You want a drink, honey?" he asked.

"No. You said the guy was drunk. It might be nothing but gossip."

"Maybe so, maybe not. I'd find out, if I were you. You stay on your toes with that guy," Hutch warned.

She thought of all the work she'd put into her marriage. And how the kids liked their school. If the story was true, her husband had lied to her-by omission-but still a lie. She felt stupid for not learning more about Dutch before she married him. The facts had to be checked out carefully. She remembered reading a newspaper article about a young mother who was shot dead by her husband as she was coming out of church, because she was planning on leaving him.

Hutch is right. I have to stay on my toes, she thought.

But what if the story was full of wild speculation about a situation that was so terrible Dutch suffered every time someone brought it up. She could understand Dutch hiding the fact he had a son, because of the boy's suicide. And a mentally ill wife must have been real hard to live with, and not something Dutch would want to talk about. The sensational parts of the story were probably nothing more than vicious gossip. Then she thought of the spankings and Dutch's hot temper.

For a moment she was angry at Hutch for telling her. Hutch must have told Edith, as well. I'm sure she made some comment about me being stupid for not knowing my husband, Michelle thought, and ground her teeth. She stabbed at the ice in Hutch's freezer with renewed vigor, then clawed several chunks forward and let them fall into the bucket with a clatter that startled the blind man lounging on the bed.

"Did you tell Edith about this?" Michelle demanded.

Hutch didn't answer until she turned and asked him again.

"I asked her if I should tell you about it," Hutch replied, his eyes now open wider, his mouth slack and oval.

"Since when did she know, or care what's best for me, Hutch?"

"Now, Michelle, calm down. Your mother's a pretty sharp gal as you know."

"Yes, she's sharp alright. And what did she think I should do?"

"Leave him," Hutch said.

"Leave him? That's what I'd expect her to say," she said. "Like mother, like daughter."

"Get an attorney and get all you can," he advised.

Michelle wished she had not asked about Edith's opinion, for her first inclination was always to do the opposite. Would staying with Dutch endanger her kids? Edith had called her bullheaded at least a thousand times. So she was-when it came to doing what Edith wanted. If Dutch's story was pitiful and deserved her compassion, she would give it. Anything to keep her tribe secure. Besides, she reasoned, if Dutch had done anything wrong would he be a respected member of the school board?

The pickup carrying Dutch, Michelle, and Debi turned into the farm's drive just as Gene was braking his bus to a stop across the road. Duke was right there to bark at the yellow bus from the yard.

"Bye, Ben," Darlene said. "See ya tomorrow!"

This irritated Pam. Darlene had been acting like her brother's best friend and wearing their mother's clothes ever since Ben stole them from her closet: a maroon sweater and a pair of black slacks, and from her dresser, the near-full bottle of White Shoulders perfume that Ben gave their mother for her last birthday.

Every single day since Ben handed over the stolen goods, Darlene had been wearing them all. Her mother's outfit looked pretty good on Darlene, but her body odor clashed with the expensive perfume, and she wore way too much of it. The deal: "Get me some of yer mom's nice clothes and some of that perfume she wears," Darlene promised, "and you'll find out what happened to D. J."

Pam and Ben were afraid to ask Darlene about her end of the bargain. Pam thought the older girl was crazy enough to return the clothes to her mother and ask her how best to clean them.

Gene was turning the bus onto the back road to Ledges when Darlene informed her uncle that she wanted to ride on through his route and go home with him in his car. The school's Winter Carnival was Saturday night, and she wanted Gene to buy her some things at the store so she could bake a cake for the cakewalk. After Gene gave his thumbs-up answer, she smiled at her own reflection in the bus win-

182

dow, thinking of what she planned to do at the cakewalk.

"Ask her about it," Pam urged.

"You ask her," Ben shot back.

Michelle met Pam and Ben at the back porch door. "Ask me what?" She smiled at them.

"Nothing, Mom. We were talking about someone at school," Pam said.

Their mother's expression changed when she saw Dutch coming toward them after parking the truck beside the barn.

He noticed his wife's furrowed brow. "Anything wrong?" Dutch said to Michelle.

"Not a thing, everything's fine," she assured him.

"Mom's acting strange," Pam whispered to Ben; both were lying on their stomachs in front of the TV watching cartoons.

"You think she knows her stuff is missing?" Ben whispered.

"No. But she saw Hutch today. That would make anybody act weird."

"You sure got him good with that Cherry Bomb," he snickered.

When Pam failed to laugh with him, and frowned instead, he asked, "What's up with you?"

"What if Darlene wants more clothes and gives us nothing?"

It snowed all night and all the next day. Dutch told Ben to shovel after the snowfall. Dutch seemed annoyed when Ben said he wanted to get a head start so the snow didn't pile up so deep and wasn't as hard to shovel.

After Dutch installed new chains on the pickup's tires he drove Michelle into Boone to shop for groceries. This was the first time she'd been alone with him since her visit with Hutch, except in bed at night, but that wasn't the time for serious talk. She'd been trying to think of a casual way to find out about her husband's son and ex-wife. Nothing came. There was no way she wanted to shake up her marriage, now, in the middle of winter, with the kids doing so well in their new school. Everyone had bad things in their past, some worse than others, she reassured herself.

"I thought I'd let the girls bake a cake or two for the carnival," she said to Dutch, who was feeling pleased with the way his chains plowed through the snow.

Dutch's green eyes squinted past the blue snow glare reflected onto his sunglasses. He lit a thin cigar, opened his wing window, and blew the initial puffs to his left. He was thoroughly enjoying the solid grip of the truck's tires, the snow packing tight under the chains on the asphalt surface of Route 23 leading to Boone.

"You ever been to one of these Winter Carnivals?" Michelle asked.

"Oh, yeah," he said, nodding straight ahead, smart and final.

This reminded Michelle of their drive to Vegas. He'd told her when he first got married he was young and stupid. It didn't work out, was all he had said. Then it had been her turn. She went on and on about her past, covering her marriage and a revealing account of all her relationships before and after Kenny. All over some 300 miles. Then he did pretty much the same thing as now: nodding occasionally; the cigar; the eyes hidden behind sunglasses.

Then the pronouncement: "Okay. I've heard it all once. I never want to hear about it again."

She had respected his request because he was an older man and knew what he wanted. They never again spoke of the past, not hers, and especially not his.

Inside the Boone IGA, Michelle was thinking again how she hadn't gotten to know any of the farm women well

184

in nearly nine months. And, even if she had, anything they might say about her husband's past would be more gossip and rumors, anyway. Until Dutch told her himself.

"There's California tomatoes and asparagus comin' next week," the store owner informed Michelle and Dutch, giving his old high school buddy a squeeze on his shoulder.

As the store owner walked away smiling, his thoughts were on Michelle and how in the world Dutch managed to land her.

Michelle thought, let it go. The school carnival was coming up. The kids were looking forward to it.

On Friday afternoon, the day before the Winter Carnival, Darlene was still wearing Michelle's stolen clothes. When Gene descended the bus steps to sort out a shoving match between two of his riders, Pam leaned across Ben to talk to Darlene. "You aren't going to wear those clothes to the carnival, are you?"

"You think I'm stupid, or somethin'?" Her mouth twisted, her eyes fierce on Pam.

"I just wanted you to know my mom was going to be there, that's all," Pam hurried to assure her.

Ben intervened on his sister's behalf. "She didn't mean anything by it, Darlene."

"Look, you want yer information about D. J.? I got it."

Darlene pulled a flat, open pack of Pall Malls from under the waistband of Michelle's slacks. Between the clear wrapper and the red label was a folded newspaper clipping that she slid out, handing it to Ben. "I was gonna bake it into a cake and surprise ya with it at the cakewalk."

Darlene was still chuckling as her uncle ran up the steps and settled himself behind the wheel.

Ben kept the clipping fisted in his hand, knowing he couldn't read it on the bus.

Gene had no idea his niece had gone into his bedroom

185

and taken the clipping that had been pressed between his Bible's pages for nearly fifteen years. In the face of repeated questions, Gene had seen no reason to tell Darlene anything regarding D. J., not since he sat in the Beal's kitchen and learned firsthand that the Smith kids were doing pretty good. He had told his niece to leave them alone, figuring she was pestering them for cigarette money. Now, he frowned. He'd seen the three kids deep in conversation.

Duke met the school bus with a flurry of barking. Ben followed his sister down the steps. When he turned, he saw Darlene's nose pressed to the window as the bus sped on its way.

"Let's read it behind one of the trees," Pam suggested.

"No. They know we're home now. They might see us."

"But I'm dying to know what it says!"

"Dutch won't start chores for a couple of hours. See that window up in the corncrib?" He pointed to the distant window in his high place, where an urban boy could be enclosed and alone, far removed from man and nature. "Meet me up there," Ben told her.

"I can't climb up there!"

"Oh yes, you can. I'll help you."

"Ben."

"I'll tell you what it says, then. After I change clothes I'm going up there, and I'm leaving it there."

Michelle was scouring the bathtub with Ajax when Pam came in with her brother. Debi sat on the kitchen floor outside the bathroom door coloring a paper doll's dress. Ben walked fast for his room, fighting the urge to read the clipping as soon as he closed his bedroom door.

"Mom, can we buy our valentines tonight instead of tomorrow?" Pam asked.

"We'll see. How was your day in school?"

"Fine." For the first time, Pam hurried up the stairs to her room.

Fifteen minutes later, Pam followed Ben across the frozen sweetcorn field. She wanted to cry out for him to wait for her, but Dutch was in his shop.

"You read it already, didn't you?" she accused, when she found him waiting for her at the corncrib.

"If I had, I wouldn't be here."

Pam tried not to look to the top of the ominous big barn until they stepped into its shadow, out of the north wind, onto crunchy snow, flat and smooth but for the footprints behind them. Pam gasped when she turned the corner and saw the ladder that climbed so high and narrow.

"Come on," Ben urged.

She did. Her leg ached with every step: right foot first, left foot hoisted up beside the right, pausing between each rung. Ben waited patiently at the top, on his knees on the cold pine platform. Pam's tongue stuck out of the corner of her mouth, her lips tight around it. She pulled her body upward with trembling hands in red, wool gloves with little white stars stitched over the backs.

"That's it. Just a couple more and you made it." Ben told her.

The last two rungs were above the level of the floor. Ben gripped his stronger left hand around Pam's biceps. Her brother's grip on her felt so secure she released her left hand from the top rung and stepped onto the platform confident she was safe from falling.

Ben walked over to the window with the missing piece of glass; the slightest breeze produced a faint whistle as it passed over the triangular gap. The hole was obvious. Dutch was sure to see or hear it one day. Ben blocked out the thought and fished the clipping from his back pocket. He sat with his back against the wall under the window, his knees chin-high.

Pam lowered herself to the platform beside him and stretched her left leg out. He unfolded the brittle paper carefully and placed it flat on his thigh, holding the tattered edges that fluttered in the cold draft from the window overhead.

"Read it out loud," he said.

She read the headline first. Ledges Incident Not Double Suicide

Pam paused and glanced at her brother's expressionless face. "Go on," he said.

A Boone County coroner's investigation has ruled 11-year-old Irving Beal's fatal fall at Ledges State Park an accident. During the inquest, Irving Beal indicated that his son was in good spirits after his mother's recent commitment to the state hospital, believing she would soon be well. On October 1, Irving Beal and classmate Eugene Rainbow were absent without permission from school, according to school authorities. Sources say the boys' teacher was too overcome by grief to attend the inquest. The coroner concluded that Irving slipped and fell off Inspiration Point while climbing with Eugene. Young Rainbow was found badly injured on the bank of the Des Moines River 300 yards from the High Bridge, located three miles southwest of Boone. Rainbow's fall from the High Bridge was called a tragic coincidence by police who speculate that Eugene must have been rushing to town for help when he fell from the bridge. Rainbow's condition at a Des Moines hospital is critical. The body of Irving Beal, Jr., was cremated; no services were held. He is survived by his father, Irving Beal of Luther.

"Read it again," Ben said.

She did.

He kept the old clipping on his thigh, the top corners of it curling down on both sides of his thumbs.

"That story doesn't make sense," Pam said.

"Why would Gene go all the way to High Bridge?"

Ben asked. "That's a long walk."

"I don't know. The police thought he was taking a shortcut to town," Pam said, "but he could have flagged down a car."

"You're right, the road's closer to Inspiration Point," Ben said.

"You think Mom knows about this?" Pam asked.

"I don't even think she knows about D. J. If she did, she would have told us."

"Yeah. You think we should show her the article?"

"I don't know," he answered, both still staring at the clipping. "Why wouldn't Dutch tell Mom about a son who died like that? Unless..."

"What?" Pam snapped.

"Unless this isn't true," he said.

Ben refolded the clipping, then stood up, pacing the platform while Pam sat and listened.

"We can't show her the article if it's not true. We've gotta go to Gene and find out. He can talk when you hold him steady."

He opened the clipping again. "D. J. didn't even have a funeral, and Dutch acts like he never had a kid."

Ben waved the clipping at Pam; they both watched the slip of paper leave his hand and float in slow-motion out onto the sea of corn, flying six feet away from the platform to fall close to the opposite wall. Pam scrambled up to her feet. They stared at each other. Then Ben began to step out into the corn.

"What are you doing?" Pam cried.

He stopped. "I've been in there before. It's okay."

Pam wanted to say let it go, but her brother wasn't going to give up searching for the truth. And she felt the same way. Maybe even more.

Ben stepped off the platform. His left boot sank fast into the dry, yellow kernels. He didn't remember going so deep so fast last time.

"Ben, be careful. Try reaching for it first."

He stretched forward but was two feet short. Then he stepped farther out. It was too late to lift his feet and go back to the safety of the platform.

"I should've gotten a rake and dragged it out," he said.

Pam's flesh crawled. Ben was out too far for her to reach him and sinking fast up to his knees, then to his waist, unable to move.

"Ben!"

She saw her brother drowning in the corn, still sinking.

"Take your belt off," she screamed.

He struggled to remove his belt, now submerged a few inches deep. When he finally pulled it off, he whipped the tongue end at the clipping, his motions making him sink deeper.

"Use the other end," Pam yelled.

It worked. The buckle raked the clipping toward him. He crumpled the clipping and tossed it over Pam's head onto the platform, sinking lower and lower. He lashed the buckle-end of the belt toward Pam, leaning with his toss. Lying on her belly out over the edge of the platform, she managed to grasp the belt. He switched his grip to his stronger left hand as Pam pulled with both of hers, inching him closer to her.

"My boots are coming off!" he cried.

"I can't pull any harder," Pam shouted.

"Just hold it as tight as you can!"

With all his might Ben made a thrusting butterfly stroke with only his head above the corn. He stretched and grabbed one of Pam's wrists and pulled on his sister's heavier body, freeing his arms. With one more lunge he made it to the lip of the platform.

Pam didn't care how much it hurt Ben, she put both her hands around his neck and clumsily got to her knees on the edge.

"Wait! On three...you pull, when I do," he said.

He dug his fingers into the cold wood and counted, "One, two, three!"

She yanked his head upward and his chest rose even with the platform. Then she changed her grip to under his armpits, tugging until they both collapsed from exhaustion on the cold wood. Both lay on their backs breathing hard, looking up to the ceiling, silently thanking God.

Ben swiped at a tear. "I'm in trouble now, Pam. My new boots are in there with my school shoes stuck inside. Dutch will kill me."

"Ben, you could have died!"

She lay there looking at her brother's face, tears streaming down her cheeks onto the platform. He patted her back.

"I'm okay," he said.

"I know!" she cried. "We'll tell Mom we were playing catch with my gloves and you went out in the corn to get them."

Pam took off her gloves and balled them like a pair of socks and tossed them into the bed of corn.

Going down the ladder after getting their story straight, Ben realized he was in even deeper trouble.

"He'll see the broken window."

Pam was too concerned with climbing down the last few rungs to worry about yet another problem.

Ben tiptoed in his socks on the frozen ground, moving ahead of Pam.

"Why did we go up there?" she said. "We need a reason."

Ben stopped. "The clipping. I didn't get it. Did you?"

Pam shook her head. Ben took off running toward the back porch, his feet numb on the rock-hard earth.

Pam kept her hands in her coat pockets.

Dutch was on the back porch when Ben came in without footwear.

"Where's yer shoes?"

Ben's words stammered from his airless throat. "I...I...lost them...in...in...the corn...in the...big barn."

"You did what?" Dutch's face turned blood-red; his eyes squeezed to slits. The boy's fear of him only angered Dutch more. He loomed over him.

"Dad...I...I..."

Pam spoke quickly, terrified by Dutch's threatening posture.

"Dad, it's my fault. I threw my gloves in the air and they went in the corn. And Ben tried to get them out for me and he got stuck."

"What the hell were you kids doin' up there?"

Again she protected her brother and took a chance by saying, "I wanted to know what it was like. If I could see all the way to Ledges."

Dutch's eyes changed at the mention of Ledges. "Get somethin' on yer feet and show me where they went in."

Ben's other shoes and Pam's were kept on the porch, lined up side by side on a layer of newspaper. He pushed his frozen feet into his cold Keds.

"You stay inside," Dutch said to Pam.

Ben looked like a prisoner on a death march when he stepped out of the back porch door with Dutch behind him. Pam started crying. All at once she had a pounding headache. What do I do? she thought. Run and tell Mom that Ben's in trouble? Tell her about the clipping? Would Dutch find the clipping? Would he see the broken window? What would he do to Ben up there...alone?

Pam rushed through the kitchen, her face flushed and wet from crying, and found her mother dusting the cosmetic containers on the dresser in the master bedroom. Michelle had just noticed that her bottle of White Shoulders was missing from its usual spot. When she saw Pam's distraught face reflected in the mirror, she dropped the soft rag she was using and spun around.

"Mom, Ben's in big trouble with Dutch."

"What happened?"

"We were up in the big barn and my gloves fell in the corn. And Ben tried to get them. He lost his boots and shoes in the corn, Mom. Dutch is really going to spank him bad."

Michelle rushed into the kitchen to look out the window to see if she could spot Dutch and Ben. On the back porch she pulled on her coat and jammed her feet into her penny loafers. She dashed over to the dark cob house. Then she checked the shop before turning into the stiff wind whipping through the sweetcorn field.

"He's not going to lay a hand on Ben. Not any more!" she repeated over and over as she followed deep tractor ruts, ice-covered and as hard as her husband's heart toward her boy.

Thirty feet ahead she gazed into the big barn's entrance. She could hear the sound of wood scraping against wood, magnified by the wide-open chamber, a space that could easily hold three combines and their pull.

She hesitated in the doorway. Dutch was just climbing onto the platform after pushing a ten-foot long wood plank up the ladder to Ben. She didn't hear sounds of trouble.

If she could have heard her son's heart pounding raw fear, she would have climbed the ladder instead of waiting at the bottom rung, listening.

Ben glanced at the balled clipping as Dutch lifted the plank under his left arm.

"Where'd you go in?" he asked.

Ben pointed to Pam's red gloves and wasn't sure they were close to the place his boots were. Then Dutch noticed the hole in the window pane. "You and Pam break that window?"

"It was broken when we came up here," Ben said,

sticking to the absolute truth.

"Damn pigeons tryin' to get at the corn," Dutch said. "It's happened before."

Ben was so relieved by his stepfather's reaction, a warm wave of blood surged through his body, driving off the chill of fear. A wave of thanksgiving that Dutch was too busy with the task at hand to look for the shard of glass that no longer lay below the broken window.

Dutch dropped the plank out from the platform and across the corn to a wall support beam. "Point to where you think yer boots are," he said.

Ben came over and just wasn't sure.

"It has to be in line with the gloves," Dutch growled, the same sound that came just before he kicked Ben to the ground last summer.

"Around there," Ben pointed.

Dutch knee-walked then crawled on his belly across the plank directly over the gloves. Ben knew it was now or never, as he backed up toward the clipping.

"I hear you had an accident," Michelle startled Ben. She stepped from the top rung as Dutch's arm plunged shoulder-deep near Pam's gloves. His mother's calm expression told Ben she remained unaware of his danger when he stepped into the loose corn. If she understood how stupid I was, she would take a belt to me herself, he thought.

Michelle watched her husband's left arm come up empty then repeat the same plunge. Again nothing. Then Dutch shifted six inches along the plank before going in again. Dutch knew why his wife had climbed to the platform.

"You think you should get a spankin' for this, Ben?" Dutch asked after another miss.

Michelle knew her husband's flushed face meant trouble; she had to tread carefully and not interfere unless she was forced to.

"Huh?" Dutch barked, demanding an answer.

Ben mumbled something, his head down and submissive.

"What?" Dutch demanded.

"I don't know, Dad."

Michelle stepped up to the edge of the plank saying nothing, her hands on her hips. Ben went for the clipping, turning his back to them and stuffing it into his front jeans pocket. Relief. Now, the boots, he prayed.

"Ben, get over here!" Dutch barked, into his fifth empty plunge.

Ben stood beside his mother.

"Point to where you went in."

He had no idea but he had to give Dutch something.

"Think boy!"

"I think...there." He pointed to the left of the plank some two feet. When Dutch crawled back to the platform, Michelle and Ben backed up. Dutch moved the plank.

He finally fished out the boots forty minutes later, after moving the board twice more to the left, then once to the right of his first drop.

Michelle stayed with her son until both stood close to the floor furnace in the living room raking their cold feet over the hot iron grate. Ben was exhausted from his near-drowning combined with worry over Dutch's reaction.

Later, Pam left Debi watching cartoons in front of the Zenith and went into Ben's room.

"You found your boots."

"Dutch did."

"He didn't spank you?"

"Because Mom was there. I put your gloves in your coat pocket."

"Did you get the clipping?" she whispered.

He nodded yes, then checked his front pocket to feel it still there.

195

"You better hide it."

"I will."

Michelle poked her head inside Ben's door, telling Pam, "No valentines tonight. Don't even ask. I'll take you tomorrow. Ben, you better take your bath now. Don't use too much hot water."

On her way into the kitchen, Michelle was mulling over what she had just said to Ben about using hot water. I never told the kids that, even when I was single and broke, she realized. I'm married to a millionaire, for God's sake...and I can't soak in a hot tub. And my kids have to share the same bath water. God, how did this happen?

That night, Dutch lay back in his recliner and smoked his pipe all the way through "The Untouchables." Michelle watched him hold the pipe's bowl for long periods, appearing to be thinking hard about something far removed from the family night of TV viewing.

At bedtime the girls giggled together, planning to buy sappy valentines at the Boone Ben Franklin to give to the kids in Pam's class. They whispered excitedly about the Winter Carnival the next night at school.

Downstairs, Ben was thinking of the wrinkled clipping he had placed under the center of his mattress. His back burned thinking about it there, as if the article was a hot coal. He thought, if Gene really tried to kill himself after his friend died at Ledges, was God punishing him for it by making his head say no for the rest of his life? Would Gene even remember what happened after falling like that?

For two hours Ben lay awake listening for any conversation behind the sliding walnut doors between his room and the master bedroom. He only heard his mom and stepdad if they were arguing about him or his sisters or money.

The next morning when Ben came out of his room the house was empty. They went without me, he said to himself. Not caring much about Valentines, he did like to get off the farm and go into town, where his mother sometimes treated them to ice cream with change she shaved from the grocery money. His mother's absence meant Dutch was here some-where, and could decide to give him a whipping now that his protector was gone.

Saturday morning cartoons weren't as funny as usual for Ben. Dutch might come in at any minute. Dutch was here and his own father was so far away. Maybe he could have been a better, braver son. Maybe he could have been nicer to his sisters. Dutch was Ben's punishment.

Actually things improved on the farm once Ben strengthened his back and hands during his hours as a labor-er. Spring was the only season he had not yet experienced. It would free him and free the red bike. He had already made up his mind never to spend another summer hacking ragweed. The heat, pollen, blisters and mosquitoes were tor-ture. It would kill his mother if he ran away from home, he knew, gazing at the cartoons, not seeing or hearing any-thing, but imagining how it would be.

He would cut through the winding road in Ledges and head north out of Boone for Canada using only gravel roads. Food, shelter and money did not concern him; work-ing for spare change would keep his mind off his mother and the girls. He would come back for them when he was bigger and stronger. He would be the rescuer. Just like in the song his mom used to sing while cleaning their apartment in Wichita, "Some day my prince will come."

On the back porch Ben pulled his school shoes from the dusty, black rubber boots and shook out a few kernels of corn. Everything was always cold: the linoleum he sat on while putting on his Keds and boots; his slender fingers on his coat's zipper; all the tools he touched as he did chores; the clear plastic that covered his bike in the shadowy cob house, where he printed BEN on the chrome over the back tire after removing his gloves. Every breath passing over his

197

lips or into his nostrils seemed to flow into his fingertips and down to his toes, keeping them numb and cold for as long as he remained outside.

He thought about practicing with his rifle, but he would lose too many BBs in the snow. If he looked like he was loafing Dutch would find something for him to do. He pulled his wool, navy-blue stocking cap over his ears, zipped his coat as high as he could and headed for Ledges and the trails he had not hiked.

On the snow-white, back road to Ledges, Ben's eyes squinted against the whiteness glaring in all directions. Not a soul passed or approached him the entire way. Half the time he spent thinking about the carnival that night, wondering if he gave Sally Robson a valentine, would she take it the wrong way and stare at him even more. She was the freckle-faced Boone girl who sat across from him in Mrs. Jorgenson's class. She wore glasses too.

He took the long way around Ledges to the back exit out of the park, following the black and gray tree line of the White and Red Oaks; the bare slender stands of Black Cherry, Black Maple and Ironwoods. He circled around where he had to take a trail, or slog along the east bank of the frozen river where large boulders stood. The glacier-smoothed stones had been carried there over thirteen thousand years before and Ben was not about to tackle them.

Deer tracks followed the same path until he took the timber steps up where the narrow trail began again, curving and winding to a fork. Which way to go? He took the one that veered right and up to one of the most spectacular spots in Ledges: a large, smooth-flat rock with a clear view over the snaky Des Moines.

Standing there, facing west, Ben pulled himself back from the slippery rock edge that topped a thirty foot drop. It isn't far to Gene's place from here, he thought. His bus driver's image had filled Ben's thoughts from the moment he looked down at the river. Now was the time to find out about D. J.'s fall. He wished he had brought the clipping with him. He could simply ask Gene if it was true.

Coming off of the slope of west Ledges into an open field a few hundred yards from Gene's place, Ben thought about turning back because he didn't want to run in to Darlene.

Gene's snow-dirty, lime-green trailer was in view now. He skirted Darlene's house, hoping not to be seen walking by her front window, where the curtains were open, revealing glass smudged with fingerprints. Gene's car was parked by the trailer's single door.

Ben knocked softly and heard heavy footsteps approach. Gene had been napping and stood off-guard a few seconds before waving Ben inside.

While he buttoned his red flannel shirt, Gene indicated that Ben should sit on one of the two folding chairs at the small kitchen table. The bus driver sat across from him, his blue eyes awake now. Ben removed his fogged glasses, thinking hard, wanting to say the right words.

"I heard a rumor that you jumped off High Bridge after D. J. fell at Ledges. Is that what happened?"

Gene's eyes widened, his head moving back slightly from its usual forward cant.

"No, no," Gene repeated, struggling to continue speaking, his head moving back and forth faster.

He stood up, wiping his mouth with his sleeve, and backed two steps to the counter end, where he wrapped his arms around his chest, struggling to force his words out. All he could do was groan unintelligibly.

"Can you write it down on paper?" Ben said.

Gene waved both hands thumbs down, not wanting ever to write things down about that day. He had never been officially questioned about it; and what good would it do now? Gene drew a big letter Y in the air in front of Ben.

"Why?" Ben said.

A thumbs up. Ben cleaned his lenses with the hem of his undershirt, then put them on.

"If I run away, are my mother and sisters in danger living with Dutch?"

Gene was beside himself: tortured by his bobbing head, his fear of losing his job, and wanting to tell the boy everything about that terrible day.

Ben watched Gene rub his forehead nervously. Then he pointed to Darlene's house. Despite his intention to leave Darlene's questions unanswered, she'd been relentless and had wormed the story out of him.

"No," Ben said. He removed his coat and hat and tossed them onto the table.

Ben's eyes were spooked as he motioned for Gene to open his arms. He had never really hugged a man besides his father. He pressed his head right on Gene's heart, tightening his arms as hard as he could around Gene's muscular back. Gene's massive hands slid up Ben's sides and held just below his shoulder blades.

They stood together for what seemed like hours, silent. Gene's head lolled against Ben's shoulder; its motion slowed, then stilled.

Gene's tears wet Ben's shirt.

"Me and D. J. skipped school and went to the High Bridge. A train came when we were under the tracks. The bridge started shakin' bad."

Gene closed his eyes, trying to escape his last minutes with D. J. He could feel the pull of D. J.'s weight on his arm; he could hear the roar of the train overhead. For the second time in days, Gene was looking into his friend's desperate eyes.

"D. J. dropped into the river and I jumped after him. I was hurt bad when I hit the water. D. J. found me and swam me over to the bank." Gene stopped.

"What happened to D. J.?" Ben urged.

Gene stammered, "I was in the hospital for a long time. I don't remember exactly. When I got home my mother showed me what the newspaper said-that I fell runnin' for help after D. J. fell at Ledges. It wasn't true. More than a year later, on Christmas Day I was walkin' by the cemetery. That's where I found D. J.'s belt. It was buckled around a fence post. I had to sit down right there where I found it and think what happened. He must've been real scared, thinkin' I might die and that Dutch was gonna get him good. So he jumped off Ledges...rather than face his dad."

"Why'd he leave his belt there?" Ben asked.

"If I lived...he knew I'd find it. If I died...he wanted to be there too...I guess...with me."

"That's why you put the Christmas tree there?"

"Uh huh."

"They got it all wrong, didn't they?"

"Yeah. My mother heard that Dutch sent D. J.'s mother away to a private hospital...and paid to keep her there with D. J.'s insurance money. They don't pay off for suicide, so I just figured to keep still. Wouldn't change anything, might help D. J.'s mom."

"Sure," Ben agreed.

"If you run off...I s'pose it'll be hard on yer mom most. Does Dutch treat you bad?"

"He beat me and my sister once when we first moved there. I'm just scared all the time to do anything wrong around him. My mom doesn't let him hit us now. I don't know if I should tell her about all this."

"Dutch might get in trouble with the law and then things could be really bad for all of you."

Gene dropped his hands from Ben's back. Ben eased away. He watched Gene's head slowly pick up motion and return to its usual rhythm.

Gene smiled at Ben, then brought him some cookies

from a glass jar. They ate cookies together across the table, Gene watching the boy's mind mulling over what to do. Too much worry for a boy, Gene thought.

After returning Gene's wave at the trailer door and declining Gene's offer to drive him home, communicated by pointing to his car and pretending to turn the steering wheel, Ben walked by Darlene's house. He suppressed the urge to tell her he wanted his mother's things back, that he knew everything about D. J. But Ben wanted to avoid trouble. So he went on his way, cutting through Ledges and onto the winding road.

He kept his eyes on the sandstone cliffs to his left, deciding that it must have been there that D. J. took his life. Ben thought Dutch must have been even meaner toward his own son in order for D. J. to do such a thing.

"I could never do that to myself," Ben said out loud. He thought, I only got spanked bad once. That's no reason to leave. Maybe Dutch is better now after what happened. It'll be okay. Then he thought of Pam. If she knew all this, she might tell Mom and really mess things up. Dutch owed the insurance company lots of money and might go to jail. If he didn't go to jail, he'd get Gene fired for sure. "It'll be okay," Ben repeated a hundred times through Ledges.

When Ben returned, Pam was signing valentines at the kitchen table, checking off names on her list of classmates. Debi had opened Ben's package of valentines and spread them across the floor.

"Balentines," Pam teased her brother.

Michelle came into the kitchen to check on the chocolate cake in the oven. "I still can't find my bottle of White Shoulders. Did you take it, Pam?"

Pam shook her head no. Debi did too.

"Ben, you better get your list and do your valentines. You have to have them for school on Monday," his mother said.

"Mom, do I have to?" Ben whined. "That's kid stuff!"

"They'll all be giving you valentines. Where's your list?"

Ben went into his bedroom and found the list of names Mrs. Jorgenson had given each student. He thought about pulling the envelope where he kept his bean money from under his mattress, taking out the newspaper clipping and tearing it to pieces. But he didn't.

Dutch's T-bird cruised into Boone at 7 o'clock that night, headed for the carnival. The parking lot was crowded with more vehicles than on any school day. The Smith kids were dressed like the rich kids they were thought to be. Much to Pam's disgust, her dress was an exact match for the one Debi wore. Their mother had some weird idea that dressing them like twins was cute. Pam had given up arguing about it; she had figured out that her mother thought buying them identical outfits was a way to avoid favoritism. Pam was just glad that her mother's odd ideas didn't include their school clothes.

When they entered the building, Darlene was checking coats, hanging them in the hallway on portable clothes racks borrowed from the high school band.

"Empty your pockets first," Pam whispered cynically to Ben.

Ben and Pam were relieved to see that Darlene wasn't wearing their mother's clothes. But Michelle, after passing her covered chocolate cake to Dutch, could smell White Shoulders heavy on Darlene when she handed over her coat. The mystery of her missing bottle was solved.

Ben didn't notice Darlene's cloying scent; he was too occupied looking beyond the open auditorium doors, where a line of boys waited to test their shooting skills at a target that lit up a red bulb when hit in the center.

Ben didn't care what the prize was, or how much it

cost to win it. The thousands of BBs he'd shagged from the dirt and grass near the feed house were going to pay off tonight. The four one-dollar bills in the front pocket of his slacks would be spent showing them all how he could shoulder the rifle left-handed and aim with his right eye behind his thick lenses. "Ass-backwards" Dutch called it. Still, Ben could shoot the pants off of his peers. He'd never told anyone that his skill with the rifle depended on pretending the target was a man.

Dutch stood in line with Ben. "Now be sure you mark them sights after a shot or two. They may be adjusted a hair off ya know," Dutch laughed quietly.

Though only hours earlier Ben had heard enough about Dutch to want to stay out of his way as much as possible, he was proud of the way the older boys in line respected Dutch's towering height and age by quieting their horseplay and mocking cruelties.

On the same stage where Ben failed as an actor and public speaker, Michelle was helping Debi roll a plastic bowling ball at plastic bowling pins, while Pam waited her turn. The new Mrs. Beal ignored the jealous looks from the women and quick looks from their husbands.

Across the room, Mrs. Jorgenson was seated behind a fold-out table preparing for the cakewalk, checking the labels on dozens of homemade cakes. She was relieved to see Ben and Dutch together. To her, an old friend was getting a second chance after losing his son.

"Bull's-eye," the man scoring the BB shoot barked after Ben took his first shot.

Ben aimed and squeezed his second shot. "Two," the man counted.

Ten out of ten bull's-eyes got Ben a pair of cheap plastic binoculars. Dutch managed eight out of ten and won a whistle.

"Where'd you learn to shoot like that?" the man asked

Ben when awarding him his prize.

"From my dad," Ben answered proudly, making sure Dutch heard the compliment.

Dutch and Ben went over to the basketball hoop and missed as many shots as they made. After Ben missed his last attempt, he turned and saw Gene on the stage helping as a pin setter for the bowling. Gene was too busy to notice Ben, though the boy had been on his mind since his visit. When it was her turn, Pam found Gene's negative head-waggling a distraction and rolled gutter ball after gutter ball.

Mrs. Jorgenson's voice boomed over the public address system; the microphone had to be adjusted, producing electronic squeals, like castrated piglets, Ben thought. Then his teacher called the cakewalkers over to stand on the twenty colored and numbered spots taped to the hardwood floor in the form of a large circle. One of the older students played a Glenn Miller record on a portable record player.

Michelle stood outside the cakewalk circle, holding the girls' hands. Debi was dancing on her tiptoes excited to cakewalk while Pam had her eyes on a cheesecake with cherries and whipped cream topping.

"Pick out a spot," Mrs. Jorgenson smiled at Debi from behind the microphone.

Debi danced on #12, a yellow circle cut from thick construction paper. Pam craned her head for her brother as she stepped onto royal blue #13. Pam thought about her daddy and dancing in Okoboji when Miller's "Sentimental Journey" began. The full circle of kids started walking slowly, stepping from one numbered spot to the next until April Rubindorf reached into a rainbow-colored box for the winning number. At the penultimate moment of silence after the needle was lifted from the record, the cakewalkers scurried onto a number each hoped was the winner.

"Number 6!" April announced. Mrs. Jorgenson delivered a cake from the table to the excited girl standing on spot #6, who then left the cakewalk for the evening, a winner. Her spot was filled by the girl at the front of a long line of mostly girls.

"That was a pineapple upside-down cake made by Mrs. Robbins," Mrs. Jorgenson told the crowd, which responded with envious sighs. Mrs. Robbins's cakes were legendary.

Again the music. It played longer this time. Pam's leg was beginning to ache, but her competitive nature kept her hobbling around and around. Michelle resisted the urge to ask her to sit and rest. Michelle kept hearing her mother's criticism, "Activity. She needs activity for her leg. Not your guilt or your misplaced sympathy."

Debi was so spry and lively behind her plodding sister, nearly stepping on Pam's heels twice. The tip of Pam's tongue stuck out of the corner of her mouth; her eyes were downward watching her heavy orthopedic shoes carefully so she didn't stumble into the cakewalker in front of her and start a domino disaster. The music stopped.

"Number 16."

No winner. Pam was angry at skinny Debi for not caring what number she was standing on, as if she couldn't care less about winning, happy to be dancing around the circle with the older kids. Pam wished she had picked a spot on the opposite side of the circle, away from her sister, where their twin dresses might be less noticeable. "Laurel and Hardy," she muttered to herself.

Dutch stood in the middle of the room talking to a friend who raised hogs near Story City. Like most people who knew Beal, he had heard rumors that Dutch had remarried. He wanted to get a look at the new young wife.

Ben, back in line for the BB shoot, returned Gene's wave from the bowling pin area. Everything's okay. I should tell Gene I'm not running away, Ben thought.

Pam stomped away from the cakewalk, headed for the

restroom, after Debi won a glazed orange chiffon cake. Pam lumbered down the hallway dragging her left leg noticeably.

Inside the girls' restroom, Pam entered one of the two stalls. When she dropped onto the black seat she could smell overpowering White Shoulders mixed with cigarette smoke.

"Hi, Pam!" Darlene was standing on the toilet and smiling at her over the divider, blowing smoke into Pam's stall.

Pam didn't like being stared at in such a private space. She was too intimidated to say what she wanted: Hey Darlene, get your ugly face and stinking smoke outta here. Instead she said, "Hello."

"Did ya read it yet?" Darlene asked.

"Yeah."

"Uncle Gene says it ain't true though."

"What did happen?"

"Uncle Gene jumped after D. J. fell off High Bridge. Then D. J. went to Ledges and jumped cuz he thought Gene was dead and knew his dad was gonna beat him. Uncle Gene says he can prove D. J. killed himself."

"Really?" Pam said as Darlene exhaled her smoke toward the ceiling before dropping the filterless butt into the toilet bowl below her feet.

"How come I don't baby-sit you guys anymore?"

"I don't know," Pam said, staring at the stall door in front of her, still not doing what she came in to do, adding, "Ben baby-sits us now. He's old enough."

Darlene finally dropped to the floor and left Pam alone in the restroom, but Darlene's words kept playing in Pam's mind. She sat thinking how those few words could get her off the farm and away from sluts like Darlene Rainbow, who smoked and made-out in more than one senior boy's car in the school parking lot during lunch.

His new binoculars were hanging around his neck by a plastic strap. Ben won a hoola-hoop for his sisters after his second perfect score. He was reverse-spinning the hoop out in front of him, returning it to himself, when Pam came over.

"Look what I won for you and Debi." He grinned. "If you can't get it around your waist, you can always play catch with it...like this."

"Shut up," Pam said. "Darlene says the newspaper story ain't true." She imitated Darlene's bucolic speech.

"What'd she say?" Ben said, flipping the hoop out again.

"That they both went off the bridge. That D. J. jumped off Ledges after he thought Gene was dead."

"Anything else?" Ben asked, curious to find out how much Darlene knew.

"She said Gene can prove it."

"How?"

"She doesn't know." Pam took hold of her brother's arm, stopping the next flip of the hoola-hoop. "Look, Ben, this could be our way out."

"Things are going better now," Ben said.

"Because he didn't spank you for losing your boots? That's because Mom was there, stupid."

"Maybe he's getting better. Mom says his dad was real hard on him. Much worse than he is with us," Ben said.

Pam took the hoola-hoop, put it around her waist and kept it going until Darlene walked over to them.

"Can I try it?" she asked.

Pam stepped out of the hoop and gave it to Darlene. Pam bristled at the attention shapely Darlene was getting from men and boys standing nearby, as she swiveled and rolled her hips. Like the slut she is, Pam fumed.

Ben carried Debi from the T-bird into the farmhouse; she had fallen fast asleep on the ride home. After Michelle put Debi's chiffon cake in the kitchen and changed her clothes, she ducked into Ben's darkened bedroom. He faked sleep at first, his face angled into the pillow, until his mother sat on his bed. She rubbed his back.

"Ben?" she whispered. "You know something about my missing bottle of White Shoulders, don't you?"

"No...I'm tired, Mom."

"Darlene Rainbow was wearing the same perfume tonight."

"I accidentally broke it. Don't tell Dad."

Ben was lying, but Michelle decided she better let it go. Maybe he had a crush on the older girl. Michelle didn't approve of his taste in women, not in the least. Still, it wouldn't due to make too much of it. That would only drive him closer to the girl.

"Okay. Good night. I love you."

She leaned over and kissed the back of her son's head. Relief brought him deep dreamless sleep that night. The perfume problem was over.

Meanwhile, Pam was wide awake. Her brain was going over all the possibilities that could have happened to D. J. and Gene. Ben had seemed vague, hiding something from her; and he was slipping into contentment. She wanted to get out of bed now and pour over every inch of the storeroom across the hall, rip open every box, look behind every drawer. Something might be there, she thought. But Dutch would hear her walking on the squeaky floor. "I can't stand this," she muttered.

Debi was snoring softly, one leg sticking out from under the covers. Pam turned her face away.

At 7 AM, when Dutch left the house to do chores, Pam's warm toes hit the floorboards beside her bed. She thought about getting her leg brace out of the box in the closet for the long walk ahead of her. She had to make up her mind about Ben. Could she count on him?

Pam creaked open the door from the stairway into the

kitchen. Michelle was surprised to see Pam awake so early on a Sunday. "What are you doing up?" her mother asked.

"I'm going for a walk. To get some exercise."

Her mother smiled. "I might just go with you."

That forced Pam's decision about Ben. "Ben and I are going, Mom."

There was just enough whining in Pam's voice for Michelle to realize that Pam wanted to be alone with her brother for some reason. Michelle knew if anything important was going on with Pam, Ben would tell her. "Okay," she said.

Ben bolted up and out of his covers when he heard Pam say something about Gene as she stood at the foot of his bed.

Pam was putting on her red boots on the icy cold back porch floor while Ben wolfed down his breakfast. He caught up with her at the end of the gravel lane, knowing now he would have to be patient with his sister's slower pace. He walked beside her instead of leading the way. If he was going to find out what she was up to, he'd have to let her choose their path.

"You're keeping something from me," Pam declared.

"What are you talking..."

"Last night at the carnival, after I talked to Darlene, you were acting strange. You know something about Gene and D. J."

"Pam, you always have to know everything."

"Because you're being dumb about Dutch." She started to imitate Ben's words at the carnival in a singsong voice, "Things are getting better now. Let's see how it goes."

"Shut up," Ben said.

"You know if Mom hadn't come up there when you lost your boots you'd be singing a different tune. With a blistered butt."

They took the easy way through Ledges, staying on

the main road. About halfway through the park, their eyes were looking up and to their right at the massive sandstone ledges, where rolling upland prairie had met towering walls of glacial ice.

"You think D. J. jumped from there?" Pam asked.

Ben jogged ahead of Pam some twenty yards, then turned to walk backwards while scanning the cliffs. "Gene might know. Why are you going to Gene's anyway?"

"To hear for myself what happened."

"I can tell you what he told me yesterday."

He figured his sister couldn't make it all the way to Gene's trailer. "There's this real neat spot I found. I'll tell you what he said there. It's near the exit, Pam. You can rest your leg. It's really neat, Pam...you'll see."

"Alright then," Pam said.

On they continued, at a turtle's pace for Ben, until they reached the western slopes of Ledges, staying on the service road through the oak and hickory forests until they took a hiking trail that veered to the west.

"Start tellin' me now. So I can get my mind off my leg," Pam said.

His sister was breathing hard and leaning her upper body more forward than usual. He told her, "When you went to buy valentines, I went to see Gene in his trailer. I told him I needed to know about D. J. and if the clipping was right."

Pam was looking down at her next step, not paying attention to the Black Maples in their winter stand or the goldenrod squirrels hiding motionless in the branches, peeking at them.

"He wouldn't write anything down, Pam. So I held him just like Darlene did."

"What did he say?"

"D. J. saved Gene when they both fell into the river. D. J. thought Gene had drowned and left him on the bank. Then

211

he went to Ledges and jumped cause he was afraid of what Dutch would do to him."

"Darlene said Gene could prove it," Pam prompted him.

"Gene found D. J.'s belt. You know...the same buckle Gene was wearing on the bus."

Pam stopped on the trail and stared into Ben's eyes. "Where'd he find it?"

"That's the creepy part. He found it on the fence at that old cemetery. The one with the Christmas tree."

Pam got big goose pimples on her arms thinking of the belt and all its ramifications-and finding it at that country cemetery. "He was so afraid of his own father he killed himself."

Ben knew it was true, but didn't want to go where she was leading him. He wanted peace. She didn't. He turned and started walking, listening for her dragging left leg to follow. It did.

Together they looked down at the old potato field now called Lost Lake. In the spring, water off the wooded slopes collected on the marshy wetland and slowly drained into the lake. It was about the size of a football field and but a few feet deep. Pam ambled down to a picnic table for a rest. Ben sat next to her on the table's top, facing the lake.

"How's your leg?"

"Not good." Pam gave her usual crooked-mouth laugh to humor her pain.

"It's not much further."

"What else did Gene say?" Pam asked.

"That Dutch collected on insurance because D. J.'s fall was ruled an accident. And D. J.'s mom was sent away to a private hospital somewhere."

"But it wasn't an accident."

"Right," Ben said.

"If we could prove it, he could go to jail," Pam said.

"Pam, don't you go snooping into Dutch's past! There's probably a lot we don't know about it. Anyway, don't you think Dutch has gotten better?"

"I told you what I think. I don't like living in that place."

Ben jumped down from the table. Pam did the same, her walk now a half-step limp. She paused at Katina Pond before she moved over the tiny bridge spanning the water.

"This is pretty even in winter, not like the city," she said.

Ben wondered whether to tell his sister he was going to run away if Dutch got mean again. He decided not to, because Pam might tell their mother just to stir up trouble between her and Dutch.

While Pam paid close attention to the unspoiled scene around her to keep her mind off her throbbing leg, Ben was thinking of the ways he and Pam influenced their mother's marriage. It wasn't a good thing to do, he knew. He suspected Pam would do anything to fill her own insecure needs. Ben usually thought of his mother's happiness before his own. Pam might choose a sandwich over her mother's well-being, he mused.

"The place I was talking about is at the top of this little hill."

"Little to you maybe," Pam shot back.

Ben took Pam's hand and pulled, walking backwards when she raised her left leg, inching up the last six steps.

He watched his sister's brown eyes scan the river left then right. Then her gaze traveled across the river to the fertile valley blanketed with whiteness except for areas where the black soil had been exposed by wind. She looked at Ben and said, "Really neat."

The flat rock at the lookout point appeared too slippery to Pam. Ben crept to within six inches of the edge to sneak a look down.

"That's too close, Ben. Get back!"

But Ben inched even closer to the grooved, down-sloping ledge of the rock to show his sister how bold he could be.

"Ben...please! That's not safe!"

He turned and smiled at Pam. His ears and cheeks were cold-red, though it was above freezing with no wind.

"Ben, I'm going to Gene's right now, if you don't get away from that ledge!"

"Okay, I'm coming. Isn't this the best place? Huh, Pam?"

"Could this be where D. J. jumped?" Her comment deflated him.

"I hope not. I'll bet he jumped from one of the big ledges along the main road."

Pam found a large rock and sat for awhile. "Mom thinks Darlene has her perfume," Pam said. "She asked me about it last night at the party."

"What did you say?"

"I told her I didn't know anything about it. But Darlene really stank."

"Don't worry. I told Mom I broke it."

"She believed you?"

"Yeah, so everything's covered."

"How did they fall off the bridge?"

"A train came by and shook them so hard that D. J. fell in the river."

"I think Mom should know about this," Pam said.

"No. What if he hurts her or somethin'?" Ben protested.

"What if he does anyway?"

"Gene will lose his job for sure," Ben said.

"Oh, so we let Dutch beat us up, just so Gene can keep his stupid job?"

"Pam, you're gonna get us all killed."

214

Pam shook her head like Gene, saying, "I'm not spending another summer on that farm, using that outhouse. It's too hot upstairs. You don't have to take a bath in Debi's bathwater...or play dolls with her in that sweatbox."

"I could complain too, you know," Ben said.

"This makes Mom look stupid when we know all these things and she doesn't."

"Maybe she does know," Ben said.

Pam smirked.

"She might!" Ben insisted.

"Not everything," Pam said.

"If he spanks us again..."

"I'm not waiting for that to happen," Pam said.

She got up gingerly and started walking back, following the trail that led them there.

"Gene really likes driving a bus, Pam," Ben called after her.

She turned toward him. "Yeah, while he's happy, we're getting our butts blistered, or worse."

"Big deal...one time you got it. All you have to do is make your bed and play dolls. I don't feel sorry for you."

"Next time he hits anybody, I'm telling Mom everything," Pam declared.

He skirted around Pam and stayed three steps in front of her, slowing his walk to match hers. On the short bridge over Katina Pond, Ben stopped, silently hushing Pam with his finger to his lips. He pointed to a stand of Eastern Red Cedar. A deer stood still as a garden statue twenty yards away, its head cocked toward them, listening.

"That's the way Gene is," Ben whispered with his hand cupped close to Pam's ear, "living quiet-like. Not hurting anyone."

Pam nodded her head and watched the deer with her brother, giving her leg a rest.

Into The Sun

February remained locked in cold storage-no more snow or sun. The first half of March was as dreary as February, except a few degrees warmer. Then, with only a week of March remaining, the sky cleared and the trickling meltdown of the coming spring began in the top layers creating mud and slush that Ben called sludge.

Michelle's face without makeup was winter white. She looked down to her feet in Dutch's truck, depressed that she was wearing Dutch's old buckled boots on her way to the dentist in Boone. Her hair, without the help of a beauty shop, had grown out dull brown. It looked like a bird's nest. "Ratty," she muttered to herself as Debi sat tight against her, listening to the school bell ringing the beginning of Pam's lunch period and Ben's study hall.

While Debi watched for her brother and sister, Michelle lamented the fifteen pounds she had put on over the winter. An old pair of denim jeans that used to be baggy on her were now squeezing her hips, legs and butt in a dozen places.

"Darlene!" Debi called out.

Michelle ignored the cigarette Darlene was lighting after exiting the school's front door and stared instead at the girl's outfit. Those are my clothes, she said to herself, watching Darlene stroll down the steps in her black slacks and maroon sweater. Michelle had looked all over for them, then assumed they had gotten lost in their move to the farm. And there they were-on Darlene Rainbow. Her mind went right to the carnival when she had smelled White Shoulders on the girl.

Michelle's forehead creased in a frown as she watched Darlene amble over to the parking lot where a boy leaned against the fender of a red Chevy. Ben might have given Darlene the perfume, if he liked her. Perfume was romantic. But not the clothes. Something strange was going on.

Ben and Pam came out together about five minutes later, not realizing that their mother has seen her missing clothes on Darlene.

Michelle said nothing about it before or after the dentist examined and cleaned her older children's teeth. Ben needed a filling. Pam needed two. If it had been entirely up to Michelle, she would have had the dentist fill their teeth immediately. However, Dutch paid the bills, so she had to get his approval before any additional dental work was done.

Michelle ended up having to pay for the fillings out of the monthly $96.90 she still received from Kenny. Dutch had said, "I feed 'em, an' buy 'em clothes, an' keep a roof over his kids' heads-he can sure as hell pay for their damn fillings!"

That Thursday night after supper, when Ben and Pam were washing the dishes, Michelle decided to get some answers. Dutch sat at his desk doing his taxes and wouldn't emerge from the master bedroom until he was finished.

Michelle left the house through the rarely used front door, leaving her purse in its customary place on the kitchen counter, hoping Dutch might not realize that she was gone. She started his truck and quietly drove off the farm in the direction of Ledges. The pickup's floor vent blew cold air that chilled her feet in her penny loafers. As she shifted to second gear, she remembered Dutch saying that Ledges flooded sometimes in the spring. He'd warned the kids that

217

this year it would flood for sure because of the heavy winter snowfall.

She turned onto Gene and Darlene's road just a ways from the park's exit. She watched for the ugly house in front of the little trailer. I'll find it, she said to herself, putting on the truck's high beams. Moments later she pulled into the dirt drive, and parked near the Rainbow's front porch. From the truck Michelle saw the changing light of a black and white TV inside the house. Lights were on inside Gene's trailer, as well. His car was parked nearby.

Darlene lay napping on the couch, wearing her father's pajamas, when she heard sharp, rapid knocking on the front door. Uncle Gene didn't have to knock. She thought the visitor was one of her boyfriends. Smiling broadly, she opened the door.

Mrs. Beal had her coat collar raised to her ears in the cold air. "Darlene, I have to talk to you about something. May I come in?"

Darlene blinked in surprise, stepping back to let her in. Michelle was going to ask if she could sit down, but could see that every possible place to sit was either covered with dirty bedding, dirty clothes, or dirty dishes.

"Just a minute," Darlene said. She raked the blanket and sheet from the couch and tossed them onto the dining room floor so Michelle could sit. Darlene flopped onto the armchair and lit a cigarette. The TV's volume was turned up high.

How could the girl sleep with it blaring? Michelle wondered. She asked, "Do you mind turning down the TV, Darlene?"

Darlene slapped the off button and went back to her seat curious to hear what Mrs. Beal had to say.

"I saw you wearing my clothes at school today. And I'm missing an expensive bottle of perfume."

Michelle scooted to the front edge of the couch, feeling food crumbs beneath her fingers when she touched the cushion. Darlene blew a cloud of blue smoke toward the ceiling. Michelle was certain she could pick up the scent of White Shoulders on Darlene now.

"I didn't steal yer stuff, if that's what yer thinkin'."

"Well then, just how did you get them, Darlene?"

Darlene knew if she did not tell the truth now any number of bad things could happen. Mrs. Beal would tell her husband, and that would be that. Revenge on the whole Rainbow family. Uncle Gene was sure to lose his job. "Ben and Pam gave 'em to me," she admitted.

"Ben and Pam gave you my things?"

Darlene blew out more smoke, down this time, nodding yes. Her eyes would not take on Mrs. Beal's unblinking gaze, even in her own territory.

"Why would they do that?" Michelle's tone was stern.

"They wanted me to find out something from my Uncle Gene."

"What?" Michelle demanded. "What did they ask you to find out?"

"Gee, Mrs. Beal, I'll give back yer things right now. I don't want no trouble about this, or for Uncle Gene either. He really likes his job, Mrs. Beal. I'll get yer stuff..."

"I don't want them. Keep them."

Michelle stood up, pacing the small area in front of the TV set. Then she sat back down on the same spot, having decided on her approach. She softened her tone, but toughened her language. "Look Darlene, you tell me right now what you know, or I'll have the sheriff pull you out of school tomorrow. Your folks will miss work. I'm sure they won't thank you for that. Of course, I can't say what my husband will do."

Michelle waited. Darlene searched for another cigarette in her empty pack. Irritated, she crushed the package into a ball and dropped it to the floor.

"Can we go for a drive so I can get some cigs?" she asked.

"Okay," Michelle said, welcoming any chance to get out of the Rainbow's filthy house.

Michelle waited in Dutch's idling truck with the heater blowing warm air onto the windshield while Darlene dressed.

Gene had seen Mrs. Beal park at his brother's house. He had watched from his dark bedroom window the whole time she was there, thinking he would go over and find out from his niece why Mrs. Beal had stopped by. Had Ben run away like he said, he wondered. Why was she waiting there? Did she want Darlene to baby-sit?

He saw his niece step off the porch wearing her dad's heavy parka. Gene thought about following them in his car, but then the truck turned north toward Boone, and he decided Darlene must have asked Mrs. Beal for a ride to town. Gene went back to cooking his supper, thinking that Dutch Beal's wife was real kind to help out his niece.

Mrs. Beal was driving 30 mph on the rural road, practically crawling. Darlene unzipped her coat and put Michelle's clothes and the bottle of White Shoulders on the seat between them.

"I said you can keep them, Darlene."

Darlene's hand nervously rattled a fistful of pennies she'd stashed in the parka's pocket. Her father kept those pennies in a coffee can in his bedroom, tossing change into the can when he came home from the graveyard shift at the plant. Darlene had already taken all the quarters, dimes, and nickels. Tonight the coffee can had been down to a few hundred pennies.

"What did Ben and Pam want to know so badly that they'd give you my things?" Michelle asked.

"I gave them an old newspaper story about Gene and D. J."

"Who's D. J.?"

"Dutch, Junior. Dutch's son. He was Uncle Gene's best friend."

Michelle looked over at Darlene's face, bent low with fear and shame. The twinge of guilt she felt for threatening the girl lasted but a moment. Michelle was heading into the dark territory Hutch had warned her about, a place full of rumors, until now. She took a deep breath to steady herself and asked, "Dutch has a son?"

"Had a son. He's dead."

"What happened?"

Darlene talked all the way to Boone. Michelle drove in a trance, trying to make sense of it all: the fall from High Bridge; D. J.'s mother in Cherokee, then some private hospital; Dutch divorcing her out of greed; D. J.'s suicide at Ledges after Gene's accident; and the bogus insurance money paid to Dutch. Over and over, Michelle's mind screamed, Why would Dutch's boy jump to his death at Ledges?

Neither Darlene nor Michelle knew the truck had just run a red light at 8th Street. Darlene didn't hear the train coming or see the flashing red signal; her eyes were focused on the truck's floor. Michelle didn't see or hear anything except Dutch's shuttered face as he told her on their honeymoon, "I've heard it all, now, I don't want to talk about the past again." They didn't know what hit them.

An eyewitness loading groceries into his car at the IGA, where Michelle had been headed, saw the pickup going no more than 20 mph over the first set of tracks. The truck didn't brake or speed up to get out of the way of the Union Pacific twin-engine diesels pulling twenty-eight cars, heading west toward the High Bridge.

The train crashed into the pickup's passenger side, killing Darlene instantly. Michelle was as near to death as anyone could be after Dutch's truck was pushed and mangled down the tracks a hundred yards before settling on its side between the two sets of railroad tracks-a spot on the Union Pacific line that had never seen a fatal accident in over seventy years.

Pam answered the phone. The man just asked for Dutch. Pam went to get her step-dad, who was busy at his desk. Ben watched the phone's receiver hanging from its cord and spinning in the air near the floor and wondered why his mother hadn't answered the call.

Pam stood by quietly as Dutch picked up the phone. They could only hear Dutch's hello...then a faint groan. Pam and Ben read bad news all over Dutch's face. He turned away and mumbled, "Oh, Jesus." After listening for what seemed an interminable period, Dutch thanked the man for calling and hung up the receiver.

"Ben," he said, "you watch the girls for me. I'll be back later on. Okay?"

"Where's my mom?" he demanded.

Pam cried, "Is Mom okay?"

Dutch was out the kitchen door onto the porch, dragging on his boots. He threw on his coat as he ran for the garage. They heard the T-bird's engine fire up and roar away without the warm-up period Dutch always gave the engine.

In downtown Boone, Dutch crossed the tracks on foot. A crowd of people were gathered around what was left of his pickup. Two firemen with crowbars were prying back the caved-in passenger door, the driver's side down to the ground.

Dutch felt nauseated, his hands trembling in his coat pockets. He knew his wife couldn't be alive the way the cab was pinched in half, as if by a giant pair of pliers. He couldn't see inside the truck. Sheriff Buell, who had called Dutch on the phone, was shining a flashlight on the area where the firemen were working.

222

"Any movement at all in there?" Dutch asked Buell.

"Nothin' yet, Dutch," Buell said.

Two red and white ambulances from Boone County hospital were parked side-by-side ready to transport. Finally the door came off the truck. A fireman waved for the ambulance crew to come over. Dutch could smell Michelle's perfume, very strong above the oil and gas and copper tang of blood.

Darlene's limp and mangled body came out first.

"That's not my wife!" Dutch shouted to Buell.

Dutch tried to look at the bloody face as the ambulance crew lifted the woman's body onto a gurney, but her blood-matted hair covered most of it.

"No ID on her," Buell announced after checking Darlene's coat pockets, finding only a handful of pennies. Buell brushed back the woman's hair and Dutch knew who it was.

"That's Darlene Rainbow. Her folks work at the Denison packinghouse," Dutch said.

"Gene Rainbow's niece?" a fireman asked Dutch.

"Yeah."

While Darlene's body was covered and carried away, the firemen were starting to get at Michelle, whose head was on the passenger side floor. Dutch's height allowed him to see the effort to free his wife.

"I gotta pulse!" a fireman called out.

"She's still alive?" Dutch cried in total disbelief.

Dutch wasn't fazed by the grisly scene covered in blood; he had seen his share of injuries and death just being a farmer. Like Michelle, he was not in-love. But he did care for her as a wife and lover. They hadn't even had time to become good friends from sharing the seasons many times over. And her kids. What am I going to do with those kids? he wondered.

A volunteer fireman joined in to help remove

Michelle's broken body from the truck as Sheriff Buell stood by with a fire extinguisher. When Michelle was freed from the cab, her eyes remained open, as if she was dead. Her beautiful face was unrecognizeable-both her cheekbones were broken and shards of glass punctured her chin in several places. She had already lost too much blood.

A fireman handed Dutch a pair of slacks and a sweater gathered from inside the truck's cab. They reeked of his wife's favorite perfume.

"She gonna make it?" Dutch asked the ambulance driver.

"If she does...she's lucky," the man said. "She a relation?"

"My wife."

"You know her blood type?"

Dutch shook his head no.

The T-bird followed the ambulance to the Boone hospital. In less than five minutes Dutch was speeding behind the same ambulance to Des Moines General where they were better equipped to handle severe injuries.

The bathroom door was open. Ben sat quietly in the dark kitchen; even tonight, fear of Dutch demanded that no lights were left on. Pam was supervising Debi's bath when Ben heard the faint sound of an ambulance screaming through the west kitchen window. Ben was to the glass first, then Pam. They knew the minute they saw the low-shining beams of the T-bird behind the ambulance. The taillights were low, spreading their red light wide like no other vehicle going north or south on Hwy. 17.

Pam took her eyes from the speeding convoy first, though she could still see the flashing red lights of the ambulance. "You know it's Mom!" she cried.

Ben turned away dry-mouthed. He stared at the vacuous rural blackness realizing he had to be strong for the girls.

"For God's sake, don't let Debi hear you," Ben whispered in anger.

Pam went to the phone. Ben stopped her hand in midair. Furious, Pam tried to bite Ben's arm. "Let go. I'm calling the police," Pam shouted.

Ben put his hand over Pam's mouth, whispering, "Wait!"

She glared at him when he dragged her over to the bathroom. He turned on the hot water and left it to trickle into the tub, creating enough noise to muffle their voices so Debi couldn't hear them in the kitchen.

Ben leaned close to the receiver as Pam asked the operator to connect her to the police in Boone. They heard the phone ring and an elderly woman's voice answered, "Sheriff's office."

"Was there a red pickup in a accident in Boone tonight?" Pam asked.

"A truck was hit by a train," the woman replied.

"Was anybody hurt?" Pam's voice was shrill, almost a scream.

"Who's calling, please?" the woman inquired.

Ben pushed down the flashhook and yanked the receiver away from Pam, who was shaking all over and weeping. She collapsed onto the kitchen floor.

Debi heard Pam's hysterical crying from the tub, stood up in her bath water and yelled for her brother or sister to come to her. Ben hurried into the bathroom, lifted Debi from the tub and wrapped her in a towel. Once she quieted, he carried her to the kitchen, sat her at the table and gave her a cookie. Then he dropped to the floor next to Pam.

"She said a red truck was hit by a train. You know it's her, Ben. Mom's dead!"

"Shut up! Don't get Debi going again!" He forked his left hand around Pam's throat, warning her. "Listen to me.

You're so smart...how come Dutch was following the ambulance if she's dead? Huh?"

Pam pulled her brother's hand down. "Ben, I'm so scared," she said, "I don't know what to do."

"We'll wait 'til Dutch gets back. You keep quiet. I mean it. I'm the boss when Mom's..." Ben stopped himself from saying gone.

Even though she outweighed her brother by twenty pounds, he was taller and stronger and in charge of her. Pam feared him when he was angry like this.

Gene was surprised when he saw his brother and sister-in-law park next to his car. They wore their bloody smocks, fresh off the killing floor, when they stepped into Gene's trailer without knocking.

Ray and Charlotte had stopped at the County Coroner's office on Carroll Street to identify Darlene's body. They had seen enough killing to be as jaded as they were. They had identified their daughter in an aura of complete calm. Gene's puzzled face told them he hadn't heard about the accident.

"Darlene's been killed," Ray said. "She was hit by a train ridin' with Mrs. Beal."

Gene backed up to his couch and fell onto it. Charlotte moved closer to him.

"What I wanna know is...what was she doin' ridin' with Beal's wife?" Charlotte barked.

Gene gave her his thumbs-down.

"Did you see her pick Darlene up tonight?"

Thumbs-up.

"Did you see or hear anything?"

He gestured no again, then Ray stepped up beside his wife.

"Sheriff thought she was givin' Darlene a ride to the store. But they drove right past," Ray said.

Gene's face had lost its color, and his head was moving faster than ever. Charlotte sat on his one easy chair and lit a Pall Mall. "She didn't suffer. That's what the sheriff said."

"She never knew what hit her," Ray added.

Gene gasped out one thing. "Mrs. Beal?"

"Ain't s'posed to make it," Ray said. "She's got them three kids, don't she?"

Gene gave a thumbs up, very worried about Ben and Pam and the little girl.

"That Beal's had a run a bad luck. First his boy and wife, and now this," Ray said as he scraped grime from under his thumbnail with a pocket knife.

"But he's gonna be payin' for my little girl. I know that!" Charlotte declared. "That fancy wife of his drove right into that train, just like she planned it. Beal's got the money, that's for damn sure. If he don't pay, I'm gettin' a lawyer on 'im."

Ray lit up one of his wife's Pall Malls at the same time she flicked her long ash into the cuff of her pant leg. Gene rubbed his moving forehead nervously, his thoughts were chaotic: Mrs. Beal, her kids, the car he promised Darlene when she graduated, D. J., and why Dutch Beal's wife had come here at night to talk to Darlene.

Dutch sat in the hospital waiting room, his legs restless, his arms crossed, while he waited for Michelle's doctor to come out of the emergency room. Dutch kept his powerful arms folded over his chest as Dr. Stemme sat down. The doctor took a deep breath.

"Well, Mr. Beal, your wife's condition is very grave. She's unconscious and she's lost a lot of blood. I don't know the extent of the damage to her brain. There's internal bleeding that's not as bad as it could be. Her right lung is collapsed, damaged beyond repair. Six broken ribs, a broken jaw, collarbone and cheekbones."

"Is she gonna die?" Dutch asked softly.

"Dr. Knoll from Iowa City is in town and I've asked him to look at her. But it doesn't look good," Dr. Stemme said.

Dutch sat without moving or speaking.

"What religion is Michelle?" the doctor inquired.

"I don't know." Dutch sighed. "Methodist, I think."

"The hospital chaplain wanted to get a priest to give her last rites, if she were a Catholic," the doctor said.

Dutch followed the doctor into the intensive care unit. Michelle had IVs going into both arms. Her face was swollen beyond recognition. As he stood beside her bed, he didn't cry. He wasn't the kind of man to say goodbye or even gently stroke his young wife's fingers. Businesslike, he told her he'd see that her kids were taken care of and that Kenny would be contacted. That was it. He left her curtained space without looking back.

Dutch called Grampa Dick and told him his daughter was near death. Dick promised he and Merle would be right down; they'd meet in the waiting room. When Dutch called Edith he thought it strange that she said she couldn't come to the hospital. Then she astonished him by asking if he wanted to make an appointment for her to work on his arm. She did say she'd call Hutch for him.

Walking to his T-bird, Dutch's thoughts were already on the $250,000 policy he carried on his wife's life. He, the beneficiary, never dreamed this time would come, and didn't think for one moment about giving Michelle's children a dime of it. The five hundred-dollar deductible on her medical policy was a drop in the bucket compared to the figure his insurance company would pay. The money part was handled. Now the hard part: telling the kids.

The farmhouse was totally dark inside. Debi slept sitting up between her brother and sister, leaning into Ben's side, on the middle of three kitchen chairs facing the kitchen's west window.

Ben and Pam were still awake at 2 AM. In the last two hours fewer cars had passed on the distant road. They could whisper now that Debi was snoring.

"God wouldn't take her away from us," Pam said.

"She's not dead. They don't drive fast like that and use sirens and flashing lights unless the person's still alive," Ben replied.

"What if she died on the way?" Pam wailed.

"Shut up. There he is. Get the stairway door. Hurry up!" Ben ordered.

Ben carried Debi upstairs and left her under the covers with Pam, then ran downstairs to quickly change into his brown and white stripped pajamas and slip under his own covers.

Dutch parked his T-bird and gave Duke a squeeze on the snout. During the drive from the hospital, Dutch's thoughts had been on another day in October, years ago, when a different sheriff, a man who knew Dutch well, came to his farm and told him that D. J. had fallen from Sentinel Rock in Ledges. The sight of his son's broken body lying motionless amongst the swirling October leaves brought...nothing. Dutch could just as well have found a calf of his trampled by the herd. And now, as his boots hit the cold back porch floor, once more he felt disconnected-emptied of all emotion.

That was not the case with Benjamin Smith. He had covered his head to feign sleep so Dutch would wait until the morning to tell him his mother had died. Ben's feet were ice cold; his face and neck were hot from worry. Then Dutch flipped on the overhead light and stood by the side of his bed.

"Ben, you sleepin'?"

Ben stayed still, his head under his covers until he felt Dutch's weight settle at the edge of his mattress, rolling Ben toward him. Dutch shook his shoulder and he turned to his step-dad with his eyes squeezed shut.

"Ben, I got some news ta give ya. I want ya to go get yer sisters and bring 'em down here so I can talk ta all of ya at once."

"Debi too?" Ben asked.

"No, yer right, let 'er sleep."

Pam could hear her brother's quick feet coming up the stairs. Her heart began pounding fast. Her brother's face without his glasses, its stark expression visible in the dim glow cast by the yard light beyond her window, warned her of what was to come. "Dutch wants to talk to us. Not Debi," he whispered.

The black lamp pole behind Dutch's recliner had only one of its three bulbs on, leading Ben and Pam to the farmer slumped in the chair.

Dutch's head hung forward from fatigue. His big hands looked tense on his lap. Pam stood behind her brother's shoulder, waiting for some indication of what their step-father wanted them to do. He curled all his fingers and motioned for them to come sit on the arms of his chair. Ben went to him. Pam followed.

Dutch started to speak. "Kids, yer mother's been in an accident. She's hurt real bad."

"She's alive?" Pam asked.

"Barely."

"Will she die?"

Dutch shrugged. "I don't know."

Ben and Pam were dismayed, unable to cry because of the messenger's remote expression.

"What happened?" Ben asked.

"She was drivin' the truck across the railroad tracks in Boone and got hit by a train. We took her to the hospital in

230

Des Moines. She's not awake."

"What's that mean?" Pam cried, alarmed.

"Yer Mom's unconscious. They can't wake her up."

"Can we go see her?" Ben's voice cracked, and the question came out a sob.

"After mornin' chores we'll go. Don't tell Debi, though. We'll drop her off at Grampa Dick's. She can stay with them 'til...later."

"Mom's going to die." Ben said.

"She could, Ben, she could," Dutch admitted.

"Let's go now to see her!" Pam cried.

"No...they won't let us see her 'til mornin'," Dutch insisted.

"What if she..." Ben stopped.

"You kids try to get some sleep. I'll getcha up after chores."

"Can Ben sleep upstairs?" Pam pleaded.

"Sure."

When Dutch heard his step-kids tramp upstairs, he reached up and turned the light off. In the dark he rubbed his hands over his sparse hair, thinking of Darlene Rainbow, wondering what was she doing with his wife.

Upstairs, Ben lay at the edge of the mattress pressed against Debi, who was breathing deeply, sound asleep. Pam knelt on the other side of the bed.

"Will you pray with me, Ben?" Pam whispered.

"No."

He turned his back to her as she recited The Lord's Prayer out loud several times.

Ben had been talking to God ever since the sheriff called Dutch. His words came from fear and anger. God, please let my mother be safe. Make things okay. Please, please. Bring her home safe. Over and over and over again through the long night of waiting. And now: How could you let this happen?

Ben cried then, storing pain in his jaws, feeling betrayed and lost, not understanding Dutch's glacial calm. He thought, I have to go. When the weather is better. I'll leave on a weekend when he's doing chores. I can't have Pam draggin' after me. She can take care of Debi.

Ben and Pam lay awake until exhaustion took them.

It would take more than the skill of Dr. Knoll from Iowa City to keep Michelle alive. Deep into the blackness of her coma, somewhere between consciousness and death, between wanting to live and letting go, Michelle experienced a moment of choice: Either let go and die-to find out-or live for a reason even more powerful than God's will.

It was more than a pulse, a breath, a brain wave traced by a machine. It was a single thought: I have to live for my kids. Somewhere in the far reaches of her brain she knew that leaving her children to be raised without her was no different than being pushed away by her own mother. No doctor could prescribe a drug so potent: I have to live for my kids.

Michelle's brain began rebuilding itself around that single purpose. One connection here, one there. Transfusions kept her vitals going while her silent mind planned and planned. She would smother her kids with affection-giving them hugs and kisses and telling them she loved them...equally. And they would learn to say I love you, too. She would never push them away. They would know their mother loved them-such a simple and natural thing-a reason to keep breathing.

All 5' 4", 140 pounds of Dr. Knoll worked like a tornado: whirling through the ICU, blowing out orders in all directions-sending doctors, nurses and interns flying about to fill them. He did this all without making eye contact. Those trained eyes had to be on his patient, looking for trouble, then a solution, before he could blink. Whatever medical equipment was needed and wherever it was to be found, he would dispatch his minions to get it without delay.

He could see the beauty of his patient beyond the cuts, abrasions, and dark bruises that covered her body. With a sterilized swab he raised and lowered her swollen lips, checking to be sure any dangling teeth were not about to lodge in her windpipe. He called a young and brash oral surgeon who might be able to save some of the broken teeth. When she was stable enough, Michelle was wheeled into a sterile room and surrounded by surgeons. They worked through the rest of the night and long into the next day.

Michelle's lung could not be saved. Once the internal bleeding had been controlled, Dr. Knoll repaired the shattered ribs, searching the patient's chest cavity carefully for fragments of bone before he closed the incision. Her head injuries needed more time for the intra-cranial swelling to subside. Dr. Knoll knew if the trauma to her brain did not show improvement once the swelling abated, she was doomed.

Debi was delivered to Dick and Merle's with her suitcase and left despite the hysterical fit she threw when she saw that her brother and sister were not staying with her. Dick and Merle each had a double shot of vodka with their tomato juice at breakfast as Debi wailed and pounded her fists on the front room floor.

Dutch and the older kids were well on their way to the hospital when the T-bird's chrome radio announced Darlene's death. Ben and Pam were stunned by the news.

"Darlene Rainbow was killed in the accident?" Pam screeched.

Dutch only nodded. Then added, after a long period of silence, "I'd like ta know what she was doin' in the truck with yer mother."

Ben shrugged his shoulders when he saw Dutch's

green eyes meet his in the rearview mirror. Ben felt his face turning red. Dutch's eyes narrowed.

"You kids have any idea why yer mother would be drivin' around with Darlene Rainbow?"

Another shrug from Ben. Dutch looked over at Pam and saw her shaking her head no. She kept it up for so long that Ben was afraid that Dutch would think it was a signal to go ask Gene. Stop for God's sake, Ben said inwardly.

By 9 AM Michelle had been in surgery with Dr. Knoll's team for over five hours. Not until 2 PM did they finish the last stitch. Dutch, Pam and Ben had sat in silence together in the hospital waiting room. Every minute Ben urgently wanted to speak to his sister about Darlene.

In the waiting room, Dr. Knoll told the family that Michelle might be in a coma for months. To be patient. No one could predict what damage had been done, he said, until she came out of it. There could be loss of speech or other senses. The good news was that her spinal cord wasn't damaged. She would be able to walk.

He said, "People can get along with one lung. That's not my concern."

"Will she die?" Pam cried.

Dr. Knoll looked into Pam's big brown eyes, liking her direct approach. "The next two to three days are critical. I'll know much more then."

"Can we see her now?" Pam asked.

"Only a few minutes," he told her. "Children aren't allowed in the ICU, but this one time I'll take you in to see your mother. I have to warn you, she looks pretty scary. No crying!"

Pam kept her hand covering her mouth to keep from blurting out the horror and shock of seeing her mother. Ben stood still. Their mother's closed eyes were the only part of her skin that wasn't bandaged. The gurgling tubes in her mouth and nostrils were too much for Ben, who dashed out of the room.

Pam gingerly raised the sheet over her mother's feet. They were covered with cuts and ugly purple-black bruises. As Dutch stood at his wife's side, Pam lightly kissed the end of her mother's big toe, whispering, "I love you, Mommy. Oh, Mommy, please don't die."

Dutch left intensive care with Pam. He took the two subdued children to breakfast at a small cafe in Huxley, on the way back to Boone. Even Pam didn't have much of an appetite as she and her brother watched Dutch finish his meal across their booth. Then Dutch outlined a plan for his stepchildren.

"You'll both stay in school. Debi can stay at Dick and Merle's. I'll call yer father and let him know he doesn't have to come back unless..."

"...she dies." Pam finished for him.

Ben looked at Dutch and knew that his stepfather thought she wouldn't last long. He dropped his eyes and tried to keep from throwing up the few bites of breakfast he'd just eaten.

"Right on time," Ben said.

The yellow school bus made the turn from Hwy. 17 toward them. Ben had gotten to the bus stop five minutes earlier than Pam on their first day back to school since their mother's accident. It was also the day of Darlene's funeral. Ben had wanted to gather some of the purple flowers growing in the shelter of the ditch near Lester's pasture, and give them to Gene to put on Darlene's grave. Ben straddled the ditch as he bent and pulled a few more of the gray-white upright stems.

"Hurry up," Pam called, "the bus is almost here!"

When he braked the bus to a stop, Gene saw that Ben was holding a bunch of Russian Sage, the same violet-blue flowers that grew wild behind his trailer. Pam got on before

235

her brother.

"Hi, Gene," Pam said.

Gene raised his hand off his wheel; he was wearing his sunglasses and a white shirt with a black tie. Ben handed him the bunch of Russian Sage with its deeply cut gray-green leaves and purple flowers.

"These are for Darlene," he said.

Gene gave a thumbs up, taking the flowers, then put them under his seat.

Pam looked over at Darlene's empty seat which was bouncing and jiggling with the motion of the bus without her on it. A sense of overwhelming guilt gave Pam an instant stomach ache. She leaned into her brother and whispered, "It's our fault Mom's going to die, just like Darlene."

"Shut up!" he hissed back.

"No, Ben, I think Mom was asking Darlene about her clothes. Darlene's been wearing the sweater a lot. Maybe Mom saw it."

"Then why didn't she ask us about it?" Ben whispered.

"Cause you lied to her about the perfume, stupid!"

"She didn't know I lied. If she had, she would have been all over me about it."

"Okay, so you explain why Mom was talking to her."

"I don't know."

"Darlene must have blabbed about D. J. You know how Mom drives when she's upset."

"So, we're to blame for the accident?" Ben whispered.

"Yes, we're the ones who started the whole thing."

"If Mom dies, I'm leaving," Ben declared. "I'm not living with Dad's wife and her kids...or staying here, either."

"Where will you go?" Pam grabbed his arm. "You can't just leave Debi and me here with Dutch."

"You won't be with Dutch. Dad will come get you." He said softly, "You'd like that."

The bus drove by Darlene's stop. Ben and Pam craned to see her house pass by the bus windows. Gene looked too. He nearly braked from habit. After watching the two Smith kids whispering together, he suspected that Ben and Pam had been talking about their mother's visit with Darlene. It had to have been about D. J. Why else would she have come at night and alone?

I never should have told Ben about him, he thought. Gene remembered the Russian Sage beneath his seat. He imagined placing the flowers on Darlene's grave today, then changed his mind. He'd plant them there to see if they'd take. Then when Ben visited Darlene, he'd see his gift year after year. Gene blinked himself back to behind his wheel. I have to be alert, he thought. Accidents happen.

School was a blur for the Smith kids. They didn't retain what they read or what was said in class. Pam wasn't the first to raise her hand in class. Mrs. Jorgenson corrected Ben's multiple-choice answers in English and History, not counting them against him. "Good - Benjamin" and "Keep up the good work" were written on his papers when returned to him. Poor Dutch, she thought, he's had some tough luck. First his son...now this.

Ray and Charlotte Rainbow's truck pulled up and parked on the gravel road behind the black hearse belonging to the Rawlins Funeral Home in Boone. Gene's car was parked several yards ahead of the hearse; it had been there for hours.

Gene had just changed back into his dress clothes after digging Darlene's five-foot-deep grave. This close to the river, five feet was plenty deep-or he would have been slinging mud. His shovel stood spiked in the dirt mound that would cover his niece. When the driver climbed out of the hearse and opened the back door, Gene waved to the man that he was coming.

Dutch's T-bird was cruising slowly toward Gene's car from the other direction. It pulled to the side of the road and stopped. Dutch stepped out of the car wearing new jeans, dress boots, and a gold corduroy sports jacket. His flannel shirt under the jacket was buttoned to the top without a tie.

Ray and Charlotte sat in their car, not liking that Dutch had come to pay his respects and help Gene lower his niece into her grave.

Gene and Dutch walked to the back of the hearse. Dutch dipped his chin down a bit, into Ray and Charlotte's windshield-receiving only blank stares in return.

Dutch, Gene and the funeral home driver carried Darlene's coffin sideways, walking forward with the length of the coffin between them. Dutch and Gene gripped the brass handles with the combined strength of four men. They made their way over the rough ground and through a break in the cemetery fence. They stepped onto flat markers and tramped over mounds of old grave sites on their beeline to Darlene's final resting place. Once at Darlene's grave, they let the coffin down gently beside the pile of earth. A few moments later, Ray and Charlotte joined them. No one said a thing, not even a prayer. The four men lowered the coffin into the fresh earth. Ray lifted Gene's shovel and began to fill the grave. Then Dutch. Finally Gene.

Ray drove his wife away, following the hearse down the road under gray-white clouds that usually meant cold rain that time of year.

Dutch would pick another time and place to quiz Gene about why Michelle was driving to Boone with Darlene that night. If it had anything to do with secrets from his past, his wife's questions would die with her. Dutch began walking back to his T-bird.

Gene looked at the Timex around his wrist; he had to be back for his run in about ninety minutes. He watched

238

Dutch's T-bird drive away from the cemetery. Then he looked down to the packing of soil he did with the back of his shovel on Darlene's grave. He used his boot to compress and level the surface around the bunch of Russian Sage Ben had given him.

Gene left the cemetery without pausing to say good-bye to his niece. He had said his goodbyes to Darlene and remembered their times together last night with his head pressed on his tearstained Bible.

Dutch went straight to the hospital. His visit was short. He entered the intensive care unit as a nurse was leaving. Nothing. No words. He wanted to ask his wife what she had been doing with Darlene Rainbow. Damn her for taking the truck without asking. He knew he was going to be sued by the Rainbows and that they would probably get the fifty thousand-dollar limit on his vehicle coverage. He wasn't sure if his farm and assets were touchable. Better go see my lawyer, Dutch thought. Just to be sure everything's covered.

A few days later, Dutch drove his prized T-bird through downtown Des Moines streets full of dirty slush. March was warming. Rain would come late this month and he'd be planting earlier than last year. Before then, he need-ed to buy a new truck. His car insurance wouldn't cover the whole price. He felt a flash of renewed annoyance at his absent wife.

He had called Kenny and let him know of Michelle's unchanged condition, that Debi was fine at Dick and Merle's, and Ben and Pam were back at school. If Michelle passed away, he had told Kenny, they were his kids and he could come and get them.

With his mind on other things, Dutch parked the T-bird and switched off the engine without thinking about it. Twenty or more times he had parked in this same spot over a span of thirty years. The space was always empty behind

Vince Braden's little office on Polk Street. Vince was a smart lawyer and had a bunch of loyal clients who kept him busy. Vince preferred to drive out to his clients' homes to consult and have important papers signed. The clients liked that about old Vince. Dutch liked the idea he could smoke a cigar in Vince's office without offending the secretary he didn't have, or another client who was never there.

Dutch smiled, lighting his thin cigar. Vince's seventy-year-old face smiled for maybe two seconds.

He said, "I'm so sorry to hear about your wife, Dutch. How is she, for God's sake?"

"Pretty much the same. In a coma. The doctor doesn't know if she'll come out of it...or what she'll be like if she does."

"How are her kids?"

"They're hangin' in there I s'pose. Back in school."

"I was talking to your wife's father a while back. Said everything was just fine."

"Dick? You talked to Dick?"

"Hutch. The blind fella. Isn't he her father?"

"Stepdad," Dutch corrected, thoroughly annoyed.

The whole town knew that Vince Braden had an after-hours drinking problem. Damn, Dutch thought, that nosy blind bastard has been pumping my own lawyer about me.

"Whatcha talk about?" Dutch inquired pleasantly.

"Oh, this and that. I don't recall all that we said."

Dutch wondered if Hutch had carried tales to Michelle. If he had, that might explain why she had gone to Darlene, sniffing around, trying to dig up the past.

Leaving Des Moines, it occurred to him that Ben and Pam rode to school on the same bus as Darlene. Who knows what they'd been talkin' about, Dutch thought. It was beginning to look like his whole damn family was out to get him. He swore under his breath and turned east, deciding to stop at Ranchers. He wanted a couple drinks at the bar while he

240

thought this out.

At the same time Dutch turned the T-bird toward Ranchers, Gene slipped Ben a note as he was getting off the bus. Ben read it outside the open bus door, then gave the driver a thumbs-up.

Brother and sister walked together down the gravel lane toward the farmhouse, skirting puddles that grew wider and deeper as the year moved closer to spring. At first, Ben didn't know if he should tell Pam about the note. But then he thought, we're alone in this together.

"Gene gave me this on the bus," Ben said, handing her the note.

Pam studied the simple map showing the winding road through Ledges. An X had been drawn in the middle of the road above the words: Meet me here at 5 today?

"I told him I would," Ben said.

"I'm going with you."

"I'm not walkin' that slow again. You can stay here."

"Not alone, Ben...with Mom not here," she insisted.

They changed into jeans. Ben went into the dark cob house as Pam waited outside. She heard him remove the sheet of clear plastic from his bike, then pushed up the kick-stand with his heel. He turned on the bike's light.

"It works," he hollered.

"Come on. Before Dutch gets back!" she shouted back.

"The tires need air," Ben said. He pushed the bike into the shop and inflated the tires using Dutch's air compressor.

Pam rode sidesaddle, facing left and gripping the inside of the chrome handlebars as Ben peddled.

Ben yelled, "Duck down, I can't see where I'm going."

Pam leaned to the left and nearly toppled them both onto the gravel lane.

"Quit steering!" He quickly swatted her hand.

241

"Why don't you just pedal and let me steer?" Pam suggested.

"No, it's my bike."

Ben gained some momentum on the gravel road leading to the back way into Ledges; now he was pedaling easier, with speed, spitting gravel and mud under his fenders. He was breathing hard.

"My butt hurts," Pam complained.

"Shut up. You wanted to come."

Ben's back and legs and lungs ached; he huffed out his words. "There's Ledges! God Pam, you weigh a ton! No wonder your leg hurts all the time."

"Shut up," she said, then asked, "What do you suppose Gene wants?"

"I don't know. Something about Darlene, maybe."

"Ben..."

"What?"

"I have to go to the bathroom."

"There's bathrooms in Ledges...just a ways more."

Ben caught his breath while Pam used the bathroom. The air felt much cooler to him. Black clouds, puffy and thick, held back rain while casting dark shadows over the land.

A car turned down the main road from the canyon entrance and stopped at the place marked by the X on the map where they were to meet. Ben could see Gene's white-blonde head moving behind his steering wheel.

Pam came out of the restroom and saw Gene's parked car. She couldn't wait to solve the mystery of this secret meeting. "Did he say anything to you? About why he wanted to meet?"

Ben shook his head no.

Love, laughter, forgiveness and patience. After nearly fifteen years, Gene's mantra had finally summoned his grief to an apex-a colliding of pain and worry that shouted go and

242

jump like D. J., or resolve and live. Do something! So he was here in Ledges. He couldn't help D. J. or Darlene. Maybe he could help Ben and Pam, and by helping them, help himself, too.

It was mostly for D. J., the best friend of his lifetime, the boy who had been old when he was still young, and so afraid of Dutch he chose to die like old animals do, isolated and alone.

Gene motioned for Ben and Pam to follow him toward the highest sandstone cliffs in the park, where the ledges were most pronounced.

"Is this where D. J. jumped?" Pam asked. Gene stopped and pointed to the summit where the ledges were the highest and gave a thumbs up. Yes, this is the place we named Long Drop, he wished he could say, this is the spot. Their place.

Ben and Pam raised their gazes to the top, raking their eyes over the vanilla ledges, thinking of D. J.'s last minutes, the windswept plunge. They tried not to imagine the impact.

Gene used his hands to signal Ben that he wanted to talk. Gene bent his knees to the ground, then he opened his long arms for Ben to come in. Pressed together, Ben could feel Gene's hot, perspiring forehead shaking against his neck.

"Come hold us, Pam," Ben murmured. "Hold his back."

Pam faltered at first, then did as her brother requested, wrapping her arms around Gene's back. Gradually Gene's head motions slowed, then became still.

"How's yer mother?" Gene asked.

"Not good," Pam said. "She might..."

"Pam, shut up," Ben warned. "She's still in a coma, Gene."

"Why was she at Darlene's house that night?" Gene asked.

"We gave Darlene some of our mom's clothes and some perfume. Mom found out about it and wanted to know why Darlene had her stuff," Ben said softly.

"Did Dutch tell yer mom about D. J.?"

"I don't think so...no," Ben said.

"You still going to run away, Ben?" Gene inquired.

"If Mom...I don't know." Ben shrugged within Gene's encircling arms.

"Don't go without me!" Pam cried.

"She's right," Gene said, "your sisters will need you. Your mother would want you to stay together."

A long pause followed.

Uncomfortable with her brother's silence, Pam inquired, "Does anybody else know your head stops and you can talk when someone holds you?"

Gene pointed his thumb down.

"I'll bet a doctor could fix it, Gene. Like Dr. Knoll, he's the one taking care of our mom," Pam said.

Gene smiled, his eyes looking across the river to the horizon, where a pinkish hue was visible in patches over High Bridge.

Dutch lit a cigar and watched out his bedroom window as Gene lifted Ben's bike out of the trunk of his car. The farmer had a few drinks in him and was feeling mean. The letter on his desk had come in the day's mail from Ray and Charlotte Rainbow's attorney in Fort Dodge. They were after Michelle for Darlene's wrongful death. And now this: Gene Rainbow dropping off those two kids. Dutch clenched his cigar so tightly between his teeth that a dribble of tobacco juice stained the corner of his mouth. He watched them walk the bike down his lane after Gene drove away.

"He's home," Pam advised her brother, referring to the closed garage door that housed the car.

"Don't say anything about D. J. if he asks," Ben said.

Pam frowned. "Why would he ask about him?"

"Because he might've seen us get out of Gene's car."

Just then, the back porch door smacked shut behind Dutch.

Pam warned, "He looks mad."

To Ben, his stepfather's legs looked flexed for a good kick. Pam limped more noticeably.

Dutch's face was blood-red. He strode toward them from the back patio with Duke pacing the space between.

"What did I tell ya 'bout ridin' the bike in the mud? Huh?" Dutch demanded.

"Dad, how's Mom?" Pam tried to deflect him.

"Get inside," Dutch ordered, without answering her, but then he called to her before she reached the patio bricks, "Pam, just what were you doin' with Gene Rainbow? Huh?"

"We went for a ride on the bike...and he gave us a ride back," she said.

Pam stood holding her breath as Dutch stared at her. After he turned away, she slid inside the back door.

"Ya don't listen ta me, do ya, Ben?" Dutch gestured toward the mud-splattered Super Chief.

"I'll clean it up real good, Dad," Ben promised.

"Take the hose to it...then dry it off with rags in the shop."

Ben had pushed his bike only a few steps when Dutch kicked him on his rump, knocking him to the ground on top of his bike. Stay down, Pam wanted to cry out, peeking from behind the porch window shade. As if Ben had heard her silent plea, he did.

Dutch stood over him. "What were you and Rainbow talkin' about?"

"Nothing, Dad."

"Yer lyin'. Get in the cob house. Yer gonna tell me why yer mother was takin' her clothes to Darlene Rainbow."

Ben had promised himself a thousand times if this

happened again, he wouldn't beg or even say a word. Dutch prowled after Ben to the cob house.

"You know why yer mother went to see that little slut, don't ya?"

Ben kept silent: no more whining or pleading; no telling Dutch he didn't know this or that, or that he was sorry and wouldn't do it again-it wouldn't work. Ben had spent too many nights going over his shame-angry at himself for every thing he had done and not done...for a thousand hours.

Pam could not watch. She listened from the porch. It scared her to hear Ben's silence. Only the sound of the belt hitting her brother's flesh, and the grunting out of air as if Dutch was crushing Ben across his lap. The sound of the belt came faster, louder. Pam knew that Dutch was trying to make her brother cry, wail, beg, something.

By nine that night, the Super Chief looked new again under its plastic cover in the dark cob house.

Ben hiked his covers over his head and breathed the same pocket of air until morning; and so did his sister.

On Saturday morning, Dutch bought a new truck. Later that day, he drove Ben and Pam to the hospital. Dr. Knoll hoped her children's presence might penetrate Michelle's coma.

One of the nurses tried to be encouraging. "I've seen patients come out of a coma just one day out of the blue, after six months, even a year."

Dutch sat in a chair at the foot of Michelle's bed in intensive care. Ben and Pam stood beside the bed's raised side rail. Pam cried as she held her mother's hand. The bandages that had covered her face had been removed. The bruising and the stitching from Dr. Knoll's work was frightening.

Dutch had just turned down Dr. Knoll's offer to transfer Michelle to Iowa City for plastic surgery on her face. Dutch had said, "My insurance doesn't cover that kind of surgery. Anyway, what if she dies? She'll look good six feet under, won't she?"

The doctor couldn't argue with that. He was being optimistic about her recovery, and thought the surgery on her face was best done now before she awoke and saw herself for the first time.

Dutch had grumbled to himself that the doctor only wanted more money anyway he could get it. If his wife ever woke up, it wouldn't matter to him one bit if she had a few scars here and there, instead of shelling out thousands of dollars to Dr. High 'n Mighty.

Ben stood there, his butt still sore and his mind on running away. Baseball would start soon. He would tell Dutch he was riding his bike to baseball practice and never look back.

Pam was thinking about her stifling routine: the boredom of school all week, upstairs alone at night, the drive to the hospital to see her beloved mother unmoving and wrapped up like a mummy, back to the farm with Dutch, her brother planning to desert her-all of it overwhelming. Her grades were slipping to Bs in school. That didn't matter.

Pam uncovered her mother's feet and tickled the bottoms to see if she'd wiggle them the slightest. Nothing.

She could see her brother's long blond eyelashes blinking behind his thick lenses. He was so like their father that way. His profile around his mouth was like looking at their mother when she was deep in thought. As the oldest, he'd cast himself in the role of helper after their father left. Ben cleaned the kids' messes without being told; he protected and nursed them all when ill; and he rarely gave their mother any trouble. To Pam, it was as if Ben had three sisters-and now the oldest might die.

Ben was thinking the same thing. If his mother died,

it was his fault. He had given Darlene his mother's clothes and perfume. If he hadn't, she wouldn't be in the hospital dying. And Darlene would be alive.

Watching the expressions crossing her brother's face, Pam knew for certain that he would run away the moment their mother died. And like their father, he would would go far away and be lost to her. Pam pictured being alone on that farm with Dutch and cringed inside. She thought of her little sister alone with those two old drunks. Oh, how she must be crying day and night! Poor Debi, Pam thought. And poor Grampa Dick and Grama Merle! She imagined Dick and Merle, drinks in-hand, wearing earplugs, watching Milton Berle while Debi rocked and wailed on the sofa.

As she left her mother's bedside, Pam's mouth twisted in a grim smile.

Friday after school, Ben took his Christmas baseball glove from his dresser drawer. He had kept it in there so he wouldn't be reminded time after time that baseball practice hadn't begun. He didn't care that the glove was stiff and foreign to his hand. He would ditch-it anyway one day.

Now, in April, the ground dried out if the spring rains stopped for two days in a row. Tomorrow was the first day of baseball practice in the field behind his school. Dutch had okayed bike-riding, even on rainy days-as long as Ben cleaned and dried the bike thoroughly afterwards. Ben's preparations to leave were working out just as he had hoped.

Pam entered his room without knocking and caught her brother on his bed counting a pile of cash. He hurriedly stuffed the money in an envelope. He had counted it five times and would wait until she left his room before returning it to its hiding place under his mattress.

He rolled his eyes when Pam sat on the end of his bed. She knew where he kept his money and that he had one hundred and eight dollars. She had stood just outside her brother's door while their mother had been helping him turn his mattress. She'd heard her mother ask Ben how much cash he had in the envelope. "Why don't you put it in the bank?" Michelle had asked. Ben had shrugged his shoulders. Even then, Pam suspected, her brother had been thinking of taking off and needing money.

"I want to visit Darlene today," Pam said. "Will you give me a ride?"

"I don't like going to that place," Ben replied.

"Please, Ben," Pam wheedled. "I feel like it's our fault."

"Yeah," he said in a moment of complete honesty, "I feel the same way."

"Maybe if we say sorry, we'll feel better and God will let Mom live."

Pam's bulbous orthopedic shoes were getting in the way of his left pedal as she again sat sidesaddle facing left. She felt even heavier to him now than the first time they rode tandem. He tried hard to keep his speed up on the flat road toward Ledges.

"I forgot how much my back hurts with you on my bike," he complained.

Pam said nothing.

Maybe the extra weight is good training for my legs, he thought, thinking of the heavy backpack he would carry when he made his escape from Dutch.

They reached the cemetery as the sun slid behind the edge of a black cloud. Ben pushed his bike through the cemetery's narrow entrance. He steered the Super Chief around the graves and dropped his kickstand on the Rainbow plot, where it sank into the ground a couple of inches before holding the bike. They stood looking down at Darlene's freshly-packed grave, the only recent grave in the cemetery. They saw Ben's bunch of Russian Sage growing on it, surrounded by pale green new grass. Gene had been there, too.

"What's your best memory of Darlene?" Pam asked.

"I don't know."

"Mine was when we danced upstairs the time she baby-sat us. Isn't it weird that now she's here?"

Ben leaned against his bike feeling guilty about his plan. He looked away from his sister's eyes knowing that he would see them every night and day on his journey alone.

"Do you think we should say a prayer for her?" Pam asked.

Ben thought, maybe Gene had wanted to say a prayer for Darlene, but couldn't say it out loud. "Sure, go ahead," he said.

Pam began, "Now I lay me down to sleep..."

He joined his sister as she recited the prayer their mother had taught them when they were little.

"Okay, let's get out of here," Ben said, kicking-up the bike's stand.

Pam followed him as he pushed his bike up the back road into Ledges-up the hill toward their special viewpoint. They stood on the flat rock together. The greens of spring were taking over the grays of winter; the river was foaming, full of run-off from melting snow that trickled in at a million places along its banks. The air was sweet again.

"The land is like a table, isn't it, Ben?"

"What do you mean?"

"All the things that are placed on it." She pointed to her examples, continuing, "The river, the barns, the animals, the trees..."

"And the roads. Let's hit it. I want to get back," Ben said.

Ben nearly said home, but that word didn't fit a house without his mother.

Pam shook her head. "I'm going to D. J.'s spot...the place Gene showed us...to the top."

"What for?" Ben asked.

"I want to see what he saw up there."

"You can't walk up there," Ben said.

"Watch me!"

Ben pedaled away, braking the bike's speed to give Pam time to change her mind as he hoped she would.

After a while, he caught up with her where the ground leveled off and the sandstone cliffs began just across from the main exit out of the park. She acted as if her brother wasn't there. As she limped along she scanned for a way up. Ben could see that her leg hurt. He rode at her walking speed, balancing by quick-turning his front wheel from side to side.

"The steps are down there." Ben pointed to the place.

Just then, they saw three boys from their school walking toward them on the road. They were ninth graders. One was throwing rocks up at the cliffs as he strolled with his buddies.

Pam was limping badly. Ben got off his bike and walked with her as they passed the boys. He turned back to the boys when one of them called out, "Gimp!" and imitated his sister's crippled walk. Ben's heart shot blood to his ears and neck. They were cruel idiots. He kept looking back to make sure that the boys were leaving the park.

"Are these the steps that lead up to the top?" Pam asked.

"You can try if you want, but you're not going to make it," he said.

Ben watched her lumber up each stone step, balancing by throwing her arms and upper body off kilter; she took every stone step with her right leg leading.

Ben walked his bike along the bottom of the sandstone cliffs, over seven stories high and straight up. He dropped his kickstand on ground full of cracks and fissures, where glaciers once moved. The sky began to rumble above the park, then rain poured down without warning.

Ben kept watching for Pam to come back down. When she didn't appear, he watched the summit expecting her to wave down to him. Then, everything came together at once-a sudden feeling like the burst of rain-the dawning that she was his best friend, too. And this was D. J.'s spot.

He drew in a deep breath before he roared in a voice he had never used as her big brother. "Pam, I'm coming!"

He was drenched before he hit the bottom step. He couldn't see in the deluge. All he could see was his sister's unhappiness: her beloved daddy leaving her behind, a limp that people laughed at, skinny cute Debi always at her side, Mom in the hospital nearly dead, nights spent alone in that upstairs bedroom-and a selfish brother. She knows I'm going without her. Why else would she be here and not stop on the way when it began to rain this hard?

"Pam!"

Already Central Iowa's ground was so saturated from the whiteness of winter the river was over its banks in Fort Dodge and flooding farms splayed off the Des Moines just north of Boone. When floodwater flowed into the park, the main road became impassable, submerged beneath a lake lapping at the 13,000-year-old cliffs.

Ben felt ten pounds heavier as the rain soaked into his jeans and shirt and poured into his boots. He still couldn't see her.

"Pam!"

The steps ended and the climb grew easier as he neared the lower ridges of cliffs and kept going, running.

She was standing on the very spot D. J. had stood during his last moments on earth, though she didn't know it. She should be sitting, not standing, Ben thought.

"Pam!" he called again.

Her arms were spread wide with her back to him. She was letting the rain pour over her near the edge of the highest cliff, one with a vanilla-colored band of ledges, four or five, stepping down its face beneath her. She had known Ben would come to her. She smiled, thanking God for it as Ben took over.

"Get back from that edge. Now!" he commanded.

When he reached out for her he was out of breath and mad. He pulled her back and flung her down to the mud. She landed on her tailbone and cried out. He watched her roll onto her side in pain. Ben stood over her madder than he'd ever been.

"You know you could've fallen, you dummy!"

"You hurt me!" she accused.

"You fall off here and Mom dies, too, you farthead! You want that? Huh? Answer me!"

"No."

She got to her knees, sinking her hands in the red mud. "My back hurts," she cried.

For all he knew, she was faking just to get his help walking down. He turned away.

Looking down at the park, he couldn't believe what he saw. The river was flowing fast from the western slopes of Ledges, covering the main road. The noise from the rain was so loud he had to lean down to Pam when he helped her to her feet and yell to be heard.

"We have to get out of here before it's too deep."

"I can't walk," she cried. "Ben, it really hurts."

"It's probably just a bruise. Put your arm around me."

Twice they slipped and landed in the mud. The second time Pam laughed at the way Ben's skinny butt had bounced while his glasses went flying off his face. When he found them, they were so muddy he folded them inside his shirt pocket before continuing downhill .

It took twenty minutes to get Pam down to the bottom stone step. Then Ben panicked. He couldn't see his bike. Water was ankle-deep where he had parked it. Not enough water to wash away the heavy Super Chief, he thought.

In the rain, he covered the whole area like a squirrel rounds a tree. No bike. The flood wasn't his danger now. Dutch was. Ben's legs, weak from hauling Pam down the cliff, felt like his rubber bands.

Pam was sitting on the bottom step wincing in pain, when Ben returned empty-handed. She had no idea he was crying until he spoke.

"My bike's gone, Pam. He's gonna kill me for sure now."

"The water must have moved it. You'll find it."

"No. I looked. It's gone. I can't go back without it."

"We've got to go, Ben. We can't stay here. I'm cold."

They headed back. The water was up to their knees for fifty yards on the main road. They hunched forward in the downpour, doing well until they tried to cross a ditch by walking across a 2-by-4. Ben went first and fell into the ditch, coming out covered head to toe with mud.

At the house, with no sign of their stepfather, Ben stripped off his clothes and rinsed the mud off at the outside faucet. They dried their clothes in the clothes dryer. Pam took her bath first. Heck with it, Ben said to himself, I'm not sharing her bath water. After fixing a supper of sandwiches, they went to bed before Dutch got back.

Dutch had been at the hospital. Dr. Knoll's nurse had called. "Your wife has been fluttering her eyelids and moaning."

"What's that supposed to mean?" Dutch asked.

The nurse didn't reply to his question. "Dr. Knoll wants to see you," she said.

It rained all day Saturday. Baseball practice was canceled. Ben spent the day upstairs in Pam's room, snapping rubber bands at the Army and Navy, while Pam read a Jane Austen novel, and Dutch did his book work downstairs at his desk. Dutch had not yet noticed the missing bike.

On the way to school Monday, Ben wasn't feeling well. That morning he woke up with his hands between his hot thighs, shivering.

The first hour after noon recess Mrs. Jorgenson noticed her favorite student nodding asleep at his desk at the back of the classroom. While his classmates' attention was on their twenty question English quiz, she felt his forehead with the back of her hand. It was so hot it alarmed her; she had to stop herself from crying out his name. She bent to his ear and whispered, "Go to the nurse's office. You know where it is?"

Ben nodded yes.

"I'll clear off your desk," she whispered.

He left the classroom without his books, but came back for them when his teacher called to him. He grabbed his coat from a hallway peg.

Pam saw him walk past her open classroom door, dragging his Keds and the weight of Dutch finding out about his bike sooner or later.

Pam watched for him the rest of the school day, but he lay on the nurse's cot after taking two aspirin with a drink of water.

Ben watched the ceiling at first. His head was burning-up and tossed like Gene's if he let it. He had to hold on and get home on the bus without calling Dutch to come get him. He imagined how he would go to his room and shiver this firestorm out with his money hidden just under him, waiting for his escape move. It was there for him to take. He would call Ernie to pick him up in his cab. He could visit his mother before he went, tell her he loved her and to please understand and forgive him. He was crying on the cot before he fell asleep.

His feverish dream: He was hiding from his father's

Christmas Eve call, looking down at his mother in the central farmyard, who was searching for him.

"If you don't have anything good to say...don't say anything at all," he called out to her.

He picked up his pump-action rifle that was lying on the platform, aimed and fired rapidly at baseball cards standing against the opposite wall. He hit them all-sending the white uniforms flying and spinning, some falling face-down and dead; others still leaning on their sides, only to be shot down in succession. He heard his mother saying, "He's off playing somewhere. I know he'll be upset he missed your call. He's doing fine, Kenny. He's turned into quite a helper for Dutch. He's got a hundred and eight dollars under his mattress and a clipping that got Darlene killed. I think he's really grown here, Kenny."

Ben squeezed the trigger: Pop. He walked over to the last fallen card. The player in the white uniform was Kenny Smith, shot through the eye. Ben smiled at his marksmanship.

The school's final bell woke Ben. His long day in hell would soon be over. He was the first passenger on Gene's bus. Gene watched him drag his feet coming out of the school, then sit against the window with his head resting against the bottom frame. Pam sat beside him.

"Ben, I'll take care of you, okay?" she said.

Gene watched them walk down the white-gravel lane as Duke barked behind the moving bus. In his rearview mirror he saw Ben's books still on the seat under the window.

Ben's fever hit 103 degrees as Pam helped him remove his shoes on the back porch. She brought him a glass of ice water, then placed a wet washcloth with two ice cubes wrapped inside on his hot forehead. He shivered and burned from the loss of his Super Chief. He would not take another beating. And he would not forego his escape plans. As long as he had his stash under him, pressed flat with the clipping inside the envelope-his ticket was still good.

Dutch didn't return until after sunset. He was drunk and feeling sorry for himself. Michelle was still in a coma, though now the respirator had been removed and she was breathing on her own, but with only one lung.

Dutch passed out on his bed in his clothes. In the next room, Ben was delirious, his hair and pillow wet from perspiration.

Upstairs, Pam prayed, "Get us through tonight, God. Bring the morning, please." She lay awake listening to rain begin to fall harder and harder as the hours ticked by.

Pam was dressed for school earlier than usual in the morning. After she heard the back porch door smack, she came downstairs into the kitchen carrying a small suitcase and wearing her heavy orthopedic shoes. She watched Dutch from the edge of the kitchen window tramping off in the rain to do chores with Duke leading the way. She picked up the phone, dialed information and got the phone number for Ernie's cab company.

She requested Ernie's cab to pick her up for a visit to her mother in the hospital. "He knows where the farm is," she told the dispatcher. "He's been here before. It's near Ledges Park. And please tell him to hurry."

Now she had to get Ben dressed. Get the money. And be ready for Ernie. She had it all planned. They would wait in the T-bird's garage for Ernie, and be gone before Dutch finished his chores.

"Ben. We gotta go. Ernie's picking us up. To take us to see Mom. Come on, Ben. Hurry before Dutch comes back."

Ben was still hot and weak all over. "I'm thirsty," he groaned.

Pam ran into the kitchen and got him some water from the tap. When she returned to his room, he was on the bed, slumped onto his side with his feet on the floor. Pam put the glass of water to his chapped lips and poured. Finally she splashed the rest onto his face, screaming, "Ben, get up! It's our chance."

"Oh God, Pam, I'm so hot..."

She put on his socks and shirt, then his pants, before running to the porch to get his shoes.

Gene's bus was closing-in on the Beal Farm. He stopped and looked down the lane for his missing passengers. He didn't honk. Pam must be taking care of Ben, he reasoned. Then, for a moment he thought of opening his door and running down the muddy lane with Ben's books just to check on them. He looked at his Timex, then again down the lane, until he heard Duke's bark approaching. He drove on.

"Help me, Ben."

Pam was trying to lift the mattress after she had been unable to reach Ben's envelope. Together they hoisted it enough to see that the envelope was no longer there.

"It's gone!" Ben cried, collapsing on the bed, his body hot and weak.

"He's got your money, Ben."

"The clipping," Ben moaned.

Alarmed, she shook him. "The clipping was with your money?"

He nodded yes, his head down.

"He knows we know about D. J. We've got to go right now."

"My rifle..."

"You can't bring that."

He picked up his rifle and stuffed a cylinder of BBs into his front pocket. Pam turned him left once out of his room, saying, "We're going out the front door."

"We don't have money, Pam."

"Ernie will drive us. We have to get away before Dutch discovers you lost your bike. He'll use it as a reason to hurt you."

They made it to the T-bird's garage, getting soaked by the rain. Ben had to help her raise the garage door; then his legs buckled, taking him down to the cold floor. He sat against the garage wall near the T-bird's rear bumper, his rifle lying beside him. Pam pleaded out loud for Ernie to come, pacing at the garage entrance. Every so often she peeked around the corner of the garage to see if Dutch was coming.

"Here comes the cab," Ben said when he heard the taxi's engine.

"Let's run to the road," Pam cried.

"No," Ben warned her, "Duke'll see us and bark."

Ernie slowed the cab, then took the service road, since the gravel lane was covered with large patches of standing water.

"He took the wrong road, Ben. Dutch'll see him."

From his tractor's seat, Dutch watched the cab coming toward his cattle yard, then turning around to the feed house. He told Duke to sit.

Ernie's windows were rolled up. His fear of the aggressive farm dog, plus the rain, made him keep his wing closed even as he smoked the last of his Camel non-filter.

Pam and Ben left the garage. When Ernie spotted them he began honking the taxi's horn as he drove from the feed house all the way to the back porch.

"Now!" Ben yelled.

They bolted for the cab in the rain. Pam, toting her suitcase, was faster today than her brother. Between the cab's wipers Ernie saw his passengers coming and nervously checked his mirrors for the guard dog. Ben looked ready for war with his rifle in one hand. Ernie reached back and opened the door behind him. The two kids scrambled in breathing hard.

"Go Ernie. Go!" Pam screamed.

The cab fishtailed in the muddy farmyard, its wheels sliding and slithering rounding the feed house. Then, Ernie braked. Dutch was blocking their way, sitting atop his tractor.

"What the?" Ernie gasped. The kids stopped breathing.

Dutch stepped down off his Farmall, smiling, wearing his work gloves, and walked to Ernie's door.

"Go, go!" Pam screamed.

Dutch jerked open Ernie's door, snapped his fingers and said, "Sic 'em, Duke."

Instantly Ernie was on his front seat screaming beneath seventy pounds of determined muscle and foaming teeth-fighting for his life as Duke snarled and chewed on his upthrown arms. Pam was screaming as Ben pushed her out the back door on the other side of the cab, abandoning her suitcase.

Dutch watched them run in the rain past the chicken coop and turn into the sweet corn field. He reached in and pulled Ernie's keys from the cab's ignition.

"Duke. Come!" he ordered.

Duke left Ernie's blood-covered chest and sat on the earth at Dutch's feet. Ernie struggled out of the front passenger door and staggered down the muddy road toward the highway. Dutch watched and waited, then said, "Go get 'im."

Duke was off, chasing the cab driver, then taking Ernie down by his throat. The dog clamped on the soft flesh until his prey was dead.

Dutch got behind the cab's wheel, started it, and backed it up all the way to the back porch, leaving his gloves on and the keys in the ignition. He noticed that he had gotten some of Ernie's blood on his overalls. He removed them there in the downpour, then checked his Dekalb cap for more blood. He balled his overalls and gloves and walked to the outhouse, where he dumped them into the hole-gone forever. He strolled to his shop in no hurry-he knew where the kids were.

He washed his hands with pumice soap outside his shop door in the rain. His eyes looked up to the window atop his big barn.

Ben was there, his fever forgotten, watching Dutch wash his hands. Dutch was looking at him and grinning as if he had him trapped. Pam was sitting on the platform holding her sore leg.

"He's gonna get us, too. What are we going to do, Ben?" Pam cried.

"Trust me," he said.

Ben began filling his rifle with BBs. He looked too weak to Pam to even lift the gun.

"Come here," he said.

"What for?"

"Just get over here," he ordered.

Pam got to her feet and went to the window.

"He's at the shop. Let me know when he's coming," Ben told her.

She watched the shop's big door, then scanned to the parked cab, then to the spot where Duke guarded Ernie's lifeless body.

"Here he comes, Ben. What do I do?"

"Quiet."

Ben dropped to his belly, the rifle barrel hardly visible at the platform's edge near the ladder. He removed his glasses and cleaned the lenses with his shirt.

Pam could find no place to hide except in the corn-where she'd drown. She crouched, making herself as small as possible.

Ben's fever was breaking-as if fear and loathing had sweated his long paralysis out of him. Now, he felt ready.

He heard Dutch's boots tramping through the mud in

the sweetcorn field. Ben gauged the height of his target at the corn crib's corner with his finger on the trigger, as the steps came closer and closer. Dutch underestimated his adversary. Pop! Bull's-eye. Ben hit Dutch's right eye dead center of the green. Dutch reeled, stumbling back toward his field.

"Got him. Right in his eyeball!" Ben shouted to Pam.

Ben hustled to the window and watched Dutch holding his right eye rushing into the back porch door.

"Pam, you have to get to the phone and call the police. Come on. Come on!" he roared.

Ben went down the ladder first, leaning his rifle against the crib's wall in the large passageway, then helped Pam down. The rain was loud around them as Pam limped behind her brother. He pointed out her route through the cattle yard.

"Wait at the gate. Don't run to the house until he leaves."

"But my leg..."

"Forget it. You can do this."

"What about Duke?" Pam cried.

"He won't chase you. You're not a stranger."

"Okay," she said. "I love you, Ben." She limped away.

"I love you, too," he said too softly for her to hear in the rain.

Ben turned, grabbed his rifle, and scurried up the ladder onto the platform over the stored corn. Back at the high window, he could see his sister stepping through ankle-deep mud in the cattle yard. He imagined he heard her clumsy black and white orthopedic shoes suctioning and sloshing through the mire. Then she fell forward, hands down into the black mud and dung that had puddled where the cattle trudged near the gate. She struggled to get up. Suddenly his attention was drawn away from his sister. Dutch was headed for his shop. Ben knew he had to distract Dutch from

Pam. He took the butt of his rifle and smashed out the high window, yelling down to Dutch, "Yes...I broke it!"

Pam was exhausted, covered with mud and cow shit, though the rain was washing some of it away. She peeked around from the cattle yard gate, terrified that Dutch would come out of his shop and discover her.

Ben's fear intensified when he saw Dutch leave his shop wearing his welder's mask with the eye-shield flipped down, his forearms covered by a pair of long welder's gloves. No target. Ben watched Dutch unbuckle his belt and whip it from his waist while he stalked toward Ben's tower on the far side of the sweetcorn field.

Pam dashed for the house after she saw Dutch go into the field, her upper body leaning forward against the force of the rain.

Ben began burying himself frantically in the sea of corn under a 2-by-4, not far from the platform and window. He dug himself deeper and deeper into the corn, piling the kernels as high and as close as possible. He had dropped his rifle and glasses over the opposite side of the platform hoping to lure Dutch that direction. He heard Dutch's boot hit the bottom rung and prayed that the rain drowned out the sounds of his digging and breathing.

Dutch climbed slowly, his belt draped over his shoulder. He was in no hurry. I've got 'em both now, he thought, two ungrateful brats who'd been snooping into his past and getting cozy with the Rainbows, trash who were threatening to take away everything he'd worked for.

When Pam reached the kitchen, the phone had been ripped from the wall. She circled the kitchen, tracking mud, out of her head about what to do. She went to the window and stared at the high window where Ben was trapped. Then an idea emerged. She ran into the master bedroom to Dutch's desk and reached into the middle drawer where she grabbed all the spare keys. She hurried out the front door.

She had forgotten about Duke. There he was. Prowling toward her. She rattled the keys in her hand and called to the dog, just as Dutch often did. "Want to go for a ride, boy?" It worked. Duke hightailed it over to Dutch's new truck and leaped into the back.

She ran for the garage in the rain. The T-bird's seat was too low for her to see over the steering wheel, and too far back for her to reach the pedals. Her hands trembled as she tried key after key, none fitting, dropping each wrong key to the floor.

"Ben," she cried, banging her fists on the steering wheel before trying yet another key.

Over Ben's head, Dutch's boots walked the platform toward the broken window. Dutch had left his gloves on the ladder's top rung and removed his welder's mask when he saw Ben's childish decoys in the corn. He walked the platform's edge, his good eye on the hunt for a clue in the corn. There. He saw it. He squinted and found one of Ben's BB cylinders poking out from just under the surface. He heard the soft whoosh of air as Ben inhaled through the narrow tube. He grinned at his little farmhand's ingenuity, then balancing his frame on the platform, he squatted. Dutch picked up a single kernel of his best hybrid, waited for the boy to breathe in and dropped it into the tube. Ben's head jerked out of the corn coughing violently.

Just as Dutch was about to drag the boy out of the corn, he heard the T-bird's horn honking. He went to the window, leaving Ben to flounder in the corn, trying to pull himself out, still coughing.

Dutch saw his precious toy fishtailing in a muddy circle around the central pole in his farmyard. The driver was laying on the horn steady as Duke barked and chased and tried to bite the tires in the downpour.

Pam couldn't find the knob that turned on the windshield wipers. Blinded by the rain, she accelerated with her right foot and braked with her left at the same time. The car bucked beneath her. One more swing around the pole and she headed for the sweetcorn field, skidding in the deep mud, burning rubber off the whitewalls in the mire, headed for her brother.

Gene turned his car onto the lane leading to the Beal Farm. Ever since he'd passed the place on his early morning route, he'd been worried about Ben. The kid had been real sick yesterday, so sick he'd forgotten his books on the bus. Gene glanced down at the books lying on the passenger seat. When he looked back at the road he gave a gargling cry and stomped on the brake pedal.

A small body covered in blood sprawled across the lane. At first Gene thought it was Ben and he bolted out of his car to kneel beside the motionless figure. The moment he saw the agonized expression on the dead man's face he rose and started running toward the farmyard.

The sound of the T-bird's laboring engine and blaring horn guided his steps. Once he recognized Pam behind the wheel, Gene raced in the same direction as Dutch's treasured vehicle. Something very bad was happening in the corn crib.

The sole of Dutch's boot pressed on the crown of Ben's thrashing head, pushing it down into the corn as Ben fought and groaned for air. He would go down here, fighting to the last, without pleading or begging. The thrust of Dutch's boot was too much. He had to let go now and sink—he must leap off the edge as D. J. had, knowing that death was better than the brutality to come. But then Ben's trembling fingers closed over the piece of glass from the broken window that he had tossed into the corn. He couldn't feel how deep his fingers were cut. With the last of his strength Ben surged upward, jabbing the shard deep into Dutch's calf muscle above his boot.

Dutch fell on his back on the platform. As he rolled

back and forth, grasping his wounded leg, he realized that someone had stepped off the top rung of the ladder and now stood over him. He looked up and stared at D. J.'s buckle sparkling at the end of the belt held like a weapon in Gene's hand. Dutch focussed on his son's initials.

"Where'd you get that belt?" Dutch demanded.

Gene's stride to Ben was swift and powerful. He yanked the boy into the air and laid him gasping on the platform. When he saw Ben's bleeding hand, Gene ripped off his flannel shirt and quickly wrapped it around the gaping wound.

"Behind you," Ben choked out, pointing with his good hand. Gene turned in time to block the rifle butt from smashing his skull.

Gene snapped the rifle away from his assailant with such power, Dutch felt as if his arm had been torn from its socket.

Then Gene hit Dutch with a left roundhouse on his right ear that knocked him sideways to the platform. Gene pounced on his chest, looping D. J.'s belt around Dutch's neck. He tightened the belt to a choke.

Gene shouted at Dutch, pouring out a string of unintelligible howls. In Gene's own mind, the words were clear.

"You see this?" Gene's thumb displayed D. J.'s initials on his buckle. "I found it on the fence at the cemetery when I got off my crutches. D. J. left it for me to find. He fell off High Bridge. I jumped after him. He saved me before I drowned."

Dutch blinked his good eye and stared up at Gene, almost as if he understood the garbled words.

Gene shoved Dutch toward the ladder, his left hand squeezing the belt, powering the farmer along the platform away from Ben with his left fist wedged under Dutch's jaw.

"You know why he jumped? Huh?" Gene screamed the words and they came out like the bawling of a maddened bull.

Dutch's heels dragged.

"He was afraid of you."

Now Gene held onto the ladder's top rung with his right hand. "You killed D. J.! Why?"

Gene held Dutch's upper body out over the platform's edge, dangling forty feet above the concrete floor. "Answer me."

Dutch groped for the ladder, but Gene's powerful grip kept him out and away and dangling.

Gene looked at his best friend's father, seeing only the fear of death. Then D. J.'s eyes flashed before him-wide and pleading-staring up at him with the same fear, as the train roared overhead. His friend's fear had turned to trust when he told D. J. he was jumping after him.

There was D. J.'s buckle fisted tight between him and Dutch...holding on...holding on...holding...

Horn blaring, the T-bird crashed into the corn crib's passageway and Gene let go of the belt. Dutch screamed, then slammed headfirst onto his T-bird's baby blue hood.

Pam scrambled out of the car and stood shrieking for Ben.

Gene showed Ben how to use the cab's radio. Ben asked the dispatcher to call the police.

When Sheriff Buell arrived, he had to shoot Duke to get near Ernie's body.

Gene and the kids had their story straight. There was no sense in bringing-up D. J.'s belt, Gene slid it around his waist and pulled his t-shirt down over it. And there was no sense in bringing up the envelope full of cash and an old clipping they had taken from Dutch's pocket.

Buell was satisfied that Gene had been checking on the kids since they missed his bus. The kids told the sheriff that Dutch had gone crazy and ordered Duke to attack the cab driver who had come to take Pam to visit her mother. Gene had saved Ben from Dutch in the corn. All three said Dutch just fell off the edge of the platform.

It all made sense to Buell, a wife in a coma, combined with the Rainbow lawsuit against him. Dutch must've just snapped, Buell thought. He told Gene to come to his office to sign a statement after they cleaned up and got Ben some stitches.

Under High Bridge late that night, where he and D. J. began their final minutes together, Gene rolled D. J.'s belt to the buckle with the clipping under it, and threw it out into the middle of the river. It sank near the spot where they fell, where D. J. might have died that day, but didn't. He gave his four-word mantra to the river. He said them the way he always did-to himself.

Ten days later, two days after Dutch's body had been cremated and his ashes taken to Wisconsin by his sister, Michelle woke up.

Dr. Knoll rushed to her bedside when he got the early morning call from the hospital. The first thing he did was introduce himself to his patient. Shortly thereafter, Michelle found herself the focus of a barrage of tests administered by her smiling doctor. Exhausted by all the attention, not to mention the poking and prodding, Michelle fell asleep-this time for a short afternoon nap.

Gene got the call from Dr. Knoll and had a substitute driver take his run. He took Ben and Pam out of school, picked up Debi at Dick and Merle's, and drove them to the hospital, where they met Sheriff Buell.

When Michelle awoke, her bed was surrounded by people. She had seen her ravaged face earlier in the day when Dr. Knoll handed her a small mirror and discussed the miracles of plastic surgery. Now, she worried that her healing wounds would frighten her children. She turned toward Pam.

Her mother's voice sounded strange to Pam, raspy and barely more than a sigh. "Don't...don't...be...scared."

Tears rolled down Pam's cheeks. "Oh, Mommy, I love you!"

"B...Ben?" Michelle sought out her son.

As he always had, Ben understood his mother without the need of explanation. "It's okay," he reassured her. "We've been to see you lots of times before this."

Michelle's eyes went to each person in turn. Pam, Ben, a nurse, Dr. Knoll and, standing at the foot of her bed, Sheriff Buell and Gene Rainbow. Michelle's forehead creased in puzzlement. Her glance went again to Dr. Knoll.

"Michelle," he began, "there's no way to say this that makes it easier, so I'll just say it straight out. Dutch suffered some kind of mental breakdown and he's dead."

Michelle gasped and turned toward her son.

"It's true, Mom. But it was an accident. He fell from the platform in the corn crib."

For ten days, Ben and Pam and Gene had stuck to their story. Brother and sister saw no reason to tell the truth now, or to upset their mother with the details of Ernie's death. The facts could wait.

Pam took her mother's hand. "Dutch was drinking," she said.

Michelle nodded and seemed to relax.

Ben thought to himself, the best lies are the ones that stick to the truth. He glanced at Gene and smiled. Gene gave him a quick thumbs-up.

"Mom," Ben said, "Gene's been staying with Pam and me at the farm. We've been doing all the chores, so the animals are okay."

"Mrs. Beal," Sheriff Buell said, "I have to ask you if Gene, here, has your permission to remain in your house

269

and supervise your two older children. Your father and his wife have agreed to keep Debi. But they say the two older kids would be too much for them."

Michelle stared at Gene, watching his head rock from side to side, watching his eyes trying to hold steady on her own.

Sheriff Buell became impatient. "If you won't give your permission, Pam and Ben will go into foster care until you leave the hospital."

"No," Michelle whispered.

"Okay," Buell replied, "I'll make arrangements for placement in foster homes tonight."

The sheriff turned to leave.

Michelle's hand shot out and grasped her son's arm. He looked at his mother's expression and called out, "Wait!"

"Mommy," Pam pleaded, "we want Gene to stay with us. He's our best friend!"

Michelle sat up in bed. "No...foster..." she said, then sank back against her pillows.

"And Mr. Rainbow is your choice of guardian while you remain in the hospital?" Buell asked.

Michelle was too tired to answer. She looked at the man standing silently at the foot of her bed and gave the sheriff a thumbs-up.

Six months later, Michelle left a hospital for the last time after extensive plastic surgery to her face performed in New York City. She did not return to the farm. Michelle had moved her children back to Des Moines. She saw her mother as little as possible, and Hutch not at all, after Pam told her what he'd done. Pam and Ben were making friends in school, now that neither gave a darn what the other kids said about them. Ben and Pam thought of Darlene often.

Mrs. Beal had inherited nearly two million dollars in

cash plus the total value of the farm which had been calculated at another two million. Her attorney settled with Ray and Charlotte for three hundred thousand dollars, and the Rainbow couple moved to Denison where they bought a nice house.

Gene continued to drive a bus for the Boone School District. After Michelle decided to move to Des Moines, she hired Gene to run the farm. One of Gene's first tasks as manager of the Beal Farm was to drive Dutch's baby blue T-bird deep into Lester's pasture, where it remained year after year, season after season, slowly turning to rust.

The End

Librarians and readers interested in
Michael Frederick titles and information
on his first book signing tour may
E-mail: mfrederick310@aol.com
or write to: Michael Frederick
PMB 246, 14245 S. 48th Street
Phoenix, AZ 85044